FRANCESCA

FRANCESCA

A novel

by

DON TASSONE

Adelaide Books
New York / Lisbon
2021

FRANCESCA

A novel

By Don Tassone

Published by Adelaide Books, New York / Lisbon
adelaidebooks.org

Editor-in-Chief
Stevan V. Nikolic

For any information, please address Adelaide Books
at info@adelaidebooks.org

or write to:

Adelaide Books
244 Fifth Ave. Suite D27
New York, NY, 10001

ISBN: 978-1-955196-44-4

Printed in the United States of America

For Liz, my hero

Contents

"Be the one who walks with the Lord."

— Shellie Palmer

Acknowledgements

I am deeply grateful to my wife, Liz, Patti Normile, Kathy Kennedy, Murray Bodo, Nina Bressau, Anna Gayford, Christine des Garennes, Andi Rogers, Lindsey Tassone, Logan Malone, Sandy Weiskittel, Dave Weiskittel, John Young, Kelly Fitzharris Coody and Ryssa Kemper for their helpful feedback and encouragement on drafts of this novel.

Preface

As I write this, our world is in the throes of a pandemic, social justice protests and economic upheaval. No one knows how it will all play out and what our "new normal" will look like.

I wrote this novel before our present crisis, but it seems fitting that it be published during this time of great change because *Francesca* is a story about transformation.

The main action is set in a not-too-distant future which, at first, might seem far-fetched. But until recently so did the idea of everyone wearing masks and social distancing.

Once in a while, someone comes along who reminds us of what's most important. The main character in this story is such a person. In times of great change, these people inspire us to think deeply about the new normal we want to create.

Don Tassone
August 2020

PART 1

Chapter 1

May 2055

Rays of the rising sun hit the Egyptian obelisk in the center of St. Peter's Square, casting a long, thin shadow, pointing like a finger toward the Basilica.

Twelve hours earlier, a newly elected pope had appeared briefly on the balcony. Now the new pontiff was about to hold a news conference, the first ever at the Vatican. Everyone was eager to learn more about this improbable new leader of the world's two billion Catholics.

Reporters jockeyed for seats or spots to stand. Their cameras, microphones and lights stood in stark contrast with the fourteenth-century, frescoed room.

At 8:00 sharp, with no introduction, the pope entered the room and stepped up to the podium, scanning the curious faces of those gathered and smiling.

"Good morning, everyone," she said with a slight Missouri drawl.

Chapter 2

They had placed a wide, wooden box behind the podium for her to stand on. Good thing. Otherwise, she would have hardly been visible.

She wore a white pantsuit, which had become her trademark. She'd worn it in public at non-religious events ever since she'd become a priest. Her linen blazer was double-breasted with white buttons. Her cotton blouse was also white, and she wore simple black flats.

Traditional clerical garb felt pretentious, and she had always liked pantsuits anyway. She'd chosen white because it was simple.

Her hair was salt and pepper, her head uncovered. Her face was thin, her nose small and sharp. She looked as petite as a sparrow.

"I appreciate you being here, especially so early in the morning," she said. "I'm from Missouri. We tend to get up early."

This sparked laughter — an unfamiliar sound lately around the Vatican.

"I just want to make a few points. Then I'll be happy to take your questions."

She pulled a single index card from her jacket pocket. There was no paper or binder on the podium. There was no teleprompter.

"First, I want to thank God for this extraordinary opportunity," she said. "I hope and pray I am worthy of it.

"Second, I want to ask everyone for their prayers — everyone here and everyone around the world. We are a family, and I know I can count on you, my brothers and sisters, in my hour of greatest need.

"Third, just a word about the new name I have chosen, Francesca. Since I was a girl, I've been inspired by St. Francis of Assisi. He lived and died not far from here. He was a simple man who devoted his life to following the teachings of Jesus. Two of my predecessors, who also took the name Francis, did the same in their own ways.

"I want to follow Jesus' teachings too. He told us to love God with all our heart, all our soul and all our mind and to love our neighbor as ourselves. This was his great commandment, and I believe it should be our focus. Guiding the Church along this path, maybe even *back* to this path, will be *my* focus as pope.

"But to be sure, we're all in this together. I've learned that leadership requires active listening. And so I'll begin my papacy by sharing my vision with the members of my family, all around the world, and by listening to you.

"I'll begin in the United States, not out of any favoritism to that country but because it's the only home I've ever known. One week from today, I'll fly to St. Louis. I expect my journey around the world will take about a month. I am very much looking forward to it.

"That's really all I wanted to say today. Now, I suspect you have some questions."

Every hand went up. Francesca smiled. In the US, she knew the faces and names of many reporters. Here, most were new to her.

Her eyes came to rest on a young woman in the front row.

"Yes?" Francesca said, extending her open hand.

"Good morning, Your Holiness," the reporter said.

"Good morning to you. What is your name?"

"Lakshmy. My name is Lakshmy."

"Good morning, Lakshmy," the pope said, smiling.

"Your Holiness, you have just taken the lead for a Church which many would say is in disarray. What do you see as your biggest challenges and how will you go about addressing them?"

"You're right," Francesca said. "We certainly have no lack of challenges. Some even speak of this as a dark period for the Church. I have a favorite quote by my great predecessor, Pope John XXIII. He said, 'If God created shadows, it was to better emphasize the light.' It may be true that the sky seems filled with clouds. But we know that behind the clouds is the sun, waiting to shine through. Sometimes all we need is a good breeze to push the clouds away and reveal our brightest and closest star. That, I think, is my biggest challenge — just to help remove those things which are keeping us from God, who is always there for us. *How* I will do that, I'm not exactly sure. But I know there is wisdom in the people, and so I'm going to begin this new journey by reaching out to them."

"Thank you," Lakshmy said.

"Yes?" Francesca said, pointing to a man in the back of the room.

"Your Holiness," he said, "you have a progressive track record. Will you continue on this path as pope, and will you be dismantling some of the measures Pope Benedict put in place?"

"If progressive means finding new ways to follow Jesus in today's world, then yes, I'll stay on that path," Francesca said. "When it comes to the contributions of those who came before me, I'm interested only in building on them."

She called on a woman in the center of the room.

"Your Holiness, as the first female pope, can you speak about what this moment means for women around the world?"

"Well," she said, smiling, "I suppose it means that, with God, anything is possible."

Again, laughter.

Reporters continued posing questions. They asked about a range of issues, from the steep decline in the number of Catholics in recent years to growing divisions within the Church. Several tried to get Francesca to comment on some of the more controversial positions taken by her immediate predecessor, Benedict XVII. One boldly asked if she and her husband would be sharing a bedroom in the Apostolic Palace.

But Francesca wouldn't take the bait. She stayed on message, about the need to return to Jesus' teachings.

After an hour, she looked at her watch and said, "I'm sorry, ladies and gentlemen, but I need to go. Thank you all for being here this morning. God bless you all. Please keep me in your prayers."

Then she stepped off the platform and disappeared from sight.

Chapter 3

One evening earlier, just before she was announced to the world as Pope Francesca, as a tailor was frantically adjusting her new vestments, Jessica Simon stood alone in the Palace of the Vatican.

Part of her was lost in God, content and grateful to be in that quiet moment.

But part of her was thinking ahead. She had already begun forming a new vision for the Church. She imagined traveling the world to share that vision and connect with Catholics everywhere. She was eager to get on with it. She imagined leaving the Vatican in a day or two.

Then she pulled out her cell phone and called her husband, Michael, who was in his hotel room just a few blocks away, watching all the excitement on TV, wondering like the rest of the world who the new pope would be.

★

Thirty minutes later, coming back inside from the balcony, Francesca was greeted by a tall, handsome, serious-looking cardinal.

"Your Holiness," he said in English with an Italian accent, "I am Cardinal Angelo Salzano. I am your Secretary of State."

He extended his hand and bowed slightly. She took it.

"Your Eminence," she said. "What a pleasure to meet you. I've heard so many good things about you."

It was more than a formality. Salzano had a reputation as a most able administrator and diplomat. As Secretary of State, he was the head of the Roman Curia, which comprises the administrative institutions of the Holy See, the central body through which the affairs of the Catholic Church are conducted. In other words, the papal bureaucracy.

"Thank you," Salzano said. "I very much look forward to working with you."

Well, Francesca thought, I might as well put him to work.

"Your Eminence, I need your help," she said. "I'd like to hold a brief news conference here at the Vatican tomorrow morning."

"A news conference?"

"Yes. Can we set it up for 8:00?"

"Of course, Your Holiness. May I ask the purpose?"

"I'd like to make a few announcements."

"Announcements?"

"Yes. For example, I'd like to fly back to the US in a couple of days to begin a world tour to share my vision for the Church."

"In a couple of days?"

"Yes. Is that a problem?"

"Frankly, yes. We have two weeks of briefings planned for you," Salzano said.

"Briefings? On what?"

"Your Holiness, there are myriad subjects and issues to review with you to help ensure you are well prepared to begin your new role."

Bureaucracy, Francesca thought. I can't escape it.

"All right," she said. "I understand the need to be briefed. But for two weeks? I think one week should be more than enough time."

"One week?"

"Yes, one week. Then I'll be leaving for the US. Your Eminence, thank you in advance for arranging a news conference for tomorrow morning. Will you let the media know tonight?"

"Yes," said Salzano, an unflappable man looking perplexed.

Chapter 4

One week later, Francesca looked out her window, holding Michael's hand, as Shepherd One landed at Lambert International Airport on a sunny Friday afternoon. She had left St. Louis just two weeks earlier. How much had changed in that short time, she thought.

Everything looked familiar, but she knew this was no longer her home. She had spent more than half her life in St. Louis, but now her place was in Rome. She knew she would be expected to live there the rest of her life. She wondered if, after this trip, she would ever return to St. Louis. She hoped so.

"Home again," Michael said, squeezing her hand.

"Yes," she smiled. "I can't wait to see Emma."

The terminal was packed with people, all of them hoping to see the new pope or shake her hand. Francesca could have been whisked through a private exit, but she insisted on walking through the main terminal. Airport security and the local authorities had cleared a path for her.

When she stepped out of the gateway, once again wearing her white pantsuit, a great wave of cheers and applause erupted throughout the terminal. People of all ages were there to welcome her home. Some held banners and signs. Some held up giant, cardboard cutouts of Francesca's head. A group of women wore white pantsuits.

Shaking hands, blessing people, kissing babies, laying hands on people in wheelchairs — it took Francesca nearly an hour to make her way through the terminal. Michael walked behind her. No one in the crowd seemed to pay him much attention, but she kept turning around to check on him. He just smiled.

At several points, someone yelled, "Speech!" But Francesca simply waved, smiled and kept walking.

At last, she, Michael and their small Vatican entourage reached the end of the terminal. Several cars were waiting for them outside. Like nearly all vehicles in the US, these were self-driving and solar-powered.

A papal assistant directed Francesca and Michael to the first car, and they got in. Two men put their luggage in the trunk, and they set off with a police escort for Benton Park, a neighborhood in southside St. Louis. For the next few days, Francesca and Michael would stay there at the home of their daughter Emma and son-in-law Lucas.

Two of the other cars headed downtown, where the others from Vatican City, all of them papal assistants, checked into the Hotel Saint Louis. From there, they would go to nearby Forest Park to oversee preparations for the outdoor Mass Francesca would be saying in the morning.

Emma and Lucas were waiting out front when Francesca and Michael arrived. Emma ran down the brick walkway to her mother, and the two embraced.

"Oh, Mom," she said, crying. "It's so wonderful to see you. Thank you for coming. And congratulations!"

"Thank you, Em," Francesca said with tears in her eyes. "I'm so happy to see you."

"Dad," Emma said, turning to her father and embracing him. "Welcome home."

"Thank you, Em," he said, wrapping his arms around her.

Lucas stepped in. He shook Michael's hand and gave Francesca a tentative hug.

"Should I call you 'Your Holiness' now?" he asked.

"That won't be necessary, Lucas," Francesca said, smiling. "Francesca will do nicely."

"Well, let me get your luggage," he said, heading to the car.

Just then, a local TV news car pulled up and stopped in front of the house. A woman and a man jumped out.

"Your Holiness!" the woman said. "May I ask you a few questions?"

"Not right now, thank you," Francesca said. "I want to spend some time with my daughter. But I'll be holding a news conference after Mass in the morning. I hope you'll be there."

"I understand," the woman said.

Her associate was videotaping Francesca as she made her way up the walk to her daughter's small, red brick house. Millions were watching his feed live.

Those watching could see the stark difference between this new pope and the last one. Gone were the robe, the staff, the red shoes, the handlers and the guards. Gone were the pomps. Here was a pope who looked more like a neighbor in the year 2055 than a regal figure from some century long ago.

For those in the Vatican used to "managing" the pope, the change was jarring. For five years, they had surrounded Benedict, mapping and charting his every move. They attended him always, planning his schedule, scripting him, dressing him, feeding him, guarding him, even changing his bed sheets every day. Benedict XVII had lived with an entourage. This was the pope the world had come to know, a stage-managed man who always seemed a few layers removed.

Francesca had never given in to such trappings. She planned her own schedule, wrote her own speeches, made her own coffee.

A small group of priests and bishops had approached her soon after she first blessed the crowd in St. Peter's Square. They were members of the Curia.

These men — and they were all men — began to tell the new pope what she now must do. She listened for a few minutes. Then she smiled and held up her hand.

"Thank you," she said. "But this is all too much. I've just talked with Cardinal Salzano, and we agreed to a series of briefings over the coming week. Here's what I'd like right now, though. Dinner for my husband and me in our apartment. Something light, please."

The Curial administrators paused for a moment. Then, undaunted, they resumed raising a host of practical considerations, from Francesca's daily vestments to security.

"I can see I am in very good hands," she finally broke in. "I know these things are all important, but let's deal with them tomorrow. Okay?"

They agreed to stand down for the moment, except for security.

"You must be kept safe," a bishop said.

"I am safe," she said. "No one has ever wanted to harm me."

"With respect, Your Holiness, it is a dangerous world. I am sorry to say that, for some, you may now be a target. Please, we must insist on security for your well-being and the good of the Church."

Reluctantly, Francesca allowed it.

Now, as she stepped inside her daughter's house, an unmarked car with tinted windows was parked at the end of the driveway. The two armed men inside would take turns sleeping and keeping watch through the night.

★

After breakfast, Emma and Michael helped Francesca put on her vestments, which had been tailored for her in Rome: her cassock, made of white silk; her mozzetta, a short cape, made of white satin; her pallium, a circle of fabric made of wool with pendants hanging down in front and back; and a stole, also made of wool.

Michael lifted a long, silver chain over her head and draped it around her neck. From it hung a large, silver cross, embossed with an intricate image of the crucified Christ. Emma placed her zucchetto, or skullcap, on her head. Finally, Michael set her black flats on the floor in front of her, and Francesca held onto his arm as she stepped into them.

Michael and Emma stepped back to look at her.

"You look beautiful, Mom," Emma said.

"Thank you. But I must admit, I feel a bit overdressed."

"Those vestments have never looked so good on a pope," Michael said with a smile.

Francesca blushed.

The three of them and Lucas got into the car that had been designated for Francesca for the weekend and took off for Forest Park, less than 15 minutes away.

A police car led the way. Another trailed them, followed closely by the car with the Vatican security guards. Residential streets and four-lane roads were lined with people waving hands, signs and banners.

The police guided them to a spot behind a large, wooden stage at the edge of the park, a gently sloping vast expanse of green space. It was only 8:00, but a crowd of tens of thousands had already gathered. Hundreds of wooden chairs had been set up in front of the stage. Beyond that, people had begun sitting on blankets on the grass.

The sun shone bright, and Francesca shielded her eyes as she got out of the car. Squinting, she saw some of the same priests and bishops who had attended her in the Vatican. She wondered if they ever got a day off.

"Your Holiness," one of them said, extending his hand. "Right this way."

She reached for Michael's hand behind her. Taking it, she followed the priest to a tent that had been set up just behind the stage.

"We will prepare for Mass here," he said.

Francesca said goodbye to Michael, Emma and Lucas. Seats had been reserved for them up front.

"I'll see you shortly," she said.

Michael blew her a kiss.

"This way, Your Holiness," the Vatican priest said as he pulled back the tent flap.

Francesca stepped inside. There she saw a familiar and most welcome face.

"John!" she cried, hurrying over to a tall, thin, older man wearing a black suit with a white, clerical collar.

As she went to embrace him, he stepped back, extending his arms, his palms up, and bowing his head.

"Your Holiness," he said.

"Oh, John. It's me, Jessica! I hope you'll still call me that."

"Okay," he said, bending down.

She allowed his momentary subservience, but then she embraced him, and he held her close.

"Welcome home," he said. "And congratulations."

"Thank you. It's wonderful to be with you again."

He was Father John Dumont. Francesca had met him nearly 50 years earlier, as a freshman at St. Louis University. He was her theology professor and the first Jesuit priest she had ever known. From almost the day they'd met, he had played a mentoring role to her. Aside from Michael, he was her most trusted advisor.

Now Father John was in his early eighties. He was frail but still active. When Francesca asked him to be one of several local priests to concelebrate this special Mass, he was delighted.

"Your Holiness," said one of the Vatican priests, looking askance at Father John, "let us go over the arrangements for Mass this morning."

Two other Curial administrators came up to her too. As they did, Francesca looked over at Father John with a mischievous smile. He smiled back and shook his head.

She was so happy to be home.

★

She stood behind the podium and looked out at the sea of people. It stretched all the way up to the Saint Louis Art Museum at the crest of the hill. It was a crowd even larger than the one in St. Peter's Square a week earlier.

The air was warm, and Francesca could feel the heat of the morning sun on her hair through her zucchetto. The podium was low, at her request, so she could see over it easily and people could see her.

Being close to people during Mass was important to Francesca. In church, she gave most of her homilies walking up and down the aisle. During the sign of peace, she went into the congregation to shake hands and give hugs. To her, people were the Body of Christ.

Today, of course, wading into the congregation would not be possible. Ready to give her homily, her eyes scanned the enormous crowd. In the front row, the face of an older woman caught her eye. She reminded Francesca of her mother. The two women made eye contact and held each other's gaze for a moment. Francesca smiled.

Then she looked out over the people and leaned forward.

"Good morning, Saint Louis!" she said, sounding more like a rock star than a pope.

Everyone broke into applause. Moments later, they were all on their feet, giving her a standing ovation. She waited for people to sit down, but everyone remained standing, and the applause seemed to get louder.

She looked over at Father John, who was sitting behind the altar to her right. He smiled, nodded and clapped his hands too.

People stayed on their feet. Finally, they grew quiet, and she began her homily.

"'Come, follow me,' Jesus said. He was speaking to us. He is speaking to us, calling us, today," she said, her voice strong and clear. "We need only—"

There was a loud, popping sound. In the crowd, fewer than 100 feet from the stage, a light flashed. A spray of red exploded in front of Francesca. Then a second pop and a second flash of light from the same spot. Another spray of red. Then the pope fell backwards, her arms thrust out from her sides, her body hitting the wooden floor hard.

People screamed. Father John sprang to his feet and ran to her. He was the first to reach her. The front of her robe was drenched in red, her arms hung limp at her sides and she lay on her back. She was unconscious but still breathing.

"Help!" the old priest shouted, gently, reverently slipping his shaking hand under her head.

The next few minutes were madness. Paramedics, at the ready, tending to her. Police officers and others converging on the gunman. Michael and Emma pushing their way through the throng of people to the stage. Most in the crowd in shock, not knowing what to do, many sobbing, some falling to their knees.

The paramedics lifted Francesca onto a stretcher and carried her down the steps to a waiting ambulance. Father John followed close behind and started to climb in behind her.

"No, Father," said one of the paramedics. "You'll need to ride separately."

"No, I must be with her. I need to give her last rites."

"Okay. Get in."

The priest squeezed in beside her and knelt down. The paramedic pulled the rear door shut.

Michael and Emma had nearly pushed their way through the crowd to the ambulance, but they were too late.

"Mom!" Emma screamed as the vehicle sped away. Sobbing, she turned and buried her head in her father's chest. He wrapped his arms around her, watching the ambulance spirit his wife away, his body shaking uncontrollably.

In the vehicle, Francesca lay still, unconscious, making no sound whatsoever, her white garments now dyed red with her lifeblood. One paramedic lifted the silver cross over her head and handed it to the priest. It was covered with blood. One paramedic pressed his palms down on Francesca's chest. The other placed an oxygen mask over her nose and mouth.

"Will she make it?" Father John asked.

"I don't know," the paramedic said.

As they raced to Barnes-Jewish Hospital, Father John said, "Oil. I need something with oil."

"Oil?"

"Yes, to anoint her."

The paramedic looked around.

"All we have with oil is petroleum jelly."

"Vaseline?"

"Yes."

"Give it to me."

The paramedic handed him a small plastic jar. Father John unscrewed the lid and skimmed the surface of the Vaseline with his thumb. He reached up to Francesca's forehead and, with his thumb, traced a cross on her skin.

"Through this holy anointing, may the Lord in his love and mercy help you with the grace of the Holy Spirit," he prayed, his voice trembling. "May the Lord who frees you from sin save you and raise you up."

Father John lay his hand aside Francesca's face. She moaned. He gently stroked her face and smoothed her hair with his fingers, as a father would his child. Weeping, he said a prayer under his breath.

★

By the time they reached the hospital, less than 10 minutes from Forest Park, Francesca had nearly bled out. Fortunately, Barnes-Jewish was a Level 1 trauma center. What's more, the best cardiac surgeons in the city, some of the finest in the country, were waiting for her.

The bullets had just missed the right atrium of Francesca's heart. One of them grazed her superior vena cava, which carries blood to the heart from the upper half of the body. The other bullet tore through the lower lobe of her right lung, damaging it badly. It also shattered her collar bone and several ribs.

The surgeons repaired the damage to her heart. The lower lobe of her right lung was beyond repair, though, and had to be removed. But they saved her life.

Chapter 5

Francesca lay unconscious in her hospital bed. Prayers and well wishes poured in from around the world. Masses were said for her in nearly every Catholic church. Local florists' vans made non-stop trips to Barnes-Jewish. Thousands of school children sent handmade get-well cards.

The papal assassination attempt dominated the news. The Mass Francesca had been saying in Forest Park was being broadcast live, and the terrifying moments of the shooting were captured by TV cameras and a thousand cell phones. The constant replay on cable news and social media made it all the more wrenching.

Within hours, though, amidst the regular updates on Francesca's condition, two other stories emerged.

The first was about the shooter: a 23-year-old man from Bulgaria named George Sokoloff, a student at the University of Houston.

As soon as he had fired the shots, Sokoloff was attacked by those standing around him. One man slammed him to the ground. Another grabbed his high-powered 9mm Glock 19 pistol. Moments later, he was in police custody.

It was reported that Sokoloff had been in the US for a year, studying international business in Houston. His background, how he had come to the US and why he was in St. Louis quickly became the focus of the other emerging news story.

★

Sokoloff grew up in Plovdiv, an industrial city in south-central Bulgaria. His family was poor. As a boy, he was often caught stealing candy from stores. The local police would take him home, where his father would beat him.

By the time he was 12, George, whose real name was Georgi, was stealing cars. When he got caught, he was thrown in jail. By now, though, his father had given up on him.

But George had someone looking out for him: the family's parish priest, Father Nikolay Manov. Father Nick, as he was called, ran a program for troubled youth. It was supported by Manov's parishioners, but most of the funding came from the head of the Catholic Church in Bulgaria, Archbishop Ivan Penov.

Penov funded these programs for troubled youth all around the country not out of compassion but self-interest. He knew those he saved could be indoctrinated. Some might be good candidates for the seminary one day. Others might be helpful to the Church, and to him, in other ways.

Penov tasked priests and bishops throughout the country with identifying the most promising of these troubled youth. He then brought them to Sofia, the Bulgarian capital, where he lived in a sprawling, Neo-Romanian mansion on the outskirts of the city.

Dozens of boys lived there too. There were no girls, though. Not because Penov took any prurient interest in boys. He simply didn't believe saving girls was worth the effort.

Father Manov brought George to Sofia to live in this special home when he was 12. He spent the next six years there.

George was handsome, smart and articulate, a poised and impressive teenager. Penov knew he could be useful in persuading priests throughout the country to send him troubled boys from their parishes. Some of these priests were uneasy about the whole scheme. But as the archbishop's earnest ambassador, George helped convince them of its value for boys like him.

The security and stability of living in Penov's special home was indeed good for George. He had a sharp mind. He was particularly good at math. George's teachers told the archbishop he had the makings of a financial man. Penov knew financial skills could come in handy for the Church in Bulgaria, so he arranged for George to study finance at Sofia University.

Penov also knew there were more than a quarter of a million Bulgarians now living in the US and a good number of them were getting rich, at least by Bulgarian standards. If he could only find a way to tap into this wealth to support the Church and his personal brand of conservative Catholicism in Bulgaria.

Penov was a hardline conservative. He despised progressives. He saw them as weak, lacking moral backbone. He felt they had lowered the Church's standards and, in the process, its stature in the world. The Church, Penov believed, was not meant for everyone. It was an exclusive club, and progressives seemed hellbent on letting just about everybody in.

There was a deep and hidden irony in all of it. Growing up in the city of Burgas, on the Bulgarian Black Sea Coast, Penov was himself a troubled youth. He had been raised by a single mother. His family was poor. As a boy, he learned to steal food from the local markets. His mother never disciplined or even questioned him because they needed the food.

By the time he was a teenager, Penov was stealing cars. He got caught only once, and he was thrown in jail. His mother couldn't afford to post bail or hire a lawyer, so young Penov spent two weeks behind bars.

Young Penov would have been stuck there even longer had it not been for his parish priest. His mother was a faithful parishioner, and the priest looked in on her from time to time. He was paying her a visit one day when she broke down and told him her son was in jail and begged him to help.

The priest went down to the jail. He told the officer in charge that Penov had served enough time, especially considering he was a minor and this was his first offense.

"You can safely hand him over to me," he said.

In deference to a man of the cloth, the officer released the boy.

It might be assumed that Penov would be grateful to the priest, but he had never liked him. He considered him soft. A priest should be stern and lay down the law, Penov thought. It was the persona he himself would one day adopt as a priest.

After Sokoloff earned his undergraduate degree in finance, Penov decided to sponsor him for an advanced degree in international business. There was only one place for him to go: the US. There, Houston had become a magnet for Bulgarians and other immigrants from Eastern Europe. The connections George could make there could be invaluable, Penov thought.

But there was another reason he liked the idea of sending his "boy" to the US. It was home to one of the most progressive leaders in the Church, Jessica Simon, the first female Catholic cardinal.

Penov considered her a simpleton, but he also knew she was a well regarded leader, and he saw her as a threat to his friend Pope Benedict XVII, who had recently elevated Penov to cardinal. It may be advantageous for conservatives like us, Penov thought, to have eyes on such a threat. And so he sent Sokoloff to Houston.

Now Sokoloff was behind bars, charged with attempted murder, with the FBI leading the investigation. Details of his ties to Penov began to emerge.

It was a shockingly dark story, which only added to the anguish Michael Simon felt as he held his wife's hand as she lay unconscious, hooked up to all sorts of tubes, in her hospital bed.

Chapter 6

At last, Francesca came to.

"Where am I?" she asked, looking over at Michael, who was sitting beside her.

"You're in Barnes-Jewish," he said, squeezing her hand and getting up to kiss her forehead. "How are you feeling?"

"Weak. I hurt. What happened?"

"You were shot, just as you were beginning your homily in Forest Park."

"Am I okay?" she asked, looking up at the IV bags hanging beside her.

"Yes. There was a lot of damage, but the doctors here took very good care of you. You're going to be okay."

"My Lord, Michael. Who did this?"

"A religious extremist. He's in jail."

Francesca closed her eyes and swallowed hard. Her mind was swirling. She tried to get her bearings, to comprehend her situation.

"How long have I been here?"

"Three days."

"Three days? How long will my recovery take?"

"They're not sure. Maybe three months."

"Three months? I can't be away that long."

"Now, Jess. There's a whole host of priests who have been hovering around while you've been sleeping. I'm sure there's at least one outside your door right now. I don't know much about the machinery of the Vatican, but I'm pretty sure these guys are keeping it running smoothly."

Francesca looked at her husband. He had dark circles under his eyes. He looked older than she had ever seen him. She squeezed his hand.

"How are you?" she asked.

"Better now."

A nurse came in.

"Good morning, Your Holiness," she said, adjusting the medications dripping into Francesca's IV. "It's wonderful to see you awake."

When she'd gone, Francesca said, "Your Holiness. That still sounds strange to me."

"Well, you'd better get used to it," Michael said. "I have a feeling people are going to be calling you that for a long time."

"I hope so."

"Me too," he said, bending down and kissing the back of her bandaged hand.

★

"I understand you gave me last rites," Francesca said to Father John, one of her first visitors.

"Yes, I did."

"So you carry your little black bag with you everywhere?"

"No. I had to make do with what they had in the ambulance."

"What did you use?"

"Petroleum jelly."

"You anointed me with Vaseline?" she said, rubbing her forehead with her fingertips.

"It was either that or Gatorade."

They laughed. She looked over at him. He was scarecrow-thin, and his face was a labyrinth of wrinkles. How blessed she felt that he was still alive. How blessed she felt to have had his guidance all these years. Not only that. He was also one of the few people she could still banter with, even when she was a cardinal.

"I'm so glad you're feeling better," he said.

"Thank you, John. Of course, they probably won't release me for another two or three months."

"What's the rush?"

"Well, this was supposed to be the first stop on a world tour."

"A world tour, huh? Tell me about that."

She knew what that meant. *Tell me about that* was his way of saying *Are you sure?*

She tried to sit up.

"Should you be sitting up?"

"Probably not," she said, easing her head back into her pillow. She sighed. "It's kind of a listening tour."

"A listening tour?"

"Yes. For people to listen to me and for me to listen to them. A chance to connect, really."

"Connection is good."

"You don't sound convinced."

He smiled.

"Well, I certainly get the idea of people listening to you. Most Catholics still don't know you. They do need to know where you're coming from. They need to understand your vision for the Church. But what do you hope to achieve by listening to them?"

"I don't know yet."

"Well, don't you think you should be clear about that?"

"John, I understand your point. But what I'm saying is that I really don't know what people are going to tell me, and I'm quite okay with that. I just want to talk with them, and I want them to know I'm listening."

"Why?"

"I want them to know they have a pope who cares enough about what they think to come to them and listen. We need to get back to following Jesus' teachings. That's what we should be about. But I don't want to just say that. I want to *see* how people react when I say it. Will they embrace my vision or reject it? I need to know."

"Not to push," he said, "but why is that important?"

"Because I can't do this by myself, John. There are two billion Catholics in the world. I need to know we're generally pulling in the same direction, and right now, we're not."

He sat back in his chair and smiled.

"You know, Jessica, I remember the day we met. Even then, you were way ahead of me. You still are. I think the cardinals have made an enlightened choice, and I think your world tour is going to be a great success."

★

The following week, Teresa Das, Francesca's spiritual director, came to the hospital to meet with her. Since Jessica's first days in the seminary, Teresa had gently guided her to tap into her own inner wisdom and deepen her connection with God. In times of trouble, Teresa had also been a source of comfort and reassurance.

In all the years Teresa had been his wife's spiritual director, Michael had never met her or even seen her. Such was the confidentiality of their special relationship. He only knew that Teresa played an important and totally unique role in Jessica's life and that, after they had met, his wife always seemed more at peace.

Now, to give them privacy, Michael went down to the visitor's lounge.

A few minutes later, Teresa knocked lightly at Francesca's door.

"Come in," she said.

She was sitting up at an angle in bed.

"How are you?" said Teresa, stepping over to her.

"I'm feeling a little better each day."

"Good."

There was a straight-backed chair next to the bed and another in the corner of the room. Teresa stepped over to the one in the corner and pulled it over near the bed.

"For the Holy Spirit," she said.

"Of course."

Teresa sat down. She closed her eyes. So did Francesca. They both sat quietly for a few moments.

Then Teresa said, "Holy one, we come into your presence, and we thank you for this day and this time together. We ask that this time together be in the service of Francesca's highest good. We ask this in Jesus' name."

"Amen," they said.

Again, Teresa was silent. She usually let Jessica, now Francesca, begin their sessions.

"I've never felt closer to God," Francesca said.

"How so?"

"Just as I was beginning my homily in Forest Park, just before I was shot, I was talking about following Jesus. When the first bullet hit me, my head snapped back. I remember looking up at the sky. I was beginning to fall backwards, but I wasn't afraid. I wasn't afraid because I could feel someone's arms cradling me. I looked over, and I saw his face. I knew him instantly. It was the man I had seen in the woods. Now he was holding me. He was carrying me in his arms. 'I've got you,' he said. I looked around. All around me were people, an endless sea of people. Some of them looked hungry. Some were naked. Some looked lonely. 'Who are these people?' I asked. 'You know them,' he said. He was walking with me. 'Where are we going?' I asked. 'To feed them,' he said. 'To clothe them, to visit them.' Then he stopped and gently put me down. I stood on my own. 'You're on the right path, Jessica, but you're not there yet,' he said. 'You must walk a little farther. Know that I am with you and that I love you.' Then he vanished, and I felt the second bullet tear into me. I remember falling backwards but nothing after that. Three days later, I woke up here. That was three weeks ago, and I still feel his presence. I've never felt closer to God and more certain that I'm on the right path."

"Thank you for sharing that with me," Teresa said. "Do you think the man you saw was Jesus?"

"Yes."

"When he said you must walk a little farther, what do you think he meant?

"I think he meant I have some very important work just ahead of me and—"

She paused. Teresa waited.

Francesca cleared her throat.

"And my path may not be much longer," she said.

★

As Francesca's condition improved and it became clear she would recover, media coverage increasingly focused on the murky connection between Sokoloff and Penov.

Sokoloff was being held and questioned in a jail in Clayton, just west of St. Louis. A local attorney, Alexander Nedkov, born in the Bulgaria, took his case.

In his initial public statement, Nedkov admitted his client had shot the pope but asserted he had acted entirely on his own. When asked why Sokoloff had done it, Nedkov said, "My client sees this new, liberal pope as a threat to Catholics everywhere, and he felt compelled to act on their behalf."

It was a brazen and incriminating thing to say. It seemed intended more to isolate the accused than defend him.

When pressed about Sokoloff's connection to Penov, Nedkov said the two had not been in touch "in a long time." He insisted Sokoloff had acted "at the behest of no one."

Likewise, Penov, through a written statement he was under pressure to make in Sofia, denied any involvement.

"I am appalled by this act of violence," he wrote. "It is most distressing to me that anyone, let alone a fellow countryman, would do such a thing. I do not know Mr. Sokoloff well, but I pray for his redemption, even as I pray for Pope Francesca's fast and full recovery."

It was a lie, but Penov knew he could get away with it. In fact, he had spoken with Sokoloff, using a burner phone, just before he left Houston for St. Louis.

But there was a code, an unwritten code, which all the boys who lived in his special home in Sofia knew well. The details of their lives there and their future interactions with Penov were "sacred." They could never be disclosed. Penov's boys even took an oath. No one had ever broken the code, and Penov was confident Sokoloff would not be the first.

Of course, that didn't stop journalists from digging in. For a while, headlines about "the Bulgarian connection" took center stage. But as Francesca got stronger and Sokoloff kept mum, these stories began to fade.

But the headlines had served a purpose, a dark purpose. With Pope Benedict gone, it had been unclear who ultraconservatives in the Church would look to for leadership. Many stories about the assassination attempt cast Penov as a new champion of the far right wing of the Church. Some even called him Francesca's "archrival."

"Sometimes a little drama is a good thing," Penov told friends in Sofia.

Chapter 7

Francesca's recovery was steady but slow. Her extensive wounds and surgery took time to heal, and she had to undergo daily physical therapy to help her move, walk and even breathe well again. After a month, she was finally able to walk slowly across her room.

Barnes-Jewish issued periodic updates on her condition, but Francesca herself remained relatively quiet. She was intent on healing, and Michael was protective of her privacy.

Yet the world was intensely interested in this new pope. The Vatican confirmed Francesca intended to continue her world tour once she was able to do so but said little more. Public interest in the tour grew. But in the absence of details from the Vatican, so did speculation about its purpose.

"Where is she going?" one headline read.

"Papal aggrandizement?" read another.

Some Catholics, especially those who listened to clerics like Penov, began to wonder about the intentions of this new pope. The only hint she had given was at her first and only news conference at the Vatican. "This was his great commandment, and I believe it should be our focus," she had said. But what did she mean by that? Was she saying the Church had *not* been following Jesus' teachings these past five years?

Opinions flew, and suspicions grew.

All the while, Francesca remained silent. Part of this was due to her condition. She was still recovering, and her doctors advised her to take it easy.

But part of her silence was due to her own hesitancy to speak out too forcefully, too specifically just yet. In truth, she had not yet charted her course as pope. Where *was* she going? Francesca herself wasn't sure.

She did issue a brief statement thanking everyone for their well wishes and prayers. She also permitted a photograph once she was able to sit up in bed. The image of her, wearing a hospital gown, looking small and wan but smiling, was seen around the world.

The world had grown accustomed to the brusque and omnipresent Benedict. Now the new pope was silent and nearly invisible, and the world was left wondering who she was and in which direction she intended to lead the largest religion on Earth.

★

One morning, Doctor Kaplan, the hospital's chief of cardiology, came to Francesca's room.

"Your Holiness," he said, "we are pleased with the improvement in your condition. But I want to let you know about something we have found since your surgery."

Francesca sat up a bit straighter.

"You have a mild heart arrhythmia. It's not necessarily dangerous, but I wanted to make sure you're aware of it because there is no history of an arrhythmia in your medical file."

"I see," she said.

"Let me ask you. Have you experienced any dizziness, chest pains or shortness of breath lately?"

"No — except for when they told me I was pope."

"That doesn't count," Kaplan said, smiling.

"Is there something I should do about this, doctor?"

"I don't think so. Not right now anyway. But I'd like to inform your physician at the Vatican. He or she may want to consider treatment at some point. At a minimum, they need to be aware."

"By all means," she said.

After Kaplan left, Michael, who had been sitting in the corner of the room, said, "You need to take this seriously, Jess. You know what happened—"

"I know," she said. "I will."

★

During the second month of her recovery, Francesca began venturing out into the hallway and visiting patients in their rooms, even bringing them Communion.

This is what she lived for, connecting with people, helping people. Seeing the light in the eyes of the other patients lifted her spirits and began to make her feel whole again.

By the end of the third month, Francesca's doctors had seen enough progress and stability to consider her release. Her wounds had either healed or were healing nicely, and she no longer needed antibiotics, as the risk of infection had passed.

Her release imminent, Francesca engaged the Curial administrators on the plan to resume her world tour. The Vatican press office then announced she would do one more event in St. Louis, a town hall meeting on the campus of St. Louis University. From there, she would fly to Los Angeles before heading to Mexico City.

The announcement revived interest in Francesca's "listening tour." Speculation about her intentions for the Church had never subsided, though. Much of it was driven by Penov.

He had been reaching out to his fellow conservative prelates, high-ranking members of the clergy, men who had also been loyal supporters of Pope Benedict XVII, some of them appointed by him. Like Penov, they were suspicious of progressives. They saw them as a threat to the authority of the Church and the power which they, as bishops, enjoyed for themselves.

To these men, the Church was an empire made up of fiefdoms, and they were the lords of those fiefdoms. After decades of liberalism, which had dispersed power among the people, Benedict had managed to reconsolidate it, and now that power was at risk.

"She's a one-worlder," Penov told these men. "Her intentions may sound noble, but she is hopelessly misguided, and we must stand against her."

Appointing conservative bishops and cardinals had been a priority for Benedict. In only five years, he had reversed the movement toward progressive leaders which had been led by his two predecessors over nearly 40 years. Now these conservative leaders sowed doubt about Francesca's intentions among the legions of priests who reported to them as well as the lay power brokers and influencers who made things happen and shaped public opinion.

It wasn't surprising, then, that questions about Francesca's intentions for the Church began to outweigh the excitement and interest in her world tour. She herself, though, was unaware until Father John brought it to her attention.

"News organizations have been running polls about you," he told her.

"And what do they say?"

"Well, overall they say most people are uncertain about your vision for the Church. Many feel the Church is in decline and that you won't be able to save it. There is growing skepticism, even cynicism, out there."

"Well, then, it's time to resume my tour," she said. "I need to rebuild people's confidence."

"A few weeks ago, I would have agreed with you," Father John said. "But now I'm not so sure."

"What do you mean?"

"Jessica, the Church hasn't had a leader the people really trusted in years. And now here you are, in St. Louis, where you've been out of sight for almost three months, and you're about to take off again. I know that listening to people is important to you. But right now, you're an absent leader, and Catholics are desperate for leadership."

"What are you suggesting?"

"I think you need to return to Rome."

"Return to Rome?"

"Yes. You've got a great vision for the Church, but you've got no plan. Stop putting it off. Lead. Stop acting like a politician."

She sighed, thinking about the implications.

★

A few days later, Francesca and Michael left St. Louis on Shepherd One. After a brief stop in New York, they landed in Rome the following morning.

Francesca had called a news conference for noon in the same room at the Vatican where she'd held her first news conference as pope three months earlier.

It was the first time she would be appearing live in public since her fateful Mass in Forest Park. The world was eager to see her again and finally learn more about her intentions.

The Vatican press office had said Francesca would be announcing "a new direction." But what did this mean? There was even some speculation that she might step down. Was she still up to the task?

Her news conference would be broadcast live around the world. The room was packed with reporters and videographers.

Precisely at noon, wearing her white pantsuit, Francesca once again stepped up on the wooden platform and looked out from behind the podium. She looked thin but strong and wore an easy smile. This time, she had no materials, not even an index card.

"Good afternoon," she said. "First, I want to thank everyone for their prayers and well wishes during my recovery. I want to express special thanks to the doctors in St. Louis who saved my life, the nurses who cared for me so well and all the medical professionals at Barnes-Jewish Hospital who helped bring me back to good health. I had a temporary setback. But I'm feeling fine now, and I'm eager to begin anew.

"As you know, I had planned to travel the world to share my vision for the Church and listen to my fellow Catholics. I still hope to do this one day. But I've decided that's not what the Church needs most right now."

Every reporter paid even closer attention.

"I believe the Church needs a rebirth," Francesca continued. "In recent days, it's become clear to me that we not only need to rededicate ourselves to following the teachings of Jesus. We need a bold new plan for how we're going to do that together. And so I've decided to convene Vatican III."

A loud murmur rippled through the room.

"For only the third time in our Church's history, we will undertake a major intervention in order to clarify the purpose and role of the Church in the world, to renew ourselves spiritually and to come together as one people under God.

"The only other Vatican Council in the modern age happened nearly a century ago. We'll have to figure out what Vatican

III looks like, but Pope John XXIII left us a pretty good blueprint. Vatican II consisted of four sessions, which took place over three years. I envision Vatican III consisting of three sessions. I think we can conduct these sessions in two years, maybe even 18 months. Today we can bring people together virtually, and our need to set a new course for the Church may be even greater and more urgent than it was a century ago."

She paused and looked around the room. Everyone was silent, looking at her, waiting to hear more.

"In a way, I am just beginning my papacy. Just before I was shot in St. Louis, I said Jesus is speaking to us. He came for all of us, and he is calling all of us to follow him. I am certain of that. But *how* we follow him, as one people, is up to us. That will be the focus of Vatican III. It is sacred work, and I ask for your prayers as we enter into it together.

"Now, I'll be happy to take your questions."

PART 2

Chapter 8

June 2001

"Jessie, are you ready?" Mary Hanks called to her daughter upstairs.

"I'll be right down, Mom!"

Like every kid, Jessica Hanks loved summertime. Summer days were like chocolate sundaes. But for six-year-old Jessica, this particular summer day was extra special because she would get to spend it with her mother.

Sitting on the floor of her bedroom, she fumbled with her shoe laces. Her fingers were shaking. Her whole body was buzzing with excitement.

"Now you boys mind your father today," Mary Hanks said.

Her two sons, both older than Jessica, sat at the kitchen table, eating bowls of cereal with their father. Neither of them looked up.

"Boys, your mother is talking to you," David Hanks said.

"Okay, Mom," said the older boy.

"Okay," said the younger.

Jessica skipped through the kitchen doorway. She was wearing a purple T-shirt, blue jeans and pink tennis shoes. She was tiny with short brown hair and sparkling blue eyes.

"Would you like some breakfast, Jessie?" her father asked.

"No, thanks. I already ate."

He smiled.

"You're an early riser, even on Saturday."

"I couldn't sleep."

"Well," her father said, "you two have a good time today. You're doing God's work."

Doing God's work. It wasn't the first time Jessica had heard those words. She wasn't sure what they meant, but they made her feel good inside.

"Ready?" her mother said.

"Ready," said Jessica, taking her hand.

★

Jessica had heard her mother talk about working in a food pantry many times. She knew it was where poor people went, but she wasn't sure what happened there. She wondered if it was like the pantry in her kitchen.

They hadn't driven very far when her mother pointed to an old, red-brick building as they coasted past it.

"There it is," she said.

"That was it?"

"Yep. The Well of Life."

"It looks like a house."

"It used to be. They made it into a food pantry a few years ago."

"That's a big food pantry!" Jessica said, still imagining the pantry in her kitchen.

"Yes, it is. We're lucky to have all that space."

"Where are we going?" Jessica said as they turned the corner.

"I'm going to park on a side street. I don't want to block the front door. That's where people park to get their food."

Mary Hanks parked her SUV. Jessica unbuckled herself from her booster seat, and her mother held her hand as she climbed out. They held hands walking down the uneven, crumbling sidewalk past a row of narrow, wooden houses.

Jessica noticed how little space there was between the houses and how the shallow front yards were mainly dirt and weeds. There was hardly any grass, and there were no flowers anywhere. This is nothing like my neighborhood, Jessica thought.

As they walked by a pale yellow house, a dog inside started barking loudly. Jessica squeezed her mother's hand. They walked faster.

When they reached the food pantry, they went around to the back. Mary Hanks unlocked the door and pulled it open, and Jessica followed her inside.

Cardboard boxes were stacked high and wide. There were no interior walls. Only boxes, with a gap through the middle.

"This is the storage room," her mother said. "Let's go out front."

Jessica followed her mother through the gap. On the other side was a large room. On one end was a kitchen. On the other, a wall with two interior doors, which were closed. Half a dozen long tables, with benches, took up the space in the middle.

"Good morning, Mary," said an older woman standing at the sink.

"Good morning, Claire. This is my daughter, Jessie."

"Hello, Jessie," the woman said. "I've heard wonderful things about you."

Jessica smiled and looked up at her mother.

"Well, she's a pretty special little girl," her mother said. "She's even giving up her Saturday to help us out."

"Good for you," Claire said. "I'm glad you're here."

Mary explained to her daughter what they would be doing: getting food ready in the kitchen and serving it to people who would come in throughout the day for a meal or to pick up food or both.

Soon, two men joined them. Mary introduced them. The older one was named Jim. The younger one, a teenager, was named Matt.

"I see you have your mother's good looks," Jim said.

"Thank you," said Jessie, smiling up at her mother.

They all went over their roles for the day. Jim and Matt would unpack and box up food. Claire would cook and clean. Mary and Jessica would put food on plates and bowls and drinks in cups and serve them to guests. Jessica liked how they called people "guests."

The place opened at 9:00. To get ready, Jessica helped her mother set out plates, bowls, cups and silverware on the counter. Jessica felt like they were getting ready for a party.

The first guests were a young family of four. Jessica was surprised. She was expecting homeless people. She had envisioned old men in ragged clothes.

The children, a boy and a girl, were about her age. They wore jeans and T-shirts, which looked clean and in good shape.

"Good morning," Mary said with a smile.

"Good morning," the young mother said.

"How can we help you today?"

"We were hoping for a hot breakfast."

Jessica noticed the father lowered his head as his wife spoke.

"Of course," Claire said from the kitchen. "What would you like?"

They ordered scrambled eggs, toast, cereal and orange juice. The father also asked for a cup of coffee.

Jessica poured orange juice into four glasses. Her mother poured coffee into a plastic mug.

"What kind of cereal would you like?" Jessica asked the little girl.

"Do you have Frosted Flakes?"

"Yes," Jessica said, reaching for the box.

Jessica filled the girl's bowl, then the bowls of the others with cereals of their choice.

"Why don't you have a seat?" Mary said. "We'll bring your eggs and toast over when they're ready."

As the family made its way to a table, Jessica's mother patted her daughter on the back and said, "You're doing great, Jessie."

"Thanks, Mom."

As she helped her mother butter toast, other guests came in. Some were indeed older men in shabby clothes, but there were other families too. Some were there to pick up food. But most ordered something to eat, then took food with them as well. Serving food kept Mary and Jessica busy until early afternoon.

Finally, there was a lull.

"Let's take a break for lunch," her mother said.

They fixed themselves some peanut butter and jelly sandwiches and took them over to a table. A family of five was sitting there.

"May we join you?" Mary said.

"Of course," the mother said.

Jessie sat down next to a girl who was about her age.

Over lunch, Mary and Jessica learned that the father of this family had lost his job about a year ago. Until then, they had lived near the Hanks. Jessica thought the girl looked familiar. Now they were renting a place just down the street. Jessica wondered if they had grass in their yard.

Over the balance of the afternoon, most guests came in to pick up food. Only a handful, mainly men who were alone, ordered food to eat there. When they did, Mary and Jessica joined them. Mary asked about them, and most of the men seemed happy to talk.

At 5:00, the crew of volunteers straightened things up and got everything ready for morning. Claire, Jim and Matt all shook Jessica's hand when they said goodbye. She was not used to grown-ups shaking her hand. It made it her feel special.

On the way home, Mary said, "Well, what did you think?"

"I think there are a lot of hungry people in our town."

"More than you thought?"

"Yeah. And I guess I didn't expect to eat with them."

"Well," her mother said with a smile, "that's the best part. Sometimes people feel alone. They need more than food. Sometimes they need someone to talk to. And when you can be there for them, well, I think that's what Jesus would do."

Jessie thought about that. To her, Jesus had always been a character in a book in school or a name she recited in church, a bearded man with long hair who lived long ago and far away. She had never thought about him being in a food pantry in Springfield.

"Mom, didn't you think that one man, this afternoon, looked like Jesus?"

"Jessie," she said, "that *was* Jesus."

Chapter 9

Her father had explained the Lake of the Ozarks was actually a reservoir, created by impounding the Osage River. But to Jessica, it was just a big lake. More important, it meant summer vacation.

The drive there from Springfield took less than an hour and a half. But for Jessica, it seemed like an eternity. That was partly because she had to sit between her brothers in the back seat. They always managed to claim "window seat" first.

But the trip seemed long mainly because she couldn't wait to get there. To Jessica, going to "the lake" every summer meant living in a big, beautiful house, cruising around in a pontoon boat, roasting marshmallows by the campfire at night and, best of all, spending time with her dad.

Like many men and women climbing the corporate ladder, David Hanks spent more time at work than he wanted. He knew he was shortchanging his family, and he tried hard to spend less time at work. But for the most part, he failed.

Except for two weeks every summer. That's when he was able to unplug, when his family finally came first.

When Jessica was eight, David took his family to the lake in early July. It was the first time they would be there to celebrate the Fourth.

That year, the holiday fell on a Thursday, which meant the celebration would last all weekend. Every day, there were parties on and around the lake. Every night, there were fireworks. David took his family out on the pontoon boat each night to watch the colorful light show. One night, Jessica lay on a cushioned bench on the boat and fell asleep looking skyward, her hands still tucked behind her head.

When they got back and docked, David scooped her up and carried his little girl to bed.

★

Maybe it was because his sons played sports and Jessica didn't that David spent more time with the boys. Or maybe it was simply because he knew Jessica was being very well taken care of by Mary.

But he loved his daughter beyond words, and it made his heart ache not to have more time for her. Now the prospect of spending the day with her filled his heart with joy.

David Hanks was the head buyer for Bass Pro Shops, which was based in Springfield. He had interned there during college and worked there since he graduated, more than 20 years earlier.

He'd grown up in St. Louis. He was a city boy. Books, TV, video games — these were his world. The closest he got to nature was playing baseball.

His advisor in college told him it would be a good idea to do at least one internship, but he kept putting it off. Finally, in the late spring of his junior year, David decided he would go for it.

By then, Bass Pro Shops was the only employer in the area still offering a summer internship. It was in purchasing. He applied.

When the interviewer asked about his experience outdoors and he answered honestly, David figured it was all over. He was shocked to get a call the next day offering him the position. He gladly accepted.

For him, that internship changed everything. That summer, one of the Bass Pro executives took all the interns to Lake of the Ozarks one weekend. It was the first time David had ever been in a boat, ever fished or hiked, ever slept in a tent, ever cooked over a fire. He fell in love with all of it.

It was also an opportunity for him to get acquainted with the products he'd been buying for Bass Pro. Now fishing rods, backpacks and hiking boots weren't just images on his computer screen. They were real, and he began to understand how important they were to enjoying the outdoors.

That weekend, David began to feel a connection with nature and to think about the creative force behind it. For the first time, he saw himself as part of creation.

He had grown up Catholic but never felt comfortable in church or considered himself "religious." Now, as he walked in the woods, he felt part of something sacred.

After that weekend, he began to spend time outdoors, and he knew he had to go to work for Bass Pro so he could help others experience the outdoors too.

And after that weekend, David Hanks began to know God.

★

Jessica was sitting in an oversized armchair in the family room of their vacation home, looking out at the lake, when her father came downstairs.

"Good morning, Jess," he said. "You're up early."

"I was too excited to sleep."

Her sweet smile warmed his heart.

"Have you had breakfast?"

"Yes. I had a bowl of cereal."

"Let me grab some coffee. Then we'll get going."

Mary had prepared a lunch for them. Peanut butter and jelly sandwiches, apples, cheese sticks, granola bars, juice boxes, water bottles — they were all waiting in paper bags in the refrigerator. Together, Jessica and David carefully stowed them in his backpack.

They left through the front door. As they headed down a stone walkway to their car, Jessica slipped her hand into his, and he felt his heart melt.

★

They had been hiking for about an hour, up and down gently sloping trails, winding along the water and deep into the woods.

"Should we take a little break?" he said.

"Sure."

He spotted a fallen tree just off the trail.

"Let's sit here," he said, taking her hand as they stepped through a patch of Mayapples.

It was an oak tree, splintered at the base. It stretched at least 50 feet along the forest floor. David found a flat spot on the trunk. He picked his daughter up and gently lowered her onto it. Then he pulled off his pack, swung his leg over and sat down facing her.

"Hungry?" he said.

"Yes — and thirsty."

He pulled their lunch bags out of his pack.

"Apple or fruit punch?"

"Apple, please."

"Here you go."

"Thank you."

Then he reached in and pulled out two granola bars.

"Chocolate chip?"

"Yes, please."

He was impressed by her manners. Mary's done such a good job, he thought.

David had spent precious little time alone with his daughter lately. Sitting a few feet away from her, face to face, he was surprised to see how her looks were changing. Her cheek bones were more pronounced. She had Mary's thin nose, Mary's slender face, Mary's brown hair.

But she had his blue eyes. He was struck by just how similar their eyes were — a translucent shade of bright blue. Looking into his daughter's eyes, David felt as though he were looking into his own eyes.

They made small talk, as fathers and daughters sometimes do. He asked about school, what her favorite subjects were. Social studies and religion, she said.

She asked him whether he used to walk in the woods with his father when he was a boy.

"No," he said. "Grandpa was too busy, and I really wasn't that interested in nature."

"But you love it now."

"Yes, I do."

"What changed you, Dad?"

He had never told his children about his experience in the woods during his internship in college. But since Jessica asked, he went ahead and told her everything.

She sat spellbound. Then she said, "Is that why you don't go to Mass with us?"

"That's part of it. The prayers, the songs, even the priests — they don't do much for me. But beyond that, that's not where I find God."

"Where do you find him?"

"I find him in the world, Jess," he said. "God lives in the world. He lives here in the forest. He lives in people like Mom, who feed his children. He lives in you and me. God is in the world, Jess. He is all around us."

"I love you, Dad," she said.

"I love you too, Jess," he said, his eyes welling with tears.

He wiped his eyes. She had never seen her father cry. To her, he had always been a rock. He even felt a little distant. Now, though, she felt so close to him.

Jessica never mentioned his tears or their conversation that day to anyone, not even her mother. But for the rest of her life, his words about God living in the world would echo in her mind.

Chapter 10

Jessica stole away to the deep woods behind her house whenever she could. She was drawn to the woods, especially after her hike on vacation with her father.

She liked to sit on a big, flat rock overlooking a stream and watch the water fall into a still pool below. Sometimes when she was quiet, birds would glide down to the edge of the pool. She liked to watch them dip their beaks in the water and throw their heads back to swallow it.

Birds had always fascinated her. They seemed so free and happy, always singing. She imagined that, if she were an animal, she would be a bird.

One warm spring afternoon when she was nine, Jessica was exploring a new trail in the woods when she heard a sound up ahead. She stopped, thinking it might be a squirrel or a deer.

Then she heard the soft crunch of footsteps, human footsteps. She froze, unsure what to do. Then everything was still. I must have been hearing things, she thought.

She decided to keep going. Just ahead, the trail veered to the right. As she made the turn, she looked up and saw someone on the trail about 20 feet away. It was a man. His back was to her. He was walking ahead of her.

Again, Jessica froze. Her parents had taught her to steer clear of strangers. She was afraid. She felt like running.

But then the man turned around, and she looked at his face. He had a kind look about him. His skin was dark, his eyes were brown and he was smiling. He had long, black hair and a beard. He was wearing a light brown robe and sandals. She had never seen this man before, yet he seemed so familiar.

She felt her heart pounding in her ears. She was about to turn around when the man said, "Peace be with you."

His voice was warm and gentle. It calmed her. She caught her breath and felt her heartbeat slowing. She no longer felt afraid.

"Who are you?" she said.

He smiled.

"You know me."

"Why are you here?"

"Because I love you, Jessica."

She wondered how he knew her, how he knew her name.

He began to turn around. She did not want him to leave.

"Where are you going?" she said.

"Follow me," he said, looking back at her as he stepped forward.

She hesitated. She knew she should not be going with a stranger. But there was something so very appealing about this man, and she felt an urge to follow him.

But just as she took a step, he began to vanish. She took another step, and he was gone.

She stood there for a moment, wondering what had just happened, if maybe the whole thing had been a dream. She had had wild dreams at night. They always frightened her, but now she was filled with a sense of peace.

She stood there a little longer, hoping the man might come back, might materialize again. When he didn't, she turned around and walked back home.

On the way, she thought about the man she had seen. In her mind, she could hear him saying, "Because I love you, Jessica." She had always felt loved, but now she felt loved in a new way. It was not so much a feeling as it was discovering some new reality.

Over dinner that evening, Jessica said nothing about her encounter in the woods. She knew telling her parents would only upset them, and she was still trying to figure it out herself.

In the coming days and weeks, Jessica turned the image of the man over and played back his words in her mind countless times. She wondered what he was doing there, how he knew her and why he looked so familiar. She wondered where he was going and why he wanted her to follow him. She wondered why he had disappeared and whether he would ever appear to her again.

She hoped he would.

Chapter 11

"I just know you're going to win," Jessica's friend Maddie said.

"Me too," said her friend Hannah. "Everybody's going to vote for you."

"I hope you're right," Jessica said.

"You'll be a great president," Maddie said.

Jessica smiled. She was naturally modest, but she knew she was well liked. Even the pretty girls liked her because, with a face so plain, they didn't see her as a threat. The boys liked her too because, all of a sudden, she'd grown breasts.

But the other kids liked Jessica long before she had boobs. She was kind to everyone. At lunch, she shared her food. When one of her classmates was sick, she would send an email with well wishes. She never had a harsh word for anyone and never raised her voice. She was like a saint — a petite, blue-eyed, 12-year-old saint with boobs.

She was also a news junkie. She caught the news online or on TV every day. She had developed a keen interest in politics too. Over breakfast one morning, she was browsing headlines and came across a story that horrified her — about the US President defending the practice of waterboarding Muslim prisoners.

"That's so awful," Jessica said. "It's just wrong."

"I agree," her mother said. "Maybe you should run for President one day."

"Maybe I will."

She soon got her chance — to run for class president, that is. Her friends urged her to run, and she decided to go for it without giving it much thought. She supposed it might be fun to be president of her seventh grade class. As far as what she'd actually *do* as president, she figured she'd have the whole summer to figure that out.

Her only competitor was Ethan Stone. He was handsome and athletic, popular with boys and girls alike. Everyone knew Ethan was not very smart. Some called him slow. But like Jessica, he was good to everyone. He was even known to defend the smaller kids on the playground. So his campaign theme, "Stand Up to Bullying," seemed genuine.

Jessica didn't have a campaign theme. She saw no need. Everyone liked her. Everyone knew she was smart. Surely, she thought, that would be enough to win.

But she lost — and by a lot. Jessica congratulated Ethan, and she smiled as classmates offered words of consolation. But inside, she was dying. She felt humiliated. She cried when she got home that afternoon, telling her mother what had happened.

"Oh, honey," she said, embracing her. "It's okay. There'll be more elections."

"No, there won't. I'm not running for anything ever again!"

She ran up to her room, slammed her door and threw herself on her bed.

She was lying there, texting friends, when her father got home. He came upstairs and knocked on her door.

"May I come in?"

"Yeah."

"Mom told me what happened," he said, sitting down at her desk.

"Yeah. It sucks."

"Yeah, it does."

"It's not fair, Dad."

"What's not fair, Jess?"

"It's not fair that Ethan won."

"Why?"

"Because I would have made a much better president."

"I'm sure you would have made a terrific class president," he said. "But let me ask you something. Why do you feel you would have made a *better* president than Ethan?"

She sat up. Her face was red.

"You know!"

"No, Jess. I don't. Why?"

"Because, well, he's slow."

"Slow? You mean he's not very smart?"

"Yeah, Dad. He's not very smart."

"Well, then, why do you think he won?"

"Because he made that stupid promise."

"What promise?"

"To stand up against bullies."

"I see. And what did you promise?"

"I didn't promise anything."

"Why?"

"I didn't need to. Everybody knows me. Everybody likes me."

"Everybody loves you, Jess. But when it comes to politics, that's not enough. People need to know what you stand for."

She glared at him.

"Jess, do you know what a platform is? I mean in politics."

"No."

"A platform iswhat you say you stand for. When you're running for something, it's important to tell people what you stand for."

"But to stand up to bullying? I mean, who's *not* for that?"

"That might be true, but Ethan called it out. He ran on it, and that obviously meant something to your classmates. I'd say that's pretty smart."

Jessica knew he was right. Now she was upset with herself. Her eyes filled with tears.

Her father got up, sat down next to her on her bed and put his arms around her.

"It's okay, Jess," he said. "You'll win next time, I know."

"Thanks, Dad," she said, giving him a hug and wiping her eyes.

He got up and walked to the door.

"Mom's making a chicken casserole tonight. Your favorite."

"Thanks, Dad. I'll be down in a minute."

He closed the door. Jessica drew her knees up, wrapped her arms around them and put her head back against her padded headboard.

She closed her eyes and thought about what her father had said. A platform, she thought. Next time, I'll have a platform.

Chapter 12

As a new freshman at Springfield Catholic High School, Jessica sat in religion class and listened to her teacher, Mr. Mulcahey.

"Today we're going to begin to learn about the saints," he said. "Not just any saints, but mystics. Does anyone know what a mystic is?"

No hands went up.

"A mystic," Mulcahey said, "is someone who has an experience of union with The One. The One may be God. It may be Mother Earth. It may be the cosmos."

The students looked confused, but Jessica thought of the man she'd seen in the woods near her house five years earlier. She thought of him often.

Since then, she had hiked in the woods many times, always hoping to see him again. She wanted to talk with him. She wanted to know him. She wanted to know how he knew her.

Jessica still hadn't mentioned her vision to anyone. She was afraid no one would understand. Especially now, as a self-conscious teenager, she was afraid of what people might think of her.

But she had prayed that her vision would eventually make sense.

"Over the next 10 weeks, we're going to learn about the lives of 10 mystics," Mulcahey said. "The first one will be St. Francis of Assisi."

To Jessica, St. Francis was a concrete statue in her mother's flower garden. She knew nothing of the real man.

Mulcahey proceeded to tell the story of the little man from Assisi. Jessica was enthralled.

When he got to the part where Francis heard Jesus speaking to him from the cross in the chapel of San Damiano, she thought of the man who had spoken to her in the woods.

In an instant, Jessica realized it was Jesus who had appeared to her. It was Jesus who had told her to follow him.

Mulcahey continued telling the story of St. Francis. But Jessica couldn't hear him. She could hear only the voice of a man she had once heard in a woods which now seemed to come from within.

Chapter 13

"I think you should go for it, Jessie," her brother Brandon said.

"Absolutely," said her other brother Zack. "You'll win."

"No question," said her mother.

"You'll need a platform," her dad said, giving her a knowing smile.

Jessica loved Easter. This Easter, she loved having her brothers home from college and the whole family together again. She had loved sitting next to her father in church that morning, and now she was loving their big brunch at home.

And she was loving her family's positive reaction to the idea of her running for senior class president.

"I've been thinking about that, Dad," she said. "I've been thinking about a platform of serving others."

"Serving others, huh?" he said. "What does that mean?"

"Good question," she said. "I've given that a lot of thought. 'Serving others' can't be just a warm and fuzzy idea or a campaign slogan. It has to be real. So I'm going to give my classmates three ways they can get involved in the community."

She went on to describe programs to feed the hungry, renovate houses and visit the sick and elderly.

"Sounds great," her father said. "Do you think your classmates will go for it?"

"I know they will."

"You do?" said her mother.

"Yes," Jessica said. "I've asked around. A lot of kids really like it. They feel we've become selfish. They like the idea of serving others but aren't sure how to get involved."

"We're doing that at SLU," Zack said, referring to St. Louis University, where he was a sophomore. "Even I'm getting involved."

"That's big," Brandon said. "Must be a way to meet girls."

"Well, there *are* a lot of girls involved," Zack said with a grin.

"Jess, I'm impressed," her dad said. "Sounds like you've really done your homework and you've got a strong platform and a great plan. I'm proud of you."

"You guys want to hear my kick-off speech?" she said.

"Do we have a choice?" Brandon said. "Just kidding. We'd love to hear it, Jessie."

★

What Jessica had heard by asking around proved true. The idea of serving others, simple as it was, resonated with her classmates. She won the election handily, beating four other contenders.

Being a political junkie, Jessica had read Doris Kearns Goodwin's *Team of Rivals*, about how Lincoln reached out to his political adversaries and turned them into allies. She thought she'd try to do the same with the four classmates she beat.

She met with each of them and asked if they would own a specific part of the plan to serve others in the community. All four said yes. In fact, they seemed pleased to be asked.

The five of them met once a week that spring and once a month that summer. By the time school started in the fall, Jessica and her "team of rivals" were signing up seniors to volunteer to work with a dozen different programs in Springfield.

Seeing and hearing about what the seniors were doing, some juniors and even sophomores began asking how they could get involved too. "Serving others" had become cool.

By the end of that school year, Springfield Catholic High School had become a *tour de force* in the community, with Jessica as its spirited leader. There was even a front-page feature about her in the *News-Leader*, Springfield's daily newspaper. She was careful to give credit to her four "co-captains" and insisted on including them in the photo.

In a special presentation before the entire student body, the Mayor of Springfield gave Jessica the key to the city. She accepted it alongside her beaming co-captains.

★

One evening, about a week before graduation, Jessica was stretched out on the sofa in her family room, studying for a final exam. Her dad came in from the kitchen.

"Hey, Dad."

"Hey, Jess."

He sat down in his recliner, slipped on his reading glasses and opened the newspaper.

"You know I've still got people at work coming up to me and mentioning that story about you in this paper," he said. "You've kind of made me a celebrity at the office."

"Well, you know the back story," she said.

He looked over and shook his head.

"You started it," she said.

"How?"

"You told me I needed a platform."

"I did? When?"

"Six years ago. Remember?"

"Oh, yeah."

"That was a low point for me, Dad. I was crushed when I lost that election. But if I hadn't lost, you might never have told me about having a platform, and I might have missed out on one of the most important things I've ever learned."

"That's very kind, Jess, but it was all you."

He went back to reading his newspaper, unaware that she was staring at him, feeling deeply grateful that he was her father. She hoped that she might be lucky enough to find a man like him one day who would believe in her and love her enough to always tell her the truth.

Chapter 14

Helping people in the community and her abiding vision of Jesus deepened Jessica's spirit. At the same time, her experience as class president fueled her interest in politics.

Both religion and politics lit her up. For Jessica, picking a college which embraced and embodied both was easy. It was SLU, a small, Jesuit college in downtown St. Louis.

Zack had had a great experience there. He'd told Jessica about the Jesuit philosophy of "being a person for others" and all the ways SLU students were involved in the community. After touring the campus, Jessica knew this was where she belonged.

Picking a major was much harder. Theology or political science? Both felt right to her.

As high-energy and hard-working as Jessica was, she wasn't particularly ambitious. She didn't think much about a career per se, but she wanted to make sure whatever major she picked would be useful — not for advancing her career, but for helping the world in some way.

One thing Jessica had learned about herself is that she had a lot of capacity. So when she was accepted by SLU, she declared majors in both theology and political science.

★

One Saturday in mid-August, David and Mary Hanks drove Jessica three and a half hours from Springfield to St. Louis and helped her move her stuff into Marguerite Hall.

When they were finished, they hugged their daughter and said goodbye. Mary and Jessica were tearful. David was stoic.

But once they drove away and rounded the corner, David pulled into a parking space, put his head in his hands and cried like a baby.

★

"Welcome to introduction to theology," said Father John Dumont, a tall, thin, pleasant-looking man.

Jessica guessed he was about 50.

"We're all meeting each other for the first time today. So before I go over our syllabus, why don't we get to know each other a little bit?"

He told everyone to form a circle with their desks, then go around and introduce themselves.

"Tell us your name, where you're from, a little about yourself and one thing you hope to get out of this class," he said.

Father John led off. He grew up in Iowa, became a priest at 26 and had been teaching theology at SLU for a decade.

"My purpose is to serve God," he said. "That's why I'm here."

Jessica was struck by the simplicity of that statement and the conviction with which he expressed it. She admired that.

As for the class, he quoted a poet and said he hoped to "give not of my wisdom but rather of my faith and my lovingness."

Jessica smiled. She liked this man already.

When it was her turn, Jessica briefly introduced herself. Several students smiled when she mentioned her double major. One said, "Don't those cancel each other out?"

Everyone laughed.

Father John stood up.

"Mr. —" he said.

"Sullivan. Eric Sullivan."

"Thank you, Eric," Father John said. "We'll go over the rules of the road for this class in a few minutes, but let me share two of them now. We always show everyone respect, and we don't talk out of turn."

"Yes, Father."

"Please," the priest said, turning to Jessica, "tell us what you hope to get out of this class."

"I want to understand the value, if any, of theology."

He gave her a quizzical look.

"The value of theology?" he said.

"Yes."

"Well, Jessica, I must say I find that a little curious coming from someone who has declared theology as her major."

"I understand."

"Well, you must think it has *some* value."

"I don't know."

"I'm sure you know that theology is the study of God," he said. "How can studying God *not* have some value?"

"Maybe it does. But I'm not interested in studying God."

"You're not?"

"No," she said. "I want to learn how to follow Jesus, how to bring God to life in the world."

"I see," said Father John. "I think you're talking more about religion than theology."

"Maybe so," she said. "And then when I learn about that, I want to figure out how to put it together with politics."

Father John laughed. Some of the students laughed too. Jessica looked taken aback.

"Jessica," he said, stepping over to her, "I'm not laughing at you. I'm laughing with delight! I'm delighted that is what you hope to get out of this class because I share your interest, and I'm looking forward to learning with you."

"Thank you, Father," she said, feeling relieved.

As class was adjourning, Father John asked Jessica if she could stay for a moment. She wondered if he was upset.

He was sitting on a table in the front of the room. She came up to him.

"Jessica, I'm very intrigued by what you said about what you hope to get out of this class," he said. "I've been teaching this course for 10 years, and no one has ever said anything quite like that."

"I hope that's a good thing," she said with a smile.

"It's a very good thing. I'd love to learn more about what you mean about bringing God to life in the world. Would you be open to having coffee with me in the student center sometime?"

"I'd love to," she said.

★

Over the next four years, Jessica and Father John had coffee countless times. Religion and politics were frequent topics.

But when it came to bringing God to life in the world, Jessica did much more than talk. She volunteered in soup kitchens and homeless shelters in the inner city, within blocks from SLU.

By the end of her freshman year, Jessica was recruiting other students to join her in this work. As a sophomore, she founded a group called Students Fighting Poverty. These students worked in soup kitchens and food pantries. On cold days, they sought out homeless people and brought them to shelters.

Students Fighting Poverty became one of the most popular student groups at SLU. Organizing it and working alongside her fellow students in the community became Jessica's main focus outside the classroom. It was her way of bringing God to life in the world.

By the time she was a senior, Jessica was thrilled about the positive impact Students Fighting Poverty was having in the inner city. She also loved seeing how the experience made her fellow students think more about others, not just themselves. Working with the poor grounded them. It deepened them.

In a real way, leading the group was a blend of politics and religion. Jessica loved both.

This was great for Students Fighting Poverty, which would be her legacy at SLU. But as graduation approached, for Jessica, which path to take, politics or religion, was still an open question.

Chapter 15

"What do you think I should do, Dad?"

"Do you mean right now or longer term?"

"Either."

Jessica had just graduated and moved back in with her parents. It was a temporary arrangement, but she was feeling uneasy. Not that she didn't feel welcome and even comfortable. Her mother did her laundry, even cooked for her, and that evening her father had come home early for dinner. But after living away for four years, as much as she loved that house, it just didn't feel like her place anymore.

"Are you leaning more toward politics or religion?" her father said.

"That's my dilemma, Dad. I'm kind of on the fence."

"I told her she can work with me at the food pantry while she figures it out," her mother said.

"But I've done that, Mom," Jessica said. "I mean I know it's important, but I want to try something new."

"Let me make a suggestion," her father said. "Don't feel obliged to make a big choice just yet. Take some pressure off yourself. Go ahead and try something new. Experiment. Maybe that will help you decide."

"Like what?"

"Well, I've got some friends at city hall. Why don't I ask if they know of any openings?"

City hall. Of course, she thought. She'd done an internship with a state senator in St. Louis during college but hadn't even thought of pursuing a government job in Springfield.

"Sure," she said. "Go ahead and ask. It can't hurt, I guess."

★

The next day, David Hanks called his friend, Ben Groh, Springfield's city manager. As it turns out, Groh was about to advertise for a new clerk because his longtime clerk was about to announce her retirement.

"I'll be posting the job next week," Groh told him. "If Jessica wants to apply, I'd be happy to consider her. And if she just wants to talk about what it's like to work in government, I'd be happy to grab coffee. Have her call me."

David called Jessica right away and told her about the pending job and Groh's generous offer.

"Jess, you've got to check this out," he said. "At least have coffee with Ben. It'll be a good connection for you. See where it leads."

"Thanks, Dad," she said with a lilt in her voice. "I will."

I'm 22 years old, she thought. I wonder when I'll stop depending on Daddy.

Never, she hoped.

★

A few days later, Jessica met Groh at The Coffee Ethic in downtown Springfield. They had attended the same father-daughter dances when Jessica was a girl, but neither one remembered the other, although he did recall hearing about the work she'd led in the community her senior year in high school.

She guessed Groh was in his mid-50s. He was a plain-looking man with thinning gray hair, a round face and wire frame glasses. Maybe it was because she had just finished a course in twentieth-century American history, but Jessica thought he looked a lot like Harry Truman.

"Did you bring your resume?" Groh said, getting right to the point in Trumanesque style.

"Yes," she said, handing it to him.

He skimmed it. He asked about her internship with Missouri State Senator Nasheed. Jessica had managed a pretty big project for Nasheed. She explained what she'd done and the results. Groh was impressed.

He asked how she had managed that on top of her heavy coursework. Her short answer was "discipline." Now he was even more impressed.

He told her a bit about the job. She asked good questions and took notes. Groh liked what he was seeing already.

"I hope you'll apply," he said. "I think you'd do a great job, and you'd learn a lot about how city government works."

He suggested she take a civil service test, a requirement for all applicants. She took it the following day. She aced it.

The next day, Groh called Jessica to let her know the job was about to be posted. She watched for the post, then applied right away.

Jessica liked Groh. He seemed both sharp and caring. She could see herself working for such a person. She also liked the idea of working in a position that would help her understand the inner workings of city government up close.

But she was a bit put off by the title of clerk. She'd just graduated *summa cum laude* from a well-regarded university.

Many of her former classmates were starting out as managers. Jessica was thinking about vying for a position which some might consider a glorified secretarial job.

She called Father John for his advice.

"Sounds great," he said. "What's the issue?"

"Well," she stammered, "I just wonder if I should aim higher?"

"Aim higher?"

"Yeah. I'd be a clerk. That sounds a lot like a secretary."

"Ah. You think this role is beneath you."

"Well—"

"Jessica, did I ever tell you what my job was when I was in the seminary?"

"No."

"Cleaning bathrooms."

"Cleaning bathrooms?"

"Yeah. In the seminary, we all had a job. Some guys washed dishes. Some guys cut grass or raked leaves. I cleaned bathrooms. It was considered the worst job of all. Everybody had one job each semester. Then you'd get a new job. But after my first semester, I asked to clean bathrooms again."

"You did? Why?"

"I was a bit full of myself in those days. Cleaning bathrooms grounded me. It kept me humble."

"So you think I should go for this job?"

"Yes, I do. In fact, I can't think of a better way to learn how government really works at the local level."

"And stay humble?"

"Yeah," he chuckled. "That too."

★

Jessica was invited to interview. She met with Groh, the retiring clerk, a woman named Debbie Wallace, and the city's HR manager. A few days later, Groh called her.

"We got more than 50 applications and interviewed a dozen people," he said. "You were the clear winner. I'm calling to offer you the job, Jessica. We'd love for you to come work with us."

"I accept," she said. "Thank you."

Jessica was thrilled. She had never had a job with so much responsibility. She thought of it as her first "real job."

She took her parents out to dinner that night to celebrate and thank them for all they had done to enable this moment.

Two weeks later, Jessica started as the new clerk for the city manager of Springfield. Debbie Wallace had been in the job for 30 years. She agreed to stay on for a few weeks to help Jessica learn the ropes. Good thing because there was a lot to learn.

In fact, Jessica had underestimated the complexity of the position. Twenty-six department heads reported to Groh. Helping coordinate his work with each of them was itself a full-time job.

But Groh expected even more of Jessica. As soon as she got her bearings, he had her running intradepartmental projects, leading meetings and writing reports. He hadn't expected these things from Wallace, but he knew Jessica was capable.

She delivered, but it really stretched her. Her days were long. She never slept so well. So much for cleaning bathrooms, she thought.

★

Serving as Groh's clerk gave Jessica a fast and clear-eyed understanding of what city government really does and how it does it.

Soon she realized much of what she'd studied in political science in college was theoretical, politics at a macro level. It was mainly about policy. She'd never really thought much about the politics behind getting roads repaired or rezoning a plot of land.

At first, Jessica thought about these things as trivial and boring. She had no interest in bureaucracy. But the more she learned, the more she began to appreciate the skill involved at the department-head level in getting seemingly simple things done, things that were important to people.

She also began to notice differences among Springfield's department heads, especially with regard to how they approached their work. Some of them acted like owners. Others acted like they were just doing a job. Jessica noticed the "owners" got better results. She began to see that, when it comes to getting things done, personal leadership matters.

Her position also made Jessica visible. Over her first few months on the job, she seemed to be everywhere in the four-story municipal building. She always seemed pleasant, poised and eager to help. People liked working with her.

She made a point of having lunch or coffee with someone new to her every week. It was a piece of advice her father had given her based on his own experience.

"Always network," he said. "You'll get new ideas, and your connections will lead you to interesting new places."

One day, she was having lunch with Jennifer Todd, who was in charge of the city's planning and development department. "Have you ever thought of running for office yourself?" Todd said. "The city could really benefit from a bright, young person like you."

"I've never really thought about it," Jessica said.

"Well, four city council positions will be open next year. Think about it."

Jessica was flattered. After lunch, she got back to work and didn't give the idea much more thought. But that evening, she began imagining what her platform might be, and her heart began to race.

Chapter 16

Within six months, Jessica had changed what people in Ben Groh's sphere expected from his clerk and begun to make a name for herself around city hall.

After her lunch with Jennifer Todd, Jessica began thinking hard about running for city council. The more she thought about it, the more intriguing and appealing the idea became to her.

At the same time, she was self-aware enough to know that, at 23, she might not be taken seriously. In her heart, she was unsure she had what it took to be a city councilwoman.

Once again, she turned to her mentor.

"What do you think?" she asked Father John.

"I think it's a long shot."

"You think I shouldn't do it?"

"I didn't say that. I don't know a lot about politics. But I'd say that, realistically, at 23, with relatively little experience, you're going to need something pretty compelling to persuade people to vote for you."

"Like a big idea?"

"Yeah."

"Well, I've been thinking about that," she said. "Based on what I've seen, I think the city is doing a pretty good job for its residents. But there's one big exception: social services."

"Social services?"

"Yeah. I think Springfield can and should be doing a lot more for people in this area. I think a lot of voters would be surprised to know there's such a big gap between what the city provides and what people need. I think filling that gap could be the focus of my campaign."

"Sounds to me like you're talking about bringing God to life in the world," Father John said.

"Something like that."

"I say go for it."

★

Jessica announced her campaign for an at-large council position on a frigid Saturday morning in January of 2018 at a homeless shelter in downtown Springfield.

"This shelter, the only shelter for the homeless in our city, can currently serve 25 people a night," she said to the small group of reporters, friends and family members gathered. "It's estimated there are 10 times that number of homeless people in our community. The executive director here said she had to turn away dozens of people last night alone. It was 15 degrees last night. Who of us would turn a brother or a sister out into that kind of cold?

"I think we can and must do better. Today I am announcing my candidacy for the at-large city council position here in Springfield next year. The focus of my campaign will be serving others in need. Springfield is doing so many things well, but social services is one area where we have room for major improvement.

"I'm talking about providing food for the hungry, shelter for the homeless, job training, subsidized housing, adoption assistance and mental health services. I'm also talking about lobbying government officials at the county, state and even federal levels to make sure Springfield is getting its fair share of public funds earmarked for social services.

"Over the next year and a half, I aim to raise awareness about what we need to do to improve our support for the most vulnerable among us. I'll be asking for people's ideas and sharing my own ideas. Springfield is a wonderful community. My campaign is about making it an even stronger community for everyone."

There was light applause.

"What are you proposing specifically?" a reporter asked.

"Well, I'd begin by creating of a department dedicated to social services," Jessica said. "Many cities our size have such a department. We need one in order to get a handle on our citizens' most critical needs when it comes to social services and then to develop a specific plan for delivering those services as efficiently as possible. That might sound pretty basic, but it's work we haven't yet done."

"Won't that cost money? Will you have to raise taxes?"

"The city of Springfield enjoys a budget surplus," Jessica said. "I don't think we'll need to raise taxes for this. However, I do think we might need to shift some existing resources."

"You just graduated from college," another reporter said. "What do you say to voters who might be concerned about your lack of experience?"

"I was helping my mom over at the Well of Life food pantry when I was six years old," Jessica said, smiling at her mother. "Now I'm helping the city manager get things done here in Springfield. I believe I can contribute even more to our community as a member of city council, and I'm hoping voters will give me that chance next November."

"The election is almost two years away," the reporter said. "Isn't your announcement a little early?"

Jessica smiled.

"Right now, I have no organization and no money," she said. "I know it's going to take time to build this campaign. I also want to talk with as many voters as I can. I'll still have my day job too, so I'd say I'm going to need every minute of the next 22 months."

★

That she did. Right after she announced her candidacy, Jessica began recruiting volunteers to work on her campaign. They helped with everything from creating a website to lining up meetings with churches, non-profits and county government agencies.

Jessica had to take a lot of these meetings on her lunch hour, after work or on the weekend. On Saturday afternoons, she walked through neighborhoods, knocking on doors and talking with anyone who would talk with her.

When she chose to focus her campaign on improving social services, Jessica knew the need was there, at least on paper. But it was her conversations with people in their homes that showed her just how great that need was.

She was amazed to learn how many Springfield residents were living just above the poverty line. An older woman who invited Jessica into her apartment said she would offer her something to eat but she hadn't been to the store in a while. One mother told her she could afford only one meal a day for herself and her children.

It broke Jessica's heart to hear from people who were clearly struggling with depression and other mental health issues but who had no idea how to get help. There are some things, she thought, some people just can't do for themselves.

She met with groups and talked with people throughout 2018 and into the summer of 2019. She raised money and secured endorsements, including from her old boss, State

Senator Nasheed. But until Labor Day, she kept her campaign low-profile, "listening and learning," as she told her father.

Then the more public phase of her campaign began, including participating in several "meet the candidate" events sponsored by the League of Women Voters.

Jessica thoroughly enjoyed these events. She was a good speaker, and after meeting with so many local residents for the better part of two years, she had gripping stories to share to help make her case for the need for better social services in Springfield. She was earnest and compelling.

Jessica was one of seven contenders for two at-large council positions. One was an incumbent. That fall, a poll by *The Springfield News-Leader* showed Jessica among the top three candidates.

The Sunday before election day, the *News-Leader* endorsed her for one of the at-large council positions.

"That's going to clinch it for you," Groh told her.

He was right. Jessica got the second-most votes for the at-large positions. She'd won.

When the news broke on election night, dozens of Jessica's supporters who had gathered at her "campaign headquarters" — the dining room of the Well of Life food pantry — were ecstatic.

"Thank you," Jessica said amidst cheers. "Thank you all. In a real way, my campaign began right here, 18 years ago, when I was six, helping my mom prepare food for people in our community who were hungry. I want to thank everyone who made this outcome possible tonight. But at the top of that list is my mother, who taught me everything I know about bringing God to life in the world."

★

The morning after the election, Jessica's win made headlines in Springfield.

But by the following morning, another story was making headlines all over the world.

While most Americans were still sleeping, at the Vatican, Pope Francis was announcing his decision to allow women to be ordained permanent deacons in the Church.

It seemed a small step, but Jessica knew it was significant. She called Father John to get his take.

"Francis is a reformer," he said. "He probably wants to allow women to become priests, but he knows he can't do that just yet. Allowing women to become permanent deacons is a stepping stone, not just for women, but for the pope. It's a way for Francis to bring Catholics along with him. He's a visionary, but he's also a pragmatist. The great leaders are both."

About to take on her first big leadership role, Jessica hoped she would be a good leader too.

Chapter 17

When she decided to run for council, Jessica had talked with Ben Groh about her need by law to resign as his clerk if she were to win. Now that she had won, he asked her to work with HR to lead the search for her successor.

"You're leaving big shoes to fill," he told her. "Whoever I hire, I want to make sure you approve."

It was a heady time for Jessica. An exciting new job and a change of scenery too. She could now afford her own place. She found a small loft apartment in downtown Springfield, just a few blocks from the city building. She was grateful to her parents for letting her live with them, but it felt good to finally be out on her own.

Jessica had been talking about a social services department for so long that it almost seemed like a reality. But now she needed to make it happen, and so that become her first order of business as the newest member of council.

She'd given the idea so much thought, and done so much research, that drafting a proposal was easy. Until she got to the resources needed.

At that point, she realized she had no idea how much the programs called for in her plan would actually cost or where the funding would come from. She thought about asking Groh but didn't want to appear to be naive. So she consulted her dad.

"You'll need to do some benchmarking," he said. "Talk with the people who are managing social services in other cities, cities about our size."

Jessica identified 10 cities around the country and called the heads of their social services departments. They told her how much they were spending. But their budgets were all set, so they couldn't really help her figure out where she was going to get the initial funding for Springfield's new department.

One point they all made, though, is how important it is to focus on a few critical areas.

"When budgets get tight, social services usually get cut," one director told her. "Make sure you're focusing on the most important needs in your community. You can't help everybody in everything."

It was good advice. Jessica picked hunger, mental health and job skills training as the initial focus areas for the new department in Springfield. She estimated annual funding for this work, including payroll and benefits for two people, would run about $2 million.

She knew the city didn't have an extra $2 million laying around. She knew she would need to be creative.

Establishing a social services department had been the centerpiece of her campaign. Jessica figured anyone who had cast a vote for her was in favor of this new department. The voters had spoken. She assumed it was now a priority for the city.

The vast majority of the city's budget went to its 26 departments. Jessica thought it was reasonable to expect these existing departments to kick in a small fraction of their budgets to fund the new department, at least initially, until an annual budget could be established.

So she included this in her proposal and scheduled time for a public hearing. She considered running her plan by Groh, but she was eager to move ahead and didn't want her old boss to think she was indecisive.

★

Jessica knew she would face new challenges as a city councilwoman. But she never imagined a pandemic would be one of them.

Covid-19 hit just as Jessica had finished developing her proposal for the new department. At first, no one seemed to know what to do. The US President convened a task force which provided general guidance. But for the most part, the President deferred to governors to decide how best to deal with the pandemic at the state level, and each state took its own approach.

In Missouri, the governor declared a state of emergency and ordered social distancing statewide. He also recommended wearing masks but stopped short of mandating them.

In Springfield, city council adopted an ordinance requiring people to wear face coverings in public spaces, with only a few exemptions.

At first, everyday life seemed to grind to a halt as people struggled to figure out the "new normal." In Springfield, many people began working from home. This included city employees and elected officials.

Given all this change, Jessica thought about delaying her proposal. But with the pandemic, even more people will be hurting, she thought. Why wait? We should get on with it.

So she emailed her proposal to the department heads, her fellow members of council, Groh, the mayor and the city finance manager.

Within minutes, she began to get responses. The first was from Bill Davidson, who was in charge of the public works department. He'd spent much of his career in the construction business. He was known for his colorful language.

"What in the Hell is this?" he wrote. "Scrap this thing. Rethink it. In the meantime, you won't be getting a penny from me!"

Other department heads began responding too. In less earthy language, they also told Jessica no. Most objections were about the money.

"I'm not going to cut my budget for your pet project," one wrote.

Jessica was sitting at her desk in her apartment. Her heart was pounding. She felt dizzy. This isn't happening, she thought. I have a mandate for this project from the voters. How can there be so much resistance? How could I be so far off the mark? Is my career in politics over? Her head was spinning.

Her cell phone rang. She didn't recognize the number. Feeling skittish, she picked up.

"Hello?"

"Hello, Jessica. This is Charlotte Brown. I'm calling about your proposal on social services."

Brown was the city's lead attorney. She had a no-nonsense reputation. Jessica had met her but didn't know her well.

"Yes," Jessica said.

"I'd like to talk with you about it."

Her voice was firm but warm.

"You would?"

"Yes. How about over coffee tomorrow morning?"

"That would be good."

"The Coffee Ethic at 10:00?"

"That sounds good."

"Great," Brown said. "By the way, I suspect you're going to get some pushback on your proposal. But that doesn't mean it's not important. We'll talk about that."

"Okay," Jessica said. "Thank you."

★

The following morning, Jessica got to the coffee shop a little before 10:00. Charlotte Brown was already there.

She was tall and thin with piercing green eyes and short blond hair with subtle streaks of gray. She was wearing a navy blue swing coat and a navy blue mask. As Jessica approached her, Brown extended her elbow.

"Good morning," she said.

"Good morning," Jessica said, giving her an elbow bump.

"I don't think I've seen you since you started on council," Brown said. "Congratulations again on your big win."

Jessica wasn't sure whether to call her Charlotte or Ms. Brown.

"Thank you," she said.

They ordered their coffees and brought them to a table near the back. The place was nearly empty, so there was no risk of sitting too close to others. The two of them sat down about six feet apart.

"So I want to talk about your proposal," Brown said, taking her mask off and pulling some neatly folded papers from her coat pocket.

Jessica took off her mask too.

"I know," Jessica said. "It's awful."

"Why do you say that?"

"Just about all the department heads have rejected it."

"That's because you're after their money."

"I didn't know where else to get it."

Brown sipped her coffee.

"May I give you a suggestion?"

"Of course."

"Whenever you're proposing a big idea, especially if it involves money, make sure you vet it with people first, before you make a formal recommendation."

"Yes," Jessica said. "I realize now I should have done that."

She felt like a fool.

Brown sipped her coffee as she looked over Jessica's proposal.

"Let me ask you something," she said.

"Sure."

"How did you pick these three focus areas for social services?"

"They're the areas of greatest need in Springfield."

"I see. And how do know how much programs in those areas are going to cost?"

"I estimated."

"Jessica, your proposal has merit, but it's very general, and you're not going to fund it by asking for money that's already been approved for other purposes. There's a process for making a budget request."

Jessica felt like crawling under the table.

"Jessica, getting the money is the easy part. You've got to build support for your proposal and not just inside city hall. You need the community's input and buy-in."

"But I already have a mandate from the voters."

"You ran a good campaign. But there's a difference between *campaigning* for office and *serving* in office."

"Yes. I'm learning that."

Brown smiled a small smile. She looked at Jessica as a mother might look at a daughter in need of instruction.

"Jessica, you're a councilwoman now. You've got to lead. But that doesn't mean simply pushing your ideas through."

"I understand. I'd welcome any suggestions you have."

"Okay. Commission a task force to study the problem and recommend the best ways to tackle it. I mean specific ways. Then put price tags on them. Once you've done that, I'll go with you to the finance director, and we'll get the money. Once you have that money, *then* you can hold a public hearing and ask council to vote on it."

What Brown was proposing made perfect sense to Jessica. It was so obvious now.

"Thank you," she said.

"You're welcome."

"May I ask you something?"

"Sure."

"Why are you doing this for me? I mean you didn't have to ask me here this morning."

Brown finished her coffee.

"Do you know that one in every four Springfield residents lives in poverty?" she said.

"Yes."

"Growing up, I was one of those people. We do need a department of social services. It's long overdue. But I suggest you start by addressing poverty. That's the biggest issue here. Focus on that."

"That makes sense," Jessica said.

Brown looked her in the eye.

"You're going to help a lot of people, Jessica. You just need to take a step back and start over. That's okay. We all make mistakes. I know you'll learn from this one."

"Thank you, Charlotte."

"You're most welcome. Keep going. Just let me know how I can help."

In the following days and weeks, Jessica thought a lot about that meeting with Charlotte Brown. Not just her good advice but how she delivered it and how that made her feel. Others had dismissed her proposal and made her feel small. Brown took time to understand. She was respectful and discrete. She encouraged Jessica and lifted her up.

That's the kind of leader I want to be, she thought.

Chapter 18

Never having convened a task force, Jessica turned once again to her father for advice.

"Just make sure it represents a good cross section of interests in the community," he said. "Make it small. Be clear about your objective. Take charge but don't micromanage. And make sure everything is wrapped up in six months."

"Why six months?"

"Any longer and you'll lose momentum."

"Thanks, Dad."

Reflecting on the advice from both her father and Charlotte Brown, Jessica began to see a theme emerging. Focus.

★

Jessica identified five sectors of the community she wanted to make sure were represented on her task force: religious organizations, non-profit agencies, the city, the county and business. After two weeks, she had recruited representatives from each of these sectors, including one of her fellow members of council. Because most people were working from home, this meant lots of phone calls, emails and Zoom meetings.

The following week, she convened her full task force for the first time by Zoom. She thanked everyone for agreeing to serve, then clarified the main problem and their challenge — poverty in Springfield — and advanced a specific objective.

"I think we should recommend ways we can reduce the number of people living in poverty in Springfield by 25% within five years," she said. "I know that's aggressive, but I think it's feasible. Thoughts?"

This is how Jessica engaged the members of her task force: offering her ideas, seeking their ideas and making sure there was consensus along the way.

They agreed on next steps and timing, and Jessica assigned roles. She was impressed by the enthusiasm and knowledge of each of the members of the group.

But one member in particular got her attention: Michael Simon, a young business analyst for O'Reilly Auto Parts, which was based in Springfield.

He was earnest and nerdy-looking, with curly black hair and horn-rimmed glasses, but he had great ideas for how they could "dimensionalize" the problem of poverty in Springfield. Jessica had never heard that word, but she could tell Simon knew what he was talking about. She put him in charge of defining the problem and its root causes.

She was impressed by all the task force members. But she felt an attraction to Michael. She especially liked the slow and deliberate way he talked. It was very different from the way she talked, which Father John had once jokingly called "fluid."

Within two months, the task force had taken a hard look at local poverty, done an audit of current work aimed at addressing the problem, benchmarked what had been working well in other cities and developed options for tackling the problem in Springfield.

The members then voted on the most promising options and defined the cost of each of them. Job skills training emerged as a big idea. Finally, they considered the best way to organize to get the job done. After five months, they were ready to form all of this into a plan, with a budget.

Jessica shared a draft of the plan in person with Ben Groh. The proposal called for $1.2 million in new funding for the first year. Groh told her this was a non-starter and advised her to trim it below $1 million.

"Why?"

"Optics," he said. "Any new program that costs more than $1 million causes fights to break out around here. You don't need that. Propose something just shy of a million. You can request budget increases over time."

Jessica shared that feedback with the task force. It caused them to cut two programs and the administrative position they had envisioned. Tough choices, but they brought the budget down to $900,000.

Jessica then met with Charlotte Brown to go over the final draft of her proposal.

"Looks great," she said.

"Including the budget?"

"Yes," she said with a smile. "Nice work."

"Thanks. It was a team effort. Are you still up for joining me to talk with Bob Jeffries about securing the funding?"

"Absolutely."

They met with Bob Jeffries, the city's finance director, by Zoom two days later.

"No problem," he said. "We're projecting a budget surplus next year. We'll pull this money from that. But then you'll have to come up for review annually."

"We can do that," Jessica said.

"Thanks, Bob," Brown said. "You've been very helpful."

It took Jessica two more weeks to meet virtually with her fellow members of council and the mayor to discuss her draft proposal. After that, she decided to share it by email with the department heads. Not for their approval but to make sure they were current — and knew they wouldn't be asked for money this time.

They appreciated the gesture and complimented Jessica on her work. Even Bill Davidson expressed support, in his own unique way.

"Damn!" he wrote in reply. "You did rethink this thing. Good job."

★

In September, as Missourians continued to battle the coronavirus, the governor, who had urged residents to wear masks but refused to wear one himself, announced he and his wife had tested positive for Covid-19.

"Sounds like the governor needs to walk the talk," David Hanks told his daughter.

At first, his comment sounded trite to Jessica. But the more she thought about it, and the more Missourians got infected and died, the more she appreciated how important it was for leaders to lead by example, to "walk the talk."

It was a lesson not lost on Jessica.

★

Jessica set up a public hearing for her proposal for early October. It was a virtual meeting. About 75 people logged on.

Jessica had posted the proposal online in advance. She started the meeting by running through the highlights of the plan, then opened the floor to comments and questions.

One resident asked whether the plan was striking the right balance between immediate assistance for those in need versus job skills training. Another asked if the goals were realistic. Another questioned the need to establish a new department.

Jessica was ready for these questions because they were among the very questions the task force itself had debated. She gave clear and succinct answers, and several task force members chimed in to back her up.

Michael Simon was particularly articulate and compelling on the need for more job skills training. He even shared data from half a dozen cities where investment in this area was paying off. He also talked about what the local business community was doing to hire more of these newly trained residents.

The public hearing was scheduled for an hour. It was over in 45 minutes.

★

During that month of October, Pope Francis made big news again, twice.

First, he issued a new encyclical, technically a letter to all bishops of the Church, but in reality a message to the world. It was called *Fratelli Tutti* or *All Brothers.* It was about the need for greater human fraternity. In it, Francis took aim at systems at odds with social friendship, including market capitalism, which he called "perverse."

Second, he expressed support for same-sex civil unions, the first pope to do so.

Both moves sparked both praise and controversy. Some of the pope's critics felt he had again strayed into politics and thus gone too far. Some of the loudest criticisms came from within the Church.

"With respect, the Holy Father would do well to stick to religion," said one US bishop.

Once again, Jessica called Father John to get his take.

"The pope wants us to put our faith into action," he said. "God lives in the world. Remember?"

Until then, Jessica had struggled with whether she should pursue politics or religion. Now, reflecting on what Pope Francis was *saying* and what she was *doing* to help address poverty in Springfield, she began to understand how these two paths might naturally come together.

★

Jessica honed her proposal to establish a department for social services based on input from the public hearing. She then sent it to council.

In early November, almost exactly a year after she was elected, all eight members approved it — at city hall with everyone wearing masks and sitting six feet apart. That timing was critical because there was just enough time for the funding to be included in the city's 2021 budget.

After the vote was taken, people broke into applause. Jessica was thrilled. After the meeting, the first person she sought out to thank was Charlotte Brown.

"I told you that you could do it," she said.

The members of the task force were all there too. They came up to congratulate Jessica with fist and elbow bumps. But Michael Simon leaned in and gave her a hug. For Jessica, it was the sweetest gesture of all.

Chapter 19

Jessica was relaxing in her recliner, reading a book and watching fat snowflakes float and dance outside her window, when her phone rang.

She put down her Friday night glass of chardonnay and looked at her phone. *Michael Simon* flashed up. Her heart raced. She cleared her throat, then picked up.

"Hello?"

"Hello, Jessica? It's Michael Simon."

"Hi, Michael."

"Do you have a minute?"

It's Friday night, and I'm alone, she thought.

"Sure," she said.

"Good. I'm calling for a couple of reasons."

A couple of reasons? What a nerd, she thought. But a cute nerd.

"First, I want to congratulate you again on getting your proposal approved. I meant to send you a note, but I've been pretty busy at work."

"Well, thank you, Michael. I couldn't have done it without you."

Silence.

"You said there was a second reason?"

"Oh, yeah. I was wondering if you'd like to go out to dinner sometime. I've enjoyed working with you, but I thought it might be nice to, um, get to know you a bit better."

Jessica had gone on a lot of dates, going back to high school. But she never seemed to be asked out by the guys she really wished would ask her out, guys she found interesting. Most of her first dates had never led to second dates.

Michael was the kind of guy she was hoping would ask her out. He was smart and thoughtful, confident but soft-spoken. He projected a kind of quiet power. He was also handsome in a nerdy sort of way.

"I'd like that," she said.

She could hear him exhale.

"Good. How about tomorrow evening? I know you're probably busy—"

"Tomorrow night is good for me."

"Great. What kind of food do you like?"

"I like just about everything," she said. "But I love Italian."

"Me too! How about Avanzare's?"

"I love that place."

"Great. How does sex — uh, six — sound?" he stammered.

"Six sounds fine," she said with a little laugh.

"Great. Okay if I pick you up?"

"Yes. Do you have my address?"

"Yes. I live right around the corner from you."

"Really? Cool. Well, I'll see you tomorrow then."

"Yeah. See you then. Good night."

"Good night, Michael."

She hung up, set her phone down and picked her wine glass back up.

"How does sex sound?" she said out loud with a giggle.

★

He rang her bell promptly at six.

"Hello, Michael."

"Good evening," he said.

He was wearing a navy blue overcoat, black jeans, gray suede shoes and a light blue surgical mask — and holding a single, white rose.

"This is for you," he said, handing her the flower.

"How lovely," she said, taking his gift. "Thank you."

"You're welcome."

"Won't you come in? And please feel free to take your mask off."

"Thank you," he said, stepping inside and pulling off his mask.

"Let me put this in a vase. I'll be right back. Have a seat, if you like."

She stepped into the kitchen. When she returned a few minutes later, Michael was still standing near the door, with his hands in his coat pockets. He looked nervous.

"I'll get my coat," she said.

As she went to the closet, he stepped over and helped her with her coat.

"Thank you," she said.

Her overcoat was navy blue, like his, and she was wearing black jeans too.

"Look at us," she said. "We look like twins."

"Except you're a lot prettier."

Jessica blushed. She wasn't used to compliments on her appearance.

★

She ordered ravioli, and he ordered lasagna. They both ordered a glass of Chianti.

Over dinner, Jessica learned that Michael had two younger sisters and grew up in St. Louis. He was Catholic and 26, a year older than her. He had majored in econometrics and quantitative economics, things Jessica didn't even know existed, at Washington University in St. Louis. He went to work for O'Reilly Auto Parts right out of college. He liked the company and his job as a market analyst.

"They let me gather data and crunch numbers," he said. "I just got promoted, and they pay me well."

Jessica asked about his hobbies.

"I love to hike."

"Me too. Where do you hike?"

"Anywhere I can," he said. "But my favorite place is Lake of the Ozarks."

"Mine too! We used to go there on family vacations when I was girl."

"And we used to go there when I was a boy."

They compared notes on their favorite spots on the lake. They had several in common. He'd even watched the fireworks there on the Fourth of July, possibly at the very same time Jessica and her family were watching them.

"Once, when I was a girl, I fell asleep looking up at those fireworks on a pontoon boat."

"Cute," he said with a smile.

As they were enjoying tiramisu with berries, Michael took off his glasses.

"I've never seen you without your glasses," she said.

"I don't wear them all the time."

"Well, you look good in glasses, but they hide your eyes. You have nice eyes."

"Thanks. So do you. I've never seen eyes so blue."

"Thank you," she said, blushing again.

He smiled. She felt calm and excited at the same time. She felt happy to be with this man. She wanted to get to know him, to let him get to know her. It was only their first date, but somehow she felt close to him. She wanted to reach across the table and hold his hand, but she didn't, thinking it too forward.

"Thanks for being with me tonight," he said, sliding his open hand across the table.

"Thank you for asking," she said, taking it.

That quiet confidence, she thought. It made her feel warm inside.

★

After dinner, they drove to Park Central Square, about 10 minutes away in the heart of downtown Springfield. The trees were draped with white Christmas lights, even though it wasn't quite Thanksgiving. The constellation of small lights cast a soft glow on the snow-covered grass.

"My parents used to take us here when we were kids," Jessica said as they walked through the park. "They put up a big tree closer to Christmas. It's magnificent."

"I saw that here last Christmas," he said. "It *was* magnificent."

She wondered why he'd been there last Christmas. She wondered if he was with someone.

As they walked around the square, she slipped a little on a patch of ice. He caught her, then held her hand to steady her.

"Thank you."

She didn't let go. Nor did he. They kept walking, hand in hand. It was the first time she had ever held hands like this with a man who wasn't her father. Holding Michael's hand felt so good to her. It felt so right.

Jessica was getting cold, but she kept walking just so she could hold Michael's hand a little longer.

★

He parked on the street in front of her apartment building. They went inside, took the elevator to the third floor and walked down the hall to her apartment.

"Would you like to come in?"

"Thank you, but I'd better get going," he said. "Maybe next time?"

"I'd like that."

"I had a great time tonight," he said.

"I did too."

"Good night, Jessica," he said, bending down to give her a hug.

She embraced him tightly, then stood on her toes and gave him a kiss on the cheek. His stubble was rough against her lips. She liked that.

Since the pandemic had hit, physical touch had been rare for Jessica. Hugging Michael, and kissing him, felt so good.

She locked her door, hung up her coat and sat down in her recliner. She closed her eyes and thought of Michael. She imagined embracing him and kissing him again.

Chapter 20

Jessica and Michael gave each other a long kiss as the clock ticked into 2021. As they wished each other happy new year, Jessica had no idea just how happy that year would be.

For starters, with funds now appropriated for the city's new department of social services, Jessica was now able to kick off the search for a new department head. She, Ben Groh and the city's HR manager interviewed more than a dozen candidates.

In early March, they picked a woman named Anne Archer. She'd managed both a food pantry and a job skills training program in St. Louis. She was 48, with grown children. In April, Anne and her husband moved to Springfield, and she hit the ground running in her new job.

Leading the fight against poverty, including getting this new department head in place, was Jessica's top priority. But she had been elected a councilwoman at-large. This meant she also got involved in a range of issues and projects not taken care of by the four members of council dedicated to the city's four geographic zones.

A lot of these issues and projects were mundane. Rezoning property or passing ordinances. But some were exciting. Jessica especially enjoyed helping develop the city's 2030 strategic plan.

The variety and volume of all this work stretched her. She learned a lot about how things really get done in a city, and she began to understand how much work "public service" really is.

Her days were long, but she wasn't worn down. On the contrary, she felt energized. She felt she was making a difference. She took great satisfaction in knowing that she was doing something to improve people's lives.

And as her career was blossoming, her personal life was bursting into full bloom. She'd fallen deeply in love with Michael, and being in love for the first time made everything feel new and exciting.

One Saturday in June, Jessica and Michael went to dinner at Avanzare's again. Afterwards, he wanted to go to Park Central Square.

The air was warm and filled with the sweet aroma of freshly cut grass. Nightingales and warblers sang in the trees. The setting sun cast a rose glow across the sky.

Jessica's favorite thing in the park was the fountain. Michael knew that. As a girl, she used to make wishes there and toss pennies in the water.

They walked over to it, holding hands. There, in the fine mist of the breeze-swept spray of the fountain, Michael got down on one knee, pulled out a ring and asked Jessica to marry him.

"Yes!" she exclaimed.

They held each other a long time and said I love you, and Jessica's heart was filled with joy.

★

Jessica and Michael got married the following June at Holy Trinity Church, her home parish. Father John officiated the Mass.

By then, most Americans had received the recommended two doses of one of the new coronavirus vaccines. Infection rates and deaths had fallen dramatically. Restaurants and schools were reopening. People were gathering again. At last, the pandemic was fading.

In his homily at the wedding, Father John recalled meeting Jessica during the introductions in his freshman theology class at SLU.

"So here is this tiny 18 year old, telling me it's not enough to study God," he said. "We must bring God to life in the world."

Laughter.

"Fasten your seatbelt, Michael."

Louder laughter.

When everyone was quiet again, Father John said, "Jessica Hanks, very soon Jessica Simon, is the best person I have ever known. I've never known anyone so other-centered. She doesn't just talk about bringing God into the world. She does it every day. Sometimes, I have to remind myself how young she still is and that she's just getting warmed up. Surely this is a woman destined to do great things.

"How heartening it is to know she will now be walking alongside Michael. Jessica and Michael told me, independently, that they began to fall in love on their first date, at the moment they first held hands. Jessica told me, 'His hand just felt so right.' Michael told me, 'I felt as though I could hold her hand the rest of my life.'

"My friends, God lives within us, but we are not just spirits. We are human beings, with hands and hearts. If we are lucky, very lucky, we will find someone whose hand we can hold for a lifetime. We will find someone who always holds us in their heart as we hold them close in ours. That is true love, and true love is God brought to life in the world.

"Jessica and Michael, you inspire us, and we love you. We will always be here for you. We wish you much happiness together. May God bless you and smile upon you and give you peace all the days of your life."

Chapter 21

During the first three years of her term on council, Jessica seemed to be everywhere in Springfield. There was no major project or issue she didn't touch.

She met with senior citizens, spoke to civic groups, led town hall meetings — and still had time to feed people at food pantries and soup kitchens. *417 Magazine* did a cover story on her as a local rising star. People began recognizing her on the street.

Some began talking about Jessica running for "higher office." In Springfield, that meant only two possible positions: city manager and mayor.

Ben Groh was still the city manager, with no plans to retire soon. However, Mayor Dylan Childs had been open about not running for another term. Two members of council had already declared their candidacy for mayor. Some began urging Jessica to run too.

But if Jessica was more visible in Springfield, there was one place she showed up less: at home. She had commitments nearly every evening and weekend, and Michael seldom tagged along. So he spent many evenings alone, waiting up for her. He never complained, but he sometimes seemed down.

"Are you okay?" she would ask. "You seem quiet."

"I'm always quiet," he would say.

She worried about leaving him alone so much. At the same time, she had a growing interest in running for mayor. She figured it was a way she could serve even more people. But she decided she would run only if Michael was supportive.

"I'm thinking about running for mayor," she said over dinner one night. "What do you think?"

"I think you'd make a great mayor."

"But I might have even less time for us."

He twirled his spaghetti and said nothing.

"I won't do it if you're not 100 percent on board," she said.

"Why do you want to be mayor, Jess?"

"I think I can help even more people."

He sat back in his chair and looked across the table at her.

"I love you," he said. "I do wish you were around more. But whether you're here one hour a day or all day, I'll love you just the same. If you want to be mayor, go for it."

"Really?"

"Yeah."

She came around the table, sat on his lap and gave him a long, deep kiss.

"I love you," she said.

"And I love you," he said. "I'll always love you."

That night, as they were getting ready for bed, she patted his butt, something she sometimes did before they made love. Brushing his teeth, he got his hopes up. But when he came out of the bathroom, she was already asleep.

★

In February of 2023, at the Well of Life food pantry, surrounded by a few dozen people, including Michael and her parents,

Jessica said, "Good morning, everyone. Thanks for coming out on a chilly Saturday morning. I know you're busy. I have two announcements to make. I'll keep them brief.

"First, I'm pleased to tell you the poverty rate in Springfield has dropped to 15 percent, from 25 percent, over the past three years."

Applause.

"Of course, we won't be satisfied until no one is living in poverty. But we're making good progress, and this would not be possible without the leadership of Anne Archer, who leads our social services department. Anne had worked closely with dozens of organizations and individuals throughout our community to provide assistance for those in need, especially job skills training. Over the past three years, because of this training, more than 500 Springfield residents who were unemployed have found jobs."

Applause.

"We remain committed to reducing poverty in Springfield and eventually wiping it out. I know that, under Anne's leadership, we'll continue to make great progress."

More applause.

"What's the other announcement?" someone asked.

Jessica smiled.

"Today I am announcing my candidacy for the Mayor of Springfield."

Loud applause and whistles.

"If I'm elected, I want to jumpstart the pace of our progress in reaching the goals set out in our city's 2030 strategic plan," she said. "My primary focus will be on helping ensure our continued economic growth. But I also want to make sure this growth is broad-based, that the benefits are enjoyed by all members of our community, including the poor and disadvantaged."

Jessica stayed a little longer to mingle before leaving for other appointments. She got home late that night. Michael was already asleep.

★

That November, Jessica won in a landslide.

"I want to thank all my supporters, who worked so hard on this campaign," she said at a celebration that evening. "I want to extend special thanks to my husband, Michael, the great love of my life, and my parents, who taught me everything I know about serving others."

The atmosphere was festive. Everyone was thrilled for Jessica. But at one point, she looked across the room and saw Michael standing by himself. He looked lonely.

She was excited about being mayor, but she worried about the cost.

★

That Christmas, after the Hanks family dinner, Jessica was helping her mom clear the dishes.

"Mom, I can't tell you the number of times I think of the first time you took me to the food pantry to help you."

"I remember that day. You were such a big help."

"Do you remember what you told me on our way home?"

"No, I don't."

"You told me one of the men we fed that day, a man with long hair and a beard, was Jesus."

"Oh, yes. I do remember that."

Jessica paused.

"Mom, I want you to know I've seen that man again."

"You have?"

"Yes. I saw him in the woods beyond our backyard when I was nine."

"What?"

"I didn't say anything to you and Dad because I didn't want you to worry."

"Well, we certainly would have been concerned if you saw a stranger in the woods when you were nine."

"That's just it, Mom. He wasn't strange at all. In fact, he seemed familiar."

"How so?"

"I don't know. His voice. His face."

"He spoke to you?"

"Yes."

"What did he say?"

"Follow me."

"Follow me?"

"Yes. And he told me he loved me. He called me by name."

"Jessie, that's amazing. Have you shared this with anyone else?"

"Only Father John — and Michael, of course."

"What did Father John say?"

"He said Jesus is calling me."

"So you think it was Jesus who appeared to you?"

"I'm certain of it."

Mary Hanks was standing at the sink. She stared out into the darkness through the window.

"Has Jesus ever appeared to you, Mom?"

Her mother smiled.

"Yes. I see him in every face."

I know you do, Jessica thought. She felt so blessed to be this woman's daughter.

"I love you, Mom."

"I love you too, Jessie," her mother said, embracing her. "Merry Christmas."

★

David and Mary Hanks and Michael were with Jessica two weeks later, when a municipal court judge administered her oath of office at city hall.

She shook the judge's hand, hugged Michael and her parents and thanked the other city officials who had gathered before heading off for a meeting at the chamber of commerce.

"I'll try to be home for dinner," she said to Michael on her way out.

That evening, though, as usual, he ate alone.

★

The following week, Pope Francis stunned the world in announcing he would be allowing Catholic priests to marry.

"Today we are returning to a tradition dating back to the 12 apostles," he said in a rare, brief TV appearance, broadcast live from his small apartment in the Apostolic Palace. "In our church, we expect much from our priests. That is not changing. But celibacy is something even Jesus didn't expect from his apostles. I hope that by removing this rule, imposed by the Church a thousand years *after* Jesus ordained the first priests, even more men will answer the call to the priesthood."

Once again, Jessica called Father John to get his take.

"He's addressing a big problem," Father John said. "We're facing a shortage of priests like never before, and the pope knows one reason is our required vow of celibacy. He might really believe priests should be allowed to marry. But he's got a real problem, and this is part of the fix. Francis is a pragmatist."

"What's next?" Jessica said. "Female priests?"

"Probably," Father John said. "But once again, he's going to need to bring Catholics along. Once they see married priests, female priests won't seem like such a big leap."

"Do you really think there'll be female priests?"

"No question. And by the way, I think you'd make a good one."

Great, Jessica thought. No sooner am I elected mayor than something like this happens to make me wonder if I'm on the right track.

Chapter 22

Over the next few months, Jessica was busier than ever, attending meetings, giving speeches, presiding over council meetings. In early April, she gave her first quarterly report to council, an update on the strong progress she was already making as mayor.

She got high marks, but the pace and non-stop demands of the job were wearing her down. At least it'll be a short week, she thought, as Easter Sunday drew near.

For Jessica, the holiday began on Good Friday. It was a rare day off. She was enjoying a late breakfast with Michael when her phone rang. Her father's name flashed up.

"Good morning, Dad."

She heard someone crying.

"Dad?"

"Oh, Jessie. She's gone."

"What? Who's gone, Dad?"

"Mom. She had a heart attack. She didn't make it."

"Oh, Dad. You don't mean—"

"Yes. She's gone."

"Oh, Dad," she said, looking at Michael with quiet panic in her eyes. "Where are you?"

"I'm at Mercy Hospital."

"What can I do for you?"

"Call your brothers. Let them know. Then meet me here."

"Okay, Dad. I'll call them and be there as soon as I can. I love you."

"I love you too."

She hung up, then put her hand over her mouth.

"What's wrong?" Michael said.

Jessica stared at him, her face white, her eyes welling with tears.

"It's Mom. She's gone."

"Gone?"

"She had a heart attack. Dad's at the hospital. He wants me to call my brothers."

"Oh, Jess. I'm so sorry."

Michael got down on his knees and held her.

Her whole body was shaking, and she began to sob.

"No," she moaned.

Michael picked her up, carried her into the family room and gently put her down on the sofa.

"Rest," he said, kissing her forehead and wiping her tears. "Just rest for a minute. I'll call your brothers."

★

They held a reception after the funeral in the parish center at St. Joseph's. The place was packed. Jessica recognized a lot of her mother's friends, but there were many people she didn't know. She asked her dad who they were.

"They're the people your mother helped at the food pantry. They all came out for her."

Father John was there too. He sat at a table with some of Jessica's cousins while she made her way around the room with her dad. She didn't want to leave his side.

When nearly everyone was gone, Jessica was finally able to sit and talk with Father John.

"How are you doing?" he asked.

"Okay. I feel numb."

"Yeah," he said, patting her arm.

"I miss her so much. I wish I could have said goodbye."

"I understand. You were blessed to have her as your mother, and she was certainly blessed to have you as her daughter."

"I don't know if I can go on," she said.

"What do you mean?"

"I mean as mayor. It seems so unimportant now."

"I know you're hurting, Jessica. But you *will* get through this."

"I don't know, Father," she said with tears in her eyes. "I just don't know."

They sat there together for a while, saying nothing.

Chapter 23

On October 4, 2024, Pope Francis died. He was 88.

Francis had been a polarizing figure inside the Church. Progressives adored him. Hardline conservatives vilified him.

But to the world at large, Pope Francis was beloved. There was an outpouring of that love as his body lay in repose in the Apostolic Palace. Dignitaries from every nation traveled to Rome to pay their respects. Thousands thronged to St. Peter's Square for his funeral Mass on a crisp, clear Sunday morning.

Two weeks later, 120 cardinals from across the globe convened in the Sistine Chapel to elect Francis' successor. Unseen by the world was a pitched, if quiet, battle between progressives, many of whom Francis had appointed as cardinals, and ultra-conservatives, who longed for a pope more in the mold of John Paul II or even Benedict XVI.

Of course, as with most elections, the vote came down to which way those in the middle would ultimately lean. Over nearly three days, in the corridors, atriums and even chapels of the Vatican, some of the most powerful lobbyists in the world wore red robes.

The stakes were high. The prelates knew that electing a more liberal-minded cardinal would build on the progress Pope Francis had made over the past 11 years. What's more, they realized the right, strong progressive leader might be able to follow through on bold reforms Francis had talked about but did not enact — ordaining women, for example.

They also knew that a more conservative pope could reverse the tide of progressivism in the Church or at least slow it. Conservatism was still a major force in the Church. Though the Church tacked left, conservatives made up the fastest-growing group of Catholics.

Multiple candidates across the political spectrum received votes on the first ballot. But none of them was even close to the two-thirds majority required for election. Black smoke billowed from a special chimney placed atop the Sistine Chapel, indicating a new pope had yet to be chosen.

The following morning, on the second ballot, three cardinals got the most votes: Angelo Ricci of Venice, a leading progressive; Idris Musa of Lagos, Nigeria, a conservative; and Antonio Bautista of Madrid, a moderate. However, none achieved a majority of votes. Black smoke arose again.

On the third ballot, Bautista began to fade. Ricci and Musa picked up votes, but not enough for a majority. More black smoke.

By the fourth ballot, Bautista had quietly thrown his support to Ricci, who took a clear lead over Musa. However, Musa refused to yield. Black smoke again.

On the fifth ballot, Ricci emerged as the clear frontrunner, and Musa knew he had the momentum. He grudgingly signaled his support for Ricci.

On the sixth ballot, on the morning of the third day of the conclave, the cardinals, wishing to show a unified front, voted overwhelming in favor of Ricci. Inside the Sistine Chapel, applause broke out during the tabulation when Ricci reached the 77 votes required for election.

Finally, white smoke billowed from the chimney. In St. Peter's Square, the crowd roared in jubilation.

Less than an hour later, from the balcony of the Basilica, a cardinal called out: "*Annuntio vobis gaudium magnum … habemus papam*!" — "I announce to you a great joy … we have a pope!"

The crowd went wild.

Then the cardinal exclaimed, "*Franciscus Duo*!"

Moments later, Ricci, a small, middle-aged man, appeared on the central balcony of the Basilica. The name he had taken, Francis II, was a nod to his predecessor.

Like Pope Francis, the new pope donned simple, white vestments, an *homage* to their unadorned patron saint. For Francis II, the simple garments were also a reminder of growing up poor in Sicily.

"My brothers and sisters," he said to the massive crowd below, his arms outstretched, "we are one, and I love you."

★

Just a few weeks after his election, Francis II shocked the world by announcing he was removing 1,700 priests who had been credibly charged with sexual abuse of minors as well as 150 bishops and cardinals who were complicit, those in authority who had known about the misdeeds of these priests but failed to act.

"At long last," the pope said in a videotaped statement, "we are holding those who committed these wicked acts and those who harbored them to account. These men violated a most sacred trust. That was wrong. God may forgive them, but we cannot allow such men to continue to serve in any role in our Church, let alone in positions of authority.

"This episode has been our dark night. I know nothing I can do will make things right for the victims. But I am hopeful we have learned, and will continue to learn, from this most painful and destructive experience. And I am hopeful we can begin to re-earn trust and at last begin to heal."

The pope said the Church was setting up a special fund of $4 billion to cover the cost of settling all pending litigation. He said the money would come from reducing administrative costs, including consolidating dioceses and parishes, some of which would now be losing their priests and bishops.

"These are painful measures," the pope said, "but penance is never easy."

It had taken the Church more than a quarter of a century to own up to its misdeeds. There were many reasons for not coming clean sooner. Arrogance. Incompetence. Fear. Whatever the reasons, the Church had stonewalled. Church leaders offered apologies. But for what? They had never taken responsibility for their crimes, for the irreparable damage the Church's ministers had done to the lives of countless human beings. Even when individual priests were defrocked, Church leaders had never admitted they too were at fault.

Thankfully, the victims and their advocates never stopped seeking justice. They knew right from wrong, even if the leaders of their Church didn't or were unwilling to act with moral courage.

Yet despite the Church's intransigence, there was always hope: hope that the Church, which had once been a beacon of morality, would eventually do the right thing.

Now, with the stroke of a pen, the new pope had at last addressed the lingering issue behind the greatest scandal of the modern Church: taking responsibility for its own wrongdoing. At last, there was a reckoning.

The new pope received high praise from nearly every quarter. The response from Catholics "in the pews" was quite favorable. Many parishes reported that both Mass attendance and Offertory giving rose almost immediately. For the first time in 25 years, opinion polls showed an increase, not a decrease, in trust in Catholic Church leaders.

But Francis II had also created a new problem or at least exacerbated an old one. In removing so many clergymen, the already severe shortage of priests grew overnight to the breaking point. He acknowledged as much in his statement.

"I know that removing these men will further diminish our ranks," he said. "For that, I am sorry, and I take full responsibility. But I know that even as we pay a price to atone for our sins, God will bless us with more men, good men, to tend his flock. I also know filling the gap will take time. But with God's help, I am confident we *will* fill it and emerge stronger than ever."

His words proved prophetic. Even as Catholics began returning to the pews, within a few months, the number of applicants to seminaries began to rise.

Nowhere were these changes more welcome than in the US, which had long suffered a heavy share of reported pedophile priests and long beseeched Rome to take stronger action to address the crisis.

Now support for the Church in the US began to surge back. In the days after the pope's announcement, nine out of 10 American Catholics surveyed said they felt proud to be Catholic again.

As all this was happening, Jessica was paying close attention. Once again, she called Father John for his take.

"It's the most remarkable example of moral leadership I've ever seen," he said.

As she neared the end of the first year of her greatest leadership role at that point in her life, Jessica wondered where the new pope was heading and whether eventually there might be an opportunity for her to lead in the Church too.

Chapter 24

After her mother's death, Jessica decided she wouldn't run again for mayor. She told no one, not even Michael.

It's not that she felt being mayor of Springfield was unimportant. She just felt a need to switch gears and maybe try something new. After all, she was only 29.

Jessica still had more than a year left in office. If this is going to be my last term, she thought, I want to finish strong. She knew that's what her mother would want.

Following through on her campaign promises, she spent the bulk of her time on economic development, believing a rising tide in Springfield would lift all boats.

She personally led delegations to the headquarters of a range of companies considering expanding facilities or siting operations in Springfield. It paid off. She clinched several deals which added more than 2,000 new jobs and tens of millions of dollars in new tax revenue.

Then, following through on another campaign promise, she made sure those tax dollars were spent on programs which helped people across the community.

As a result, Jessica became even more popular. Everyone in Springfield assumed she would run for re-election. Only Michael and Father John knew she would not.

Despite her impressive achievements, Jessica felt unfulfilled and uncertain about her path forward in politics. She found herself thinking back to the time she'd wrestled with whether to pursue politics or religion, right after college. Sometimes she wondered if she'd made the right choice.

She also worried about Michael. He was growing even quieter. Sometimes she even worried she might lose him. In her heart, she knew she couldn't keep going as mayor without further compromising or even risking her marriage, and she wasn't willing to let that happen.

The day after her quarterly report to council in the spring of 2025, Jessica surprised nearly everyone when she announced she would not be running for mayor again.

"It's been an honor to serve this community," she said. "I am deeply grateful for the trust Springfield residents have put in me. We've done and continue to do some great work together. I'm especially proud of our work to help the poor in our community. We've made a real and lasting difference. I look forward to finishing my term as mayor by continuing to help make Springfield an even better place to live and work."

When asked why she had decided not to run again, Jessica simply cited "personal reasons." But that didn't even begin to convey the restlessness she was feeling in her soul.

Chapter 25

On January 2, 2026, Jessica attended the swearing in of her successor as mayor, a former councilman, Tyler Nelson.

Everyone there was congratulating Nelson. Rightly so. Jessica stood back and watched. For six years, she had been the center of attention in Springfield. Now she felt as though she were on the outside looking in.

That evening, Jessica and Michael had dinner at their old favorite place, Avanzare's.

"How do you feel?" Michael said.

"Free. And a little anxious."

"About what?"

"Well, I haven't been in this position for a long time. I have a wide-open field."

"Here's to wide-open fields," he said, raising his glass.

"I want to thank you for being so patient with me," she said, reaching across the table for his hand. "I'm sorry I haven't been more available to you."

"You can make it up to me," he said with a smile.

"Well, I've actually been thinking about that."

"About what?"

"About starting a family. What do you think?"

"I love that idea."

"Me too."

"But what will you do now, Jess? I mean from a career standpoint."

"I don't know, but I'm only 31. I've still got a lot of time to figure that out. For now, I think I'd like to stay home, especially if I'm going to be a mom."

"I think you'll make a great mom."

"And I know you'll make a wonderful father," she said, squeezing his hand.

★

Joshua David Simon was born at 8:17 a.m. on Tuesday, November 18, 2026, at Mercy Hospital in Springfield. Jessica and Michael were ecstatic. Her father and his parents were on hand to congratulate their children and revel in the moment.

Two Sundays later, Joshua was baptized by Father John at Holy Trinity Church.

It was a happy, but trying, time for the new parents. Josh was a colicky baby. He cried a lot and didn't begin sleeping through the night until he was nine months old. Jessica usually got up with him at night. Sometimes, trying unsuccessfully to quiet him, she would break down in tears, exhausted.

When Josh did finally begin sleeping through the night, he started crawling, giving Jessica a new challenge. He wanted to explore everything. Keeping an eye on him became a nearly full-time job, especially given he took only one nap a day.

Still, Jessica was happy with her choice to stay home. Once in a while, she would ask her father, who was now retired, to come over to give her a hand. Even he struggled to keep up with Josh.

But Jessica loved being a mother. Sometimes she would read about what Tyler Nelson was doing as mayor and felt a bit jealous. But then she would look at Josh and feel blessed to have this opportunity to be with him, an opportunity she would certainly not have if she were still mayor.

★

In her rare moments to relax during the day, Jessica began going online and reading the *National Catholic Register*, a conservative newspaper, and the left-leaning *America Magazine*, published by the Jesuits. Father John liked to call the Jesuits, his religious order, "renegade Catholics."

Jessica usually found herself much more in sync with *America,* but she appreciated the *Register's* perspective too. Both made her think.

In every issue of both publications, there was at least one major story about Pope Francis II. The *Register* was usually critical of him. *America* was usually complimentary. Sometimes their views were so divergent it was hard to believe they were writing about the same man and that both publications were affiliated with the same religion.

Jessica found Francis II fascinating. She admired his incisive way of looking at things and his decisive way of dealing with issues, as he had with the clergy sex abuse scandal. He was humble, but there was a real brilliance behind his humility.

How else could he have known to "clean house" right away as pope? He must have concluded that trust is essential for getting anything done, not to mention for healing. He must have known that, if he could begin to restore trust in the leadership of the Church, he would have a shot at advancing his agenda.

How wise, Jessica thought. How pragmatic. What a leader.

More and more, Jessica found herself thinking about the Church and her own Catholicism. Though she had long felt religious, the Church had never interested her all that much. Maybe it was because she had found its leaders uninspiring or that she simply wasn't paying attention.

Now, though, Francis II had her attention. He seemed to be remaking the Church, and this made her want to give it a fresh look.

Chapter 26

In the third year of his papacy, Francis II once again shocked the world.

"Women are playing leadership roles in every part of society," he said in a live, televised address. "As a practical matter, women have led in our Church since its beginning, but their official roles have largely been secondary. They've led quietly, often behind the scenes. Not because they're not capable of more. But because they've not been allowed to become priests.

"Today marks the end of that era and the beginning of an era of even stronger and more complete leadership in our Church. After much prayer and deep reflection, today I am announcing that women are eligible to receive Holy Orders, a sacrament which has been reserved exclusively for men for more than 2,000 years.

"At last, we invite both men and women called to the priesthood by God to answer that call. We need strong, principled, compassionate men *and* women to lead the way in our Church. I invite women to prayerfully consider entering our seminaries. I invite women who are now serving as priests in other religious denominations to prayerfully consider joining our Church. And I invite Catholics everywhere to welcome these women to our priesthood.

"Some may ask, 'Why now?' To that question, I will only say that I believe this change is overdue. But it is never too late to do the right thing. Now, happily, the Church will be able to serve God's people even more completely."

The pope's address had been announced a day in advance, but no reason was given. This had sparked frenzied speculation about the subject, but few had predicted this.

After years of rumors that women *might* be allowed to become priests, most Church observers gave such a radical change low odds. Many had given up on the idea.

The pope's remarks were not yet complete when the headlines broke. Within an hour, it was the biggest news story in the world.

Naturally, Jessica called Father John to get his take.

"I think women have been second-class citizens in our church for far too long," he said. "It's about time they be allowed to become priests."

"Why do you think he's doing this now?"

"Remember what I told you years ago about leaders seeing things as they are and taking action?"

"Yes."

"The reality is that, three years after priests were allowed to marry, the Church is still facing a priest shortage. The pope knows that. He also knows the number of Catholics is growing and that, unless he can dramatically increase the number of priests, the Church's business model, so to speak, will break. Allowing women to be ordained isn't a fix, but it will certainly help."

Then he said, "What do you think?"

"I think it's exciting," she said.

"Does it make you think differently about your own future?"

"Maybe."

★

Within days of the pope's announcement, women started applying to seminaries. In addition, scores of Episcopal and Anglican priests began asking about the process for converting to Catholicism. Mass attendance increased. Polls showed overwhelming support for the pope's decision.

But not everyone was supportive. Ultra conservative Catholics chaffed at the idea of female priests. "Jesus didn't ordain women. Why should we?" was their refrain.

Some priests felt threatened by the move. One was a young priest in Ruse, a city in northeastern Bulgaria, on the bank of the Danube River.

"This is a serious breach," Father Ivan Penov told a friend. "Soon we will be drowning in the rising waters of liberalism."

★

Reflecting on the pope's decision and Father John's perspective, Jessica realized what Francis II was doing. He was addressing a problem which he himself had exacerbated. In removing so many pedophile priests three years earlier, the pope had decimated the already-thin ranks of the priesthood globally.

While there was initially a surge in the number of new seminarians, that increase had flattened out, and the Church was again facing a serious shortage of priests.

She could hear Father John's voice in her mind. "Leaders see things as they are, and they act."

Thinking about the leaders she had read about as a political science major and the leaders she'd known and admired during her own time in politics, Jessica was beginning to see Pope Francis II as a quintessential leader.

She was also beginning to think harder about the path she had not taken. The world was changing. All of a sudden, now that women could become priests, religion looked like a much more interesting option.

Chapter 27

Despite the rigors of parenting, when Josh turned one, Jessica and Michael began talking about having another child. They had always hoped to have two children.

Just a few days before Josh's second birthday, Jessica gave birth to a girl, Emma Mary. She too was baptized by Father John at Holy Trinity.

From the start, Emma was as sweet and calm as Josh was wild. She rarely cried, and she slept through the night after only a month.

"I never imagined siblings could be so different," Jessica said to her father.

"Oh, yeah," he said. "In our family, your brothers were holy terrors. You were the easy one. You didn't cry much as a baby. You cooed. That was such a welcome change for Mom."

"I get that," she said.

★

With her kids asleep in their beds and Michael asleep beside her, Jessica lay awake, thinking about how different her daily life had become.

Not long ago, she worried about balancing the city's budget. Now her main concerns were changing Emma's diapers and keeping Josh out of trouble.

She thought about the pope's decision to allow women to become priests. She thought about Jesus appearing to her when she was a girl, saying, "Follow me."

She had done her best to follow him. Was she still following him? And if she was, where was he leading her? Where was she going?

One night, she fell asleep and dreamed she was standing in an enormous room filled with all the people and places she had ever loved. Her life, her entire world was somehow consolidated and neatly framed in this single space. She looked around and felt so content.

Then she spotted a door unlike any she'd ever seen. It was solid, yet a soft light flowed through it, as if through a window. She walked over to it and opened it. She looked out and beheld an astonishing new world she had never even imagined.

Jessica felt herself being drawn across the threshold. She looked back with longing, then forward with excitement.

Chapter 28

David Hanks retired when he turned 65. Now he came over to Jessica's house to help with the kids on Monday, Wednesday and Friday mornings. She greatly appreciated his help, especially with Josh. But even more, she was grateful to simply spend time with her father.

And he was deeply grateful to spend time with her and his grandchildren. He'd spent too little time with his own children when they were growing up. Now, at last, he had time. He told Jessica he considered it a gift from God.

One Wednesday morning, he didn't show up. Jessica called him, but there was no answer. She tried again about 15 minutes later, but there was still no answer. Worried, she put the kids in the car and drove over to his house.

When no one answered the front door, she let herself in.

"Dad?" she called.

There was no answer and no sign of her father.

She walked through the house, carrying Emma, Josh tagging along. When she got to her father's bedroom, the door was open. She went in. She could see him in bed.

"Dad?"

He didn't move.

She approached his bed. The window shades were closed, and the light was dim, but she could see his head on his pillow. He was on his side, facing her. His eyes were closed.

"Dad?"

He didn't move. She touched his shoulder. Still no movement.

Jessica sat Emma on the floor and closed the door so Josh wouldn't escape.

"Dad," she said, her voice trembling. "Dad, wake up."

But he still didn't move. She knelt down beside his bed and looked more closely at his face. It was pale. She touched his cheek. His skin was dry and cold.

"Dad," she said, beginning to cry.

She tried to roll him over on his back. When she did, his lower jaw dropped and his mouth opened a little. She bent down to see if she could hear or feel him breathe, but he was still.

"Oh, Dad!"

Josh, who had been exploring his grandfather's closet, heard his mother's troubled voice and started to come over to the bed. Jessica didn't want him to see his grandfather this way. So though she wanted to stay with her father, she scooped up Emma and grabbed Josh's hand and took them out into the family room.

Her father kept a collection of toys in the corner of the room for his grandchildren. Jessica brought Josh and Emma over to the toys, and they started playing.

She felt torn. She wanted to be with her father, to hold him. But she knew she needed to be with her children, and she didn't want them to see their grandfather as he was at that moment. They were too young to understand.

Watching her children at play, Jessica wiped her eyes, picked up her cell phone and dialed 911.

★

The coroner ruled the cause of David Simon's death a heart attack. He was 69.

They held a reception in the parish center at St. Joseph's Church after the funeral. It was not nearly as well attended as her mother's.

David Hanks had been the breadwinner for his family. His hard work had enabled Mary Hanks to do the volunteer work she so loved. Many of the people she had helped over the years had attended her funeral. Jessica knew that, were it not for her father, her mother might never have known these people, might never have been able to help them.

How good her parents were together, she thought. And how grateful she felt to have had this extra time with her father.

At the end of the long day of his funeral, Jessica and Michael put their kids to bed and got to bed themselves.

"You know, Jess," Michael said, "I was struck today that both of your parents died of heart attacks in their sixties."

"I know."

"I'm thinking about you, Jess. When was the last time you had your heart checked?"

"Oh, Michael, I'm fine."

"How do you know? I think you should see a cardiologist, just to be safe."

"Okay. I'll call and get a referral in the morning."

But the following day, Jessica got busy and didn't call her doctor. She didn't call the day after that either. Or the day after that.

Jessica knew she should call her doctor, but she kept putting it off, as other things took precedence.

Chapter 29

Jessica could hear Michael trying to deal with Josh in the family room — Josh, their high-strung four-year-old, who was now taking a medication for ADHD.

In the midst of such daily drama, Jessica had begun giving serious thought to becoming a priest. The idea seemed so ludicrous, though, that she hadn't mentioned it even to Michael.

Yet she couldn't stop thinking about it. By the day, the idea of becoming a priest felt more right. The image of the man she had seen in the woods as a girl was never far from her thoughts. Lately, she'd been hearing his voice too. *Follow me.*

One evening, after they'd put the kids to bed, Jessica told Michael about her interest in becoming a priest.

"I don't know what to say," he said.

"I know it sounds crazy."

"You're serious about this?"

"Yes."

"Where would you study?"

"Kenrick-Glennon Seminary in St. Louis. I've looked into it. It would take me six years to become a priest."

"Jess, do you know what this would mean for our family?"

"Yes. For starters, we'd have to move to St. Louis. You'd have to get a job there. We'd have to find childcare for the kids."

"Yeah. For starters."

"Maybe your parents could help."

He rolled his eyes.

"Michael, I know it would be a huge change for our family. I would do this only if you were completely on board."

He looked into her eyes.

"Is this really what you want?"

"Yes, it is. I've been praying over it, and it feels right to me. I believe God is calling me."

He closed his eyes and drew a deep breath. Then he opened his eyes, smiled and shook his head.

"Well, I guess we could take the kids to see the Clydesdales a lot more often."

"Oh, Michael."

She put her arms around him, and they sat holding each other, thinking about the mysterious new direction their lives were about to take.

Chapter 30

That summer, the Simon family moved to St. Louis. Michael was able to line up a job as a market analyst for Anheuser-Busch. They found a three-bedroom house in Clayton, just west of the city. Jessica enrolled Josh in preschool and herself in Kenrick-Glennon Seminary.

Mother and son started school on the same day in mid-August. Jessica dressed Josh in a white knit shirt and navy blue pants. She wore a white top with a navy blue sweater so they would match.

As Michael was dropping Josh at pre-school and Emma at his parents' house, Jessica was walking into the atrium of the seminary. She felt butterflies in her stomach, just as she had on *her* first day of pre-school.

She approached a table in the center. On it were a dozen or so name tags lined up in neat rows.

"Welcome," said an older man in a black cassock as he handed Jessica her name tag. "I'm Father Miller."

For a moment, she wondered how he knew who she was. Then she realized all the other names on the table were masculine.

"Good morning, Father," she said, extending her hand. "I'm Jessica Simon."

"I know," he said, shaking her hand. "We've been expecting you."

He may have said welcome, but his eyes said something else. He looked her over, as if he were sizing her up.

Jessica had seen that look as a new councilwoman in Springfield. At first, people weren't sure what to make of her. They too were sizing her up.

She understood it then. She understood it now. But she didn't like it.

"I'm the rector here," Miller said. "If you need anything at all, please let me know."

His tone was patronizing. He wants me to know he's in charge, she thought.

Miller handed her a folder of materials and a program for the day.

"You'll begin with an orientation in room 217," he said. "I'll see you there at 9:00."

"Thank you, Father."

Jessica took the stairs to the second floor and found 217. She was the first to arrive. A dozen desks were arranged in a near circle, a wooden lectern filling the gap. The desks looked like the ones at SLU, metal-framed chairs with plastic seats tucked under small tables with laminated tops. Jessica sat down at one across from the lectern.

Soon others came in. As she suspected, Jessica was the only woman in the class. She introduced herself to the men who sat down next to her.

At 9:00 sharp, Father Miller came in.

"Good morning, everyone," he said, as he strode over to a tall chair behind the lectern. He sat down, looking down at all the seminarians in the circle.

"Welcome to Kenrick-Glennon Seminary," he said. "We're delighted you're here. We hope you'll find the days and years ahead exciting and enriching and that you'll leave here fully ready for the priesthood."

His tone was arrogant. Jessica wondered who he meant by "we." It made the seminary sound like a club.

Miller went over their activities for the day. They would take two classes that morning: on theology and the Old Testament. Then lunch in the cafeteria. Then two classes in the afternoon: on Church history and world religions.

Finally, each seminarian would be assigned a spiritual director. Those directors would be available to meet briefly that afternoon.

"Then you'll all be free to go back to your rooms until dinner," Miller said.

"Well, those of you who won't be going home," he added, looking at Jessica.

He told them to go around and introduce themselves, including why they wanted to become a priest.

Jessica was amazed by the diversity of ages and backgrounds in the group. Two were fresh out of high school, but most had college degrees and many had career experiences. There was a former high school teacher, an accountant and a car mechanic. Several were married. Several said they had decided to become priests after emotional events in their lives.

Jessica's background was unique. Most of her classmates looked surprised to learn she had been the mayor of Springfield. When she said she had decided to become a priest "to follow Jesus," they looked even more surprised. Miller let out a small laugh.

"I'm sorry," he said, feigning seriousness. "That's very noble, Jessica."

She really didn't care for this priest.

★

Before their first class, a seminarian gave them all a tour of the place. The men walked ahead of Jessica, most of them in groups of two or three. But soon one of the younger seminarians spotted her walking alone and dropped back.

"Hi," he said with an Hispanic accent, extending his hand. "I'm Benjamin."

"Hello. I'm Jessica. Do you prefer Ben or Benjamin?"

"Well, a lot of people call me Ben. But I prefer Benjamin."

"Then I'll call you Benjamin."

"*Gracias.*"

"*De nada*," she said, drawing on a remnant of her high school Spanish.

"I like what you said about following Jesus," he said. "I feel called by him too."

"You do? I'd love to hear more about that."

★

Jessica found her morning classes boring. She quickly realized she'd covered much of the same material in her theology courses at SLU.

After lunch, Jessica checked in with her mother-in-law. Emma was fine. This eased her mind.

She then checked in with Michael. He had just picked up Josh and was on his way to his parents' house to drop him there for the afternoon. This too eased her mind. She missed her children.

In the afternoon, Church history wasn't much better than her classes in the morning. But world religions was a different story.

It was taught by a rabbi. His name was Edwin Goldberg. He was a small, older man. He wore a yarmulka, the skullcap worn by Jewish men as a sign of respect for God.

Rabbi Goldberg introduced himself, then began this way: "'I love you when you bow in your mosque, kneel in your temple, pray in your church. For you and I are sons of one religion, and it is the spirit.' These are the words of the Lebanese poet Kahlil Gibran. They will be our touchstone in this class over the next 10 weeks."

Now *this* is interesting, Jessica thought.

★

After that class, the seminarians gathered back in the atrium to meet their spiritual directors. Jessica had never had a spiritual director. Father John was her mentor. He'd given her excellent advice for years, including on matters of faith. She wondered why she even needed a spiritual director.

People milled about the atrium. Jessica wondered how she would know who her spiritual director was. Then she remembered she was the only female seminarian!

She saw a woman with dark hair and dark skin stepping toward her. She was small, like Jessica. As she got closer, Jessica noticed streaks of gray in her hair.

"Jessica?" she said.

"Yes."

"Hello. My name is Teresa Das," she said, extending her hand. Her voice was soft. "I'll be your spiritual director, if you agree of course."

"Hello, Teresa," Jessica said, shaking her hand. "It's good to meet you."

"Shall we go someplace we can talk for a few minutes?"

"Certainly."

They walked down the hallway until they found an empty classroom. They went in and sat in a couple of desks.

"Let me begin by asking if you know what a spiritual director does," Teresa said.

"I must confess I don't."

"Don't worry. It's a mystery to most people. Think of me as a guide, someone who can help you find and follow your spiritual direction. I'm here to help you in all aspects of your spiritual life to help ensure you're on your desired path. I'm not a mentor. I'll never offer you advice. And frankly, this is not about friendship. It's about you, not me. I'll tell you just three things about myself. I am deeply spiritual. I have been a spiritual director for many years. And you might have wondered about my name. I was born in the US. My parents came here from India. My mother was Catholic, and my father was Hindu. My mother named me Teresa after Mother Teresa, and Das is my father's family name. I am honored to carry both names."

"Your name is beautiful," Jessica said.

"Thank you. The seminary pays me for this work, at least while you're a seminarian. I take on new clients at my discretion. When the seminary offered me the opportunity to work with you, I said yes. That said, whether we work together is your choice. If we do work together, it will be up to you to initiate all contact. What we discuss, even who I am, will be confidential. We would meet here. The seminary would know we are working together, and I assume your husband would know too. But I would not anticipate ever meeting him. So that's it. What do you think?"

Jessica had never met anyone quite like Teresa. She was matter-of-fact to the point of seeming clinical. But she was clear about her role and apparently very experienced.

Jessica still wasn't sure how Teresa might help her. But after struggling for so long to find her path, she figured it would be a good idea to have a guide.

"I'd love to work with you," she said.

Chapter 31

Four years into her six years of study at the seminary, Jessica was at the top of her class academically and one of the most popular people in the place.

There was a refreshing simplicity about her. Everyone around her knew Jessica had a clear and simple vision of God as "living in the world." As their theological studies became increasingly layered, her fellow seminarians found Jessica's singular focus on following Jesus inspiring and a good reminder of why they were there.

Near the end of her first year, the *St. Louis Post-Dispatch* ran a feature story about her. Soon after that, several women enrolled in the seminary for the following semester. By her fourth year, Jessica was one of 10 female seminarians at Kenrick-Glennon. She played a mentoring role to all of them.

However, not everyone was so enamored of Jessica. Some of the more conservative seminarians were turned off by her progressive views. They saw themselves as "soldiers for Christ" and their training as "formation." They thought Jessica was soft and dismissed her as a lightweight.

What they didn't know was that, despite her pleasant demeanor and outward grace, Jessica was struggling mightily. Her studies were demanding. She was expected to spend five days a week in class and devote even more time to study at home, where another big job always awaited her.

Josh was now seven, Emma five. They could not have been more different.

Emma was quiet, sweet and thoughtful. She loved having Jessica read to her before bedtime. She'd also begun going with her mother to work at a local food pantry on Saturday mornings, just as Jessica had with her mother when she was a girl.

Josh was wild, headstrong and disobedient. It had become more and more difficult for Jessica, Michael and Michael's parents to deal with him.

When he was five, Josh had been diagnosed with ADHD. Jessica and Michael decided to engage a behavioral therapist. It didn't help. When Josh turned six, based on advice by their pediatrician, they agreed to start giving Josh Ritalin.

At first, he seemed to settle down. But soon his mood swings became more severe and unpredictable. When he began threatening other kids at school, his pediatrician increased his medication. Again, there was temporary improvement. But soon Josh became wilder than ever. He threw fits, and it took Michael longer and longer to calm him down.

When Jessica tried to help, Josh grew even more agitated. Her natural urge to comfort him seemed to set him off. Sometimes all she could do was hand him over to Michael.

One day, Jessica came home after class, and no one was there. She found a note on the kitchen table from Michael.

Out to find Josh. Emma is with my parents.
Love, Michael

Jessica called Michael.

"What's going on?"

"They called me from school to tell me Josh left after lunch and they couldn't find him."

"What? Did you call the police?"

"Yes. They've been searching for him all afternoon."

"My God, Michael. Why didn't you call me?"

"I didn't want to bother you, and I thought we would have found him by now."

Her heart sank. Not just because Josh was missing but because she realized she factored so little in his life these days that Michael didn't even call her.

"Michael," she said, her voice cracking, "please stay in touch. I'll pick up Emma."

"Okay. We'll find him, Jess."

On her way back home with Emma, Jessica's phone rang. It was Michael.

"I found him. He's okay."

"Oh, thank God. Where was he?"

"In the woods near our house."

"How did you know to look there?"

"I've taken him there on hikes. I know he likes that place."

"Thank God. I'll meet you at home."

Jessica and Emma were home when Michael and Josh got there. Jessica ran to her son, her arms open wide. But he pushed her away.

"No!" he shouted. "Get away from me. I hate you!"

Then he ran up to his room and slammed the door.

"He didn't mean that," Michael said. "He's just upset. I'll go up and see if I can calm him down."

Jessica was shaking. Emma came over and gave her a hug. "It's okay, Mommy."

Jessica felt her heart breaking. It was breaking because of Josh. It was breaking because Michael hadn't called her when he'd gone missing. It was breaking because she knew Emma had seen it all and that she was getting used to it.

Jessica and Emma went into the family room and sat on the sofa. Jessica put her arm around her daughter and tried hard not to cry. The two of them sat there quietly and listened as Josh's voice grew fainter.

Finally, Michael came down.

"Is he okay?"

"Yeah. I gave him his meds. He's asleep."

"Without supper?" Jessica said.

"He said he wasn't hungry."

The three of them went into the kitchen and warmed up leftovers. By the time they finished eating, it was dark, and Emma was ready for bed.

"Would you read to me, Mommy?"

"Of course."

"Good night, Daddy," Emma said, wrapping her arms around Michael's neck and kissing him on the cheek.

"Good night, Em," he said, squeezing her tight.

"What should we read tonight?" Jessica asked when they got to Emma's room.

"Reginald Clark!"

It was Emma's favorite poem from her favorite book, *Where the Sidewalk Ends*. Jessica pulled it from her bookshelf as Emma changed into her pajamas and brushed her teeth. When she returned, Jessica was sitting on her bed, wiping her eyes.

"Are you okay, Mommy?"

"Yes, sweetheart. Let's read."

Emma climbed into bed and slipped under her covers. Jessica opened the book to a dog-eared page and read aloud.

I'm Reginald Clark, I'm afraid of the dark

So I always insist on the light on,
And my teddy to hug,
And my blanket to rub,
And my thumby to suck or to bite on.
And three bedtime stories,
Two trips to the toilet,
Two prayers, and five hugs from my mommy,
I'm Reginald Clark, I'm afraid of the dark
So please do not close this book on me.

"I love that one," Emma said.

"Me too. Would you like to read another?"

"Yes. We have to read three."

"Okay."

Jessica read two more poems then tucked Emma in.

"Good night, sweetie," she said, kissing her daughter on the forehead. "I love you."

"I love you too, Mommy. Will you leave the light on?"

"Of course."

Jessica went downstairs and sunk into the sofa next to Michael.

"What are we going to do?" she said.

"I don't know. I feel like we need to try something new."

"I do too," she said. "I think we need to find a specialist."

"I agree."

"I'm going to take tomorrow off and see if I can find someone," she said.

"That would be great."

She looked at Michael. His face was drawn, and she noticed some gray in his hair. He seldom complained, but she knew all of this was so hard on him.

"I'll take the kids to school tomorrow, and I'll pick Emma up after school," she said. "We won't need your parents to watch her."

"Thank you," he said. "I'll let Mom know."

Jessica lay in bed that night thinking about Josh. I wish I could understand him, she thought. I wish I could help him.

She fell asleep as she did many nights, saying a prayer for her children.

★

The following day, Jessica found a child behavioral specialist named Indra Khatri at Children's Hospital in St. Louis. She set up an appointment for Michael and her to meet with him the following afternoon.

They were impressed by Doctor Khatri from the start.

"Based on what you've told me, I suspect Josh is suffering from Oppositional Defiant Disorder or ODD," he said.

"Not ADHD?" Jessica said.

"That's a possibility too," he said. "But based on the behaviors you've described, I think ODD might be Josh's primary condition. If that's the case, it's going to call for a different course of treatment."

At last, Jessica thought, someone who can help.

They set up an appointment for Josh to meet with Doctor Khatri. Michael brought him and stayed during the visit. Afterwards, Doctor Khatri told Michael he strongly suspected ODD but would need to do some tests to make sure. They set up another appointment.

The tests confirmed Josh did indeed have ODD. Two days later, Jessica and Michael met with Doctor Khatri to discuss his recommendations. They agreed to allow him to try a combination of a new type of therapy and new medications.

They saw real improvement in Josh's behavior almost immediately. He still had mood swings, but they were far less frequent and much milder. He began paying attention in school. He was much more pleasant. He even let his mother hug him again.

Jessica hoped they had found the fix. Doctor Khatri had cautioned he'd seen patients like Josh relapse. "There are no cures," he said.

But for the moment, there was only relief. For Jessica, her prayers had been answered.

Chapter 32

From the start, Jessica had been blazing a new trail at the seminary.

Acting on her longtime conviction of serving the poor, she devoted several hours a week to working in local food pantries, soup kitchens and homeless shelters and visiting prisoners.

She managed to persuade Father Miller to give her credit hours for this "fieldwork." Not just for herself, but for any seminarian who did such work in the community.

Jessica wanted academic credit so she could do the work in the community during the week, freeing her to spend more time with her family on the weekends. This way, she could graduate on time.

But it was the work itself that was most important to her. She had never forgotten her mother telling her that man she had seen as a girl in the food pantry in Springfield, the one who reminded her of Jesus, was indeed Jesus.

In the seminary, Jessica studied theology. But what good is it to learn about God, she thought, if I don't bring him to life in the world? What could be more important to my formation as a priest than to follow Jesus' great commandment?

Father Miller agreed to give Jessica academic credit for her work in the community. What's more, he began to understand the value of such work for all his future priests. His eyes and heart were opening.

By Jessica's third year, all seminarians at Kenrick-Glennon were required to spend at least several hours working in the community each week, and they were all given academic credit.

The more Miller saw Jessica in action, the more impressed he was. He also saw her potential as an ambassador for the seminary. He sent her to local high schools and colleges as a way to recruit younger seminarians.

When enrollment increased sharply with new seminarians from the St. Louis area, Miller began to send Jessica to other cities around the state too. Everywhere she went became a source of new applicants.

Jessica's presentation wasn't slick. She used no powerpoint slides and brought no promotional materials. She simply told her story, how she had been trying to follow Jesus all her life and how becoming a priest, for her, fit with that.

"The main thing," she told people, "is to listen to the voice within you because it is the Holy Spirit. Let the Holy Spirit be your guide."

She had learned that from Teresa Das.

Jessica's outreach was remarkably effective. Enrollment at the seminary, which had been relatively flat, began to spike.

Among those who noticed was Archbishop Andrew Fox. He was now the archbishop for all of Missouri after a consolidation of four dioceses several years earlier.

Under Fox's leadership, the archdiocese had tried a range of things to increase the number of priests in the state. But nothing seemed to work very well, and the need for priests throughout Missouri was growing. Just over 300 priests were trying to serve more than two million Catholics and lead more than 180 parishes and 100 schools throughout the state. Worse yet, the average age of these priests was 67. Fox's talent supply was literally dying off. The archdiocese was in desperate need of new, younger priests — and fast.

Now Kenrick-Glennon had begun filling up again.

Fox called Miller.

"What are you doing over there?"

Miller told him about Jessica. Fox hadn't met her. He asked Miller to send her over for a brief meeting.

When Miller told Jessica, she asked why.

"I suspect he wants to thank you personally," Miller said.

Jessica agreed to meet with Fox but called Father John to get his take.

When she told him, he laughed.

"Oh, Jessica. For someone so smart, you can be so naive."

"Naive?"

"Sorry," he said. "That's probably the wrong word. Fox doesn't usually ask seminarians to meet with him. He's sizing you up. Miller's right. He probably does want to thank you. And if he's in a generous mood, this might be a good time for you to ask for something."

"Ask for something? Like what?"

"I don't know. Just think about it. The ball's in your court."

She talked with Michael that evening.

"I'm nervous," she said.

"Why?" Michael said with a smile. "*He's* the one who should be nervous."

"Come on. What do you think this is about?"

"I think Father John is right. Fox is sizing you up. Jess, you're going to be a priest in less than two years, and this guy's going to be your boss, and he's never met you. You're his ace recruiter. Why wouldn't he want to get to know you?"

"Well, I hope it's that simple. You know I hate hidden agendas."

"Look, everything I've ever heard about Fox is that he's a straight shooter. I think you can trust this guy, Jess."

"I hope you're right. What do you think I should wear?"

"Now *that's* a good question," Michael said. "You want to look professional, but you want to be yourself."

"A white pantsuit?"

"Of course."

★

The following day, Jessica drove to the archdiocesan offices near downtown St. Louis. The old, brick building was grand and impressive.

Jessica parked in a visitor spot out front. She walked up the stone steps, pulled open one of the large, wooden doors and stepped into the lobby.

"May I help you?" said a middle-aged woman sitting behind a small desk.

"Yes, I'm here to see Archbishop Fox."

"I see," said the woman, her eyes scanning Jessica. "Do you know where his office is?"

"No, I don't."

"It's on the second floor. If you go down this hallway, there's an elevator. When you get out on two, turn left. You'll see glass doors. The archbishop's office is inside."

"Thank you. Is there a staircase?"

"Yes. It's near the elevator."

"Thank you. By the way, I don't think we've met. My name is Jessica Simon," she said, extending her hand.

The woman stood up, and her face softened.

"Hello, Ms. Simon," she said, taking Jessica's hand. "My name is Mary Lammert. I'm pleased to meet you."

"Thank you for your help, Mary. I hope to see you again."

"Yes. I hope so too. Have a good day."

On the second floor, Jessica pulled open one of the glass doors and stepped into a small lobby. A woman she guessed to be about her age sat behind a large reception desk. It was mahogany with a glass top.

"May I help you?" she said.

"Good morning. I'm Jessica Simon. I'm here to see the archbishop."

"Oh, yes, Ms. Simon. We've been expecting you. Right this way," the woman said, getting up.

"I don't think we've met," Jessica said, extending her hand.

"Oh, I'm sorry. I'm Kaitlyn Whitacre."

"It's nice to meet you, Kaitlyn."

"It's nice to meet you too. I've heard good things."

That put Jessica a little more at ease.

She followed Kaitlyn down the hallway. A few offices down, Kaitlyn stopped and gently knocked on the wooden doorframe.

"Your Grace," she said. "Ms. Simon is here to see you."

"Please send her in," said a disembodied voice from within.

Kaitlyn turned toward Jessica, smiled a small smile and gestured toward the voice.

"Thank you," Jessica said.

She stepped inside. The office was large with walnut paneling and dark green wool carpeting. Across the room was a large mahogany desk. Behind it sat an older man dressed in black with a white, clerical collar.

"Ms. Simon, welcome," he said, standing up.

His voice was warm. His face was soft, his hair white and wavy. He was not wearing glasses; his eyes were bright blue. She guessed he was in his sixties. At first glance, he reminded Jessica of her father.

He came around his desk and stepped over to her, extending his hand and smiling.

"Your Grace," she said, shaking his hand. "It's a pleasure to meet you. Thank you for inviting me."

"Thank you for coming. Let's sit for a moment," he said, nodding toward two armchairs. "Would you like something to drink?"

"No, thank you."

They stepped over to the chairs and sat down.

The archbishop rested his forearms on the arms of his chair. Jessica noticed his gold cufflinks and large, gold ring, set with an amethyst stone.

"So you must be wondering why I asked you here today," he said.

"Yes, I was a bit curious."

He chuckled.

"Well, I just wanted to thank you in person for the wonderful work you've been doing in recruiting new seminarians for our archdiocese. Father Miller has been singing your praises. So I wanted to meet you. I'm sorry we've not met before now."

"Thank you, Your Grace. I've loved helping support your work to increase vocations. I'm only building on the foundation you set."

"You're too humble, Ms. Simon. We haven't seen increases in enrollment like this for decades. Let me ask you: how are you doing it?"

"Well, it's simple really. I just share my personal story and invite people to listen to the Holy Spirit."

"Really? Would you mind sharing your story with me?"

Mindful of the archbishop's time, Jessica tried to keep it brief. But he kept asking her questions. He was particularly interested to know why she'd chosen a career in religion over politics.

"All my life, I've tried to follow Jesus," she said, "even when I held political office. After my term as mayor, when I was staying home with my children, I thought about becoming a deacon, but that role just didn't feel right to me. When Pope Francis allowed women to become priests, I had to ask myself if this might be a *new* way for me to follow Jesus. Honestly, I wasn't sure, even when I entered the seminary. But every day, I'm more certain I've made the right choice."

Fox listened intently. Jessica remembered Father John saying the archbishop wanted to size her up. Maybe Fox was evaluating her. But she felt he was truly listening, that he was genuinely interested in her. She felt they were simply having a conversation.

"I find your story fascinating, Ms. Simon," he said. "I believe you'll be an outstanding priest. Now, what can I do to help enable your success?"

Father John was right, she thought. The big ask.

Fortunately, Jessica had given it some thought.

"Your Grace, if I am blessed to be ordained, I would love the opportunity to become pastor of St. Joseph's Church in Springfield. I was baptized there. I went to school there. I made my First Communion there. My parents' funeral Masses were said there. St. Joseph's is a very special place for me, and it would be an honor to lead that parish one day."

"Well, I'm sure the parish would be blessed to have you as its pastor," he said. "I'll definitely keep that in mind as we make staffing decisions in the future."

"Thank you, Your Grace."

They finished their conversation, and he walked her to the door.

"I do have one request," he said.

"Of course."

"Will you please keep me in your prayers?"

"Yes, of course, Your Grace."

"Thank you," he said, shaking her hand. "And I will pray for you, Ms. Simon. Keep up the great work."

★

Jessica did indeed keep up her good work, which continued to pay off in ever-greater increases in enrollment in the seminary.

But recruiting took a lot of her time. Finding enough time for that on top of her studies and her work in the community in addition to doing her best to be a good wife and mother stretched Jessica to the point of exhaustion.

Fortunately, after five years of study, she got a reprieve when she was assigned to assist at Saints Peter and Paul Church in the heart of St. Louis.

Her course load was now relatively light, and she was able to make her work in the community part of her parish assignment. This gave Jessica more time for her family than she had had in years. She was thrilled and relieved.

At Saints Peter and Paul, she formed an instant bond with parishioners. Being there felt so right to Jessica.

"I finally know for sure I'm on the right path," she told Teresa Das.

Teresa just smiled.

Chapter 33

On a brilliant Sunday in June, in the main chapel of the seminary, 11 men and one woman, 41-year-old Jessica Simon, were ordained priests as part of a Mass celebrated by Archbishop Fox.

Jessica was the first woman to be ordained in the Archdiocese of St. Louis.

After Mass, as people headed to a reception for the new priests, Jessica hung back to give kisses and hugs to Michael, Josh and Emma, the three people dearest to her.

Then she saw Father John standing off to the side. She stepped over and embraced him.

"Congratulations," he said. "I knew you would answer his call."

"Thank you for helping me find my way," she said.

★

Two weeks later, Jessica and her family left for Springfield, where she would be the new pastor of St. Joseph's Church and make a new home and a new beginning in the city where she'd spent most of her life.

Getting in the car, Jessica felt a little like she did when she was a girl taking off for vacation, excited to experience something both familiar and completely new.

Chapter 34

Jessica returned to a Springfield that had changed dramatically since she'd left six years earlier.

Tyler Nelson was no longer mayor. The city's economic growth had slowed considerably, and the new mayor had put a premium on cost savings. As part of this, the social services department had been eliminated. Anne Archer was gone, and poverty in Springfield was on the rise.

St. Joseph's parish was feeling the impact too. It was an old church, built in 1892, the only Catholic church in Springfield's inner city. St. Joseph's had never been a wealthy parish, but it had always found a way to make ends meet and even maintain a small grade school.

Now, though, the parish was struggling financially, and its membership was dropping, in part because the average age of parishioners was now over 50. St. Joseph's longtime parishioners were departing, and not enough new, younger parishioners were taking their places.

Many parishioners had known Jessica as their mayor. Most were still getting used to the idea of female priests. St. Joseph's had not even had a female deacon. So when Jessica showed up for her first Mass there, most parishioners weren't sure what to expect.

"In a real way, this is a homecoming for me," she said in her homily. "I was baptized in this church 41 years ago. I said my first Confession here, made my First Communion here, went to school here. I loved my time here at St. Joseph's, and I've missed this place. It's so good to be back."

After her homily, parishioners gave "Mother Jessica" a round of applause. After Mass, they held a reception for her in the parish hall. They were warm and welcoming.

At the same time, Jessica could tell some parishioners were still getting used to the idea of a female priest. A few inadvertently called her Father.

In her first weeks as pastor, Jessica met with the leaders of all the parish's committees. Given the tough economy in Springfield, she wasn't surprised the parish was running a slight budget deficit. She was disappointed, though, to learn that the parish was doing little to help the community, including poor residents in the surrounding neighborhood.

In those first weeks, Jessica also met with a few of her former colleagues from city hall to get up to speed on what was going on in the community at large. Ben Groh, now retired, told her the new mayor had eliminated the department of social services based on the premise that local churches would step up to fill the gap.

"But they're tightening their belts too," he said. "Unfortunately, they're not even coming close to filling the gap."

Jessica looked over St. Joseph's budget and shared it with Michael. He quickly pointed out that about a quarter of the parish's budget was going to fund internal events, from monthly socials to Easter egg hunts. Only three percent was earmarked for the poor, a canned food drive at Thanksgiving.

Reflecting on all of this, Jessica decided the parish should be devoting much more of its budget to helping the poor in the community on an ongoing basis.

"Jesus told us 'Whatever you do to the least of my brothers, so you do unto me,'" she said in her homily that Sunday. "Many in our community are struggling. More people in Springfield are living below the poverty line by the day. I believe we can and should be doing more as a parish to help these people. I'd like to see us give 20 percent of our weekly Offertory collection to the poor in Springfield."

Loud whispers and the sound of people shifting in their seats rolled through the church.

"I know that sounds like a lot, but I think we can manage it," she said. "I'll work with our parish leaders on ways we can trim our budget. I don't expect we'll need to make any wholesale changes, but we may need to make some tough choices. I'll appreciate everyone's flexibility."

When she finished, Jessica expected at least polite applause. Instead, there was only the sound of low talk and grumbling.

Within hours, Jessica began getting nasty email messages. Posts on the parish's Facebook page were highly critical of Jessica's idea and even Jessica herself. Parishioners called her tone deaf. One called her a dictator. Several of St. Joseph's wealthiest members abruptly left the parish.

Jessica felt wounded.

"How could I have been so far off the mark?" she said to Michael.

"Honey," he said, "these people aren't opposed to giving to the poor. They just didn't see this coming. They don't feel they've been consulted."

"Well, they're right. I didn't consult them, and I guess I should have."

In her homily the following Sunday, Jessica apologized and announced she'd be holding a town hall meeting to get everyone's thinking on how the parish can and should be doing more to help the poor and disadvantaged in the community.

She held the meeting in the parish hall that Tuesday.

From the start, parishioners let her have it.

"You march in here and tell us what's best for us," said one. "How about asking us about how *we* want to spend our money?"

"We can barely afford to educate our children," said another. "And you want us to feed the poor? Isn't that what welfare's for?"

"Do you know that some of our most generous parishioners left us last week?" said another. "That's the last thing we need. Thanks a lot."

At first, Jessica tried to respond, but that only seemed to make people even angrier. So she stood there for two hours and took it. Finally, she brought it to a close.

"Thank you for sharing so openly," she said.

Parishioners stormed out.

When she got home, Jessica was shaking. She told Michael what had happened. He tried to comfort her, but he knew it was a mess of her own making. Short of reversing her decision, he wasn't sure how she was going to get out of it.

Frustrated, feeling personally attacked and in need of some good advice, Jessica texted Father John and asked if she could meet him at SLU for lunch the next day.

Sure.

Thanks. I'll be there at noon.

Then Jessica went to bed, seriously wondering if she'd made the right decision to become a priest.

★

The next morning, Jessica got her kids off to school, then drove three hours to St. Louis. She met Father John at the Billiken Grill in the student center.

Over lunch, she told him everything.

"What do you think I should do?"

He could see the pain in her face.

"First, he said, "you can't take this personally. You have to remember this is a time of great change for your parishioners. For starters, they've never had a female pastor. I suspect many of them have never even seen a female priest. Getting comfortable with that is going to take time."

"I get that. But it's hard not to take some of those comments personally."

"I understand. Now let's talk about your decision."

"Okay," she said. "I think the parish needs to step up and do much more for the poor than it has."

"Not that decision," Father John said. "I know how you feel about that. I mean your decision to hold a town hall meeting."

"What about it?"

"So your parishioners are upset about your decision to give more to the poor, and to deal with it, you give them all a microphone."

"I wanted to give them a voice."

"Okay. And now that you've done that, are you going to change your decision about the parish giving more to the poor?"

"No."

"Why?"

"Because it's the right thing to do."

"And how do your parishioners know that?"

"They can see the poor living all around us," she said, sounding a little exasperated. "They're right in the neighborhood."

"Really? Do they know these people? Have they even seen them? How many of your parishioners have ever stepped foot in a soup kitchen?"

"What are you getting at?"

"I understand wanting to give people a voice," he said. "But you made a decision. You made it for all the right reasons, but now you're acting like a politician. If you want your parishioners to see the face of poverty in Springfield, then take them to a soup kitchen and let them feed hungry people. Let them look into their eyes. You've been doing that since you were a little girl because your mother showed you the way. Now you need to show your parishioners the way. It's the only way you're going to help them understand that giving part of their weekly offering to the poor is exactly the right thing to do."

"I guess you're right," she said, looking weary.

"Jessica, let me ask you something."

"What's that?"

"I know you've always felt a kinship with St. Francis."

"Since I was a girl."

"Have you ever read the book *Francis: The Journey and the Dream*?"

"No."

"I'll send you my copy. Read it. It will give you a sense of what Francis went through in his life. In some ways, his struggles were not so different from the one you're facing now. But he never gave up, and he changed the world."

"Thank you, Father. I'll read it with interest."

"Good," he said. "Keep going."

★

When she got home that evening, Jessica sent an email to all her parishioners, inviting them to join her at the Well of Life food pantry that Saturday.

A few people replied to say they would join. Many more, though, replied with negative comments. Jessica chose not to respond because she didn't want to fuel debate. Instead, she said a prayer for everyone who replied.

On Saturday morning, she went down to the food pantry. She brought Emma with her. Soon a handful of parishioners showed up too. Jessica showed them around and assigned them tasks.

Over the course of the morning and into the afternoon, dozens of guests came in. With Emma at her side, Jessica helped many of them. By the end of the day, about two dozen St. Joseph's parishioners had been there to help too.

At Mass the next morning, the gospel, from Matthew, featured the Parable of the Talents.

> His master said to him, "Well done, good and faithful servant. You have been faithful over a little; I will set you over much. Enter into the joy of your master."

Jessica's sermon was short. She thanked parishioners for coming out to help at the food pantry the day before, then asked everyone to mindfully and prayerfully consider how they can best use their talents, their gifts.

When she finished, a middle-aged man sitting in the front row got up and strode to the lectern, where Jessica was still standing. She wasn't sure what he was doing.

"May I speak for a moment, Mother?" he asked.

"Yes," she said.

Her deacon stood up, as if to run interference, but Jessica raised her hand to call him off. A loud whisper swept through the church. Jessica sat down in her chair by the altar, and the man took her place behind the lectern.

"Yesterday morning," he said, "I went down to the food pantry. I had never been there. When I got there, Mother Jessica and her daughter were serving food to a family of four. They were still there, helping people, when I left. When I got home,

I had dinner with my family. As we ate, I wondered where that family of four was at that moment and whether they had a meal to share, and I realized I am blessed beyond measure.

"I know that not everyone in our parish is in favor of giving part of our Offertory collection to the poor. I don't know if Mother Jessica will be back at the food pantry this Saturday. But I'll be there, and I want to thank her for showing me the way, for showing us the way."

He turned toward Jessica, nodded and returned to his seat. Someone clapped. Then others started clapping. Soon everyone was clapping and standing and looking at Jessica.

She was overwhelmed. When everyone finally sat down, she looked for the man who had spoken, but he was gone.

★

A few days later, Jessica received a small package at home. Inside was the book Father John had promised.

A yellow Post-it Note was sticking up from a page near the end of the well-worn paperback. She opened it and read a paragraph that had been highlighted.

> People believed in him. They wanted to believe in the Dream, and he was proof that it *was*. His name was Francis, and he lived and died quietly and peacefully in Assisi. When the light of the spirit was dying out all over the world, this man, this little man, this one man, re-enkindled the flame.

Jessica closed the book. She closed her eyes and thought of the man who had spoken in church on Sunday and knew the light of the spirit was still burning and that she must help keep it alive.

Chapter 35

In the following weeks, more parishioners began showing up to help at the food pantry, soup kitchens, a homeless shelter and other places where St. Joseph's was now sending 20 percent of its weekly Offertory collection.

The parish did indeed have to make some tough decisions about where to cut its budget in order to afford to give so much away. But as parishioners saw for themselves the positive impact their contributions were making in the community, they began to let go of some of the things they'd been spending money on for years. As the parish thought more about others, it became less selfish.

For Jessica, it was a fresh reminder of the importance of personal leadership. It made her think harder about her role *inside* the parish too. She got involved in several groups, including a moms club. She even began teaching a social studies class for eighth graders.

For the first time in years, under Jessica's leadership, St. Joseph's balanced its budget. Giving away 20 percent of its weekly collection forced tough choices the parish had been unwilling to make or even thought about making. What many had first seen as an imposition turned out to be a blessing.

In the coming months and years, the parish embraced Jessica. Even those who had been wary of a female priest at first felt grateful to have someone so dedicated, skilled and compassionate as their pastor.

One of the small things Jessica did really endeared her to parishioners. At weddings and funerals at St. Joseph's, it had been traditional for the presiding priest to announce just before Communion that anyone not Catholic was welcome to "come up for a blessing." This was a not-very-subtle way of telling non-Catholics they could not receive Communion.

Jessica never made such an announcement at the weddings and funerals she officiated. Instead, she gave the host to anyone who came up to receive it.

When someone asked her why, she said, "Who am I to withhold the Body of Christ from anyone?"

It was a simple thing. But it was the kind of thing that mattered to people, the kind of thing that told the parishioners of St. Joseph's their pastor had courage and heart.

★

But there was a downside to Jessica's strong and engaged leadership. Once again, she was with her family less and less and just when they may have needed her most.

When the Simons moved back to Springfield, Michael was able to get his old job back at O'Reilly's. It was a step down from his position at Anheuser-Busch. He made peace with that, though, because it was a nine-to-five job. He knew that, with Jessica taking on a parish, he would need to play a larger role with their kids.

As always, Emma was low-maintenance. But Josh, who had increasingly struggled with ODD, was now a rebellious teenager. He drank, smoked pot and once ran away for nearly a week. He swore, got tattoos and threatened to drop out of school. His doctor increased his medications, but Josh was an uncooperative and sometimes belligerent patient.

The more his parents tried to help, the more Josh tuned them out. Not being able to connect with him was a source of frustration for Michael. Not being there more for him was a source of anguish for Jessica.

As much as she loved being there for her parish, Jessica felt she was failing her family. And it wasn't just Josh. She knew Michael was feeling the strain.

Jessica tried hard to make more time for her family. But her parishioners' needs only grew. Sometimes they needed her in the middle of the night and on weekends. Some were in the hospital. Some were homebound. Some were in jail. She always made time for these people, even knowing it often meant time away from her family.

Once, when she was in St. Louis for a meeting at the archdiocese, she talked with Father John about her struggle for more balance in her life. But having neither a parish nor a wife, he couldn't offer much advice.

Over time, Jessica tried new ways to be more discriminating about how she spent her time on parish activities. She focused her meeting time on parish council. She limited her work in the community to Saturday mornings. She stopped teaching social studies.

This helped, but she still got home late most days and felt spent when she got there. Josh was usually in his room and not interested in talking with her or anyone. Emma was always pleasant, but Jessica could tell she missed spending more time with her mother. Michael was increasingly quiet.

Jessica was usually in bed by 10:00. Sometimes, as she was falling asleep, she would say a prayer for all the people she had let down that day, those she simply didn't have time for, especially those dearest to her.

Chapter 36

By 2039, her fourth year as a priest, Jessica had balanced St. Joseph's budget three years in a row. In that time, none of the other nine Catholic parishes in the Springfield area had balanced its budget, and the Archdiocese of Missouri was feeling the pinch.

Once again, Jessica's work caught the attention of Andrew Fox. When he was Archbishop of St. Louis, before all the dioceses of Missouri were consolidated into one, he had balanced his budget for years, even during economic downturns.

But the dioceses Fox had inherited were on shaky ground financially, and he was now struggling to improve their financial well-being. He was also now 72 years old, just three years from mandatory retirement.

When Fox saw the results Jessica was getting at St. Joseph's, he wanted to know more. He invited her to St. Louis to meet again.

"You're doing a great job," he said.

"Thank you, Your Grace."

"Mother, one of the things I find particularly impressive is your ability to balance your budget despite giving away so much of your weekly collection. How have you done that?"

She explained "putting a stake in ground" on the 20 percent plan had helped focus the parish on its mission and "instantly enabled us to cut what was off-strategy."

"Of course," she said, "as you know, sacrifice is the heart of strategy."

Fox was not used to such business talk from his priests. He smiled and got to the point, the real reason he'd called her there.

"Mother, I'd like you to work with the pastors of the other nine parishes in the Springfield area to help them balance their budgets too."

She felt, and looked, surprised.

"I know that's asking a lot," he said. "Do you think you could do this without undue distraction from your work at St. Joseph's?"

"Yes," she said, even though she had no idea how she was going to pull that off.

★

Before she left St. Louis, Jessica swung by for coffee with Father John. She told him about her conversation with Fox.

"Unbelievable," he said.

"What? Good or bad?"

"Good, I think."

"You think?"

"Well, it depends on whether you want a much bigger job."

"I do think I can find a way to help the other pastors," she said.

"That's not what I'm talking about. Don't you see? Fox is grooming you. He wants you to be his successor."

"What? That's nuts."

"Jessica, don't be naive. Fox sees what you're doing at St. Joseph's, and he realizes very few, if any, of his other priests have your skills and experience. He's giving you this assignment as a test. If you do well, he'll have a basis to recommend you as his successor."

She looked at him and smiled.

"How did you get to be so smart?"

"I'm a Jesuit," he said with a grin.

★

Right after his meeting with Jessica, Fox sent an email to the pastors of the other nine parishes in Springfield, telling them he had directed her to work with them to develop plans for balancing their budgets for the year ahead.

"I know you'll find Mother Jessica a very helpful resource and a delight to work with," he wrote.

She called Michael on her way home. She wasn't sure how he would take the news, but he sounded surprisingly upbeat.

"We'll talk about it more when you get home," he said. "By the way, I'm making spaghetti and meatballs tonight."

"You're the best."

After dinner, once Josh and Emma were in bed, Michael and Jessica brought their glasses of wine into the family room and sat down on the sofa.

"To your new assignment," Michael said, raising his glass.

"Thank you," she said, clinking but still more than a little surprised by his positivity.

"So you said you'd like to talk more about it," she said.

"Yes, I would. Jess, I'm happy for you, and I love you. I'll always love you. But I miss you. The kids miss you. You're not here enough as it is, and now you'll be taking on the budgets for nine other parishes. I also worry about you. I see the stress you're under, and I think about your parents both dying so young. I want to grow old with you."

"I'm sorry," she said.

"No, Jess. I'm not looking for an apology here. If anything, I should have said something long before now. I've never asked you for much, but I'm going to make a request."

"What's that?"

"You're working 80 hours a week. I want you to figure out how to do your job in 50 hours a week, and that includes the new work you'll be taking on."

"Fifty hours?"

"Yeah. That's still a lot, but it would leave more time for us and more time for yourself."

"But—"

"Jess, please listen to me. There is only one of you in this world, and I'm in love with you. I need you. The kids need you. Your parish needs you, and now these other parishes will need you too. You're amazing, but you're just one person. I don't need to tell you that the Bible says your body is the temple of the Holy Spirit. You've got to take care of yourself, or you'll be no good to anyone."

"You're right," she said. "Thank you. I don't know how I'm going to do it, but I'll do my very best to begin doing my job in 50 hours a week."

"Do you want a suggestion?"

"Yes."

"Talk with Ben Groh. He's always seemed pretty balanced, and he managed a whole city. Get some tips from him."

"Good idea."

She put down her wine glass, got up and reached out for his hand.

"Let's go to bed," she said.

"Okay."

She chose not to tell him, just yet, about what Father John had said that afternoon.

★

Two days later, Jessica met Groh for lunch. She laid everything out and asked for his advice.

"Very manageable," he said.

"Really?"

"Yeah. You just have to do three things."

"What?" she said, pen in hand.

"First, decide how much time you're going to spend with each of the other pastors helping them set their new budgets. I mean how many hours a week. Second, have them take the same basic approach you're taking at St. Joseph's. What I mean is have them clarify what's not negotiable and start cutting everything else. Don't reinvent. You've got the model. Reapply it. Third, redefine your role as pastor. You've got to focus on fewer things and delegate more. If you don't, you'll never get to 50 hours a week."

She stopped writing and looked up.

"That's it?" she said.

"Yep."

"Good Lord, Ben. This makes so much sense. No wonder you were so successful."

"It's a gift," he said with a chuckle.

★

Jessica thought about holding a conference call with the pastors of the nine other churches to begin to engage them on budget planning.

But that felt bureaucratic. So instead she visited them, one by one. That took a lot more time, but it turned out to be important because each of these pastors confided in her how frustrated and helpless they felt when it came to their budgets.

They all had finance committees, usually led by parishioners who were financial professionals. But what they were all lacking were budgets that put their parish missions in the center so there was a clear sense of priority when it came to spending.

It's what Groh had meant when he said to be clear about what's "not negotiable."

"Invest in your mission," Jessica told them. "Everything else is secondary. Cut it or defer it."

It sounded so simple, but there was great power and wisdom in that advice. For starters, it helped ensure these parishes had really *thought about* their mission and what they were doing to bring it to life. It also gave the pastors a practical way to make tough choices.

What's more, now they could say the archdiocese was behind this. After all, Fox was indeed directing them to balance their budgets. There would be no more room for deficits. The rules had changed.

Within 90 days, all nine pastors had developed and submitted balanced budgets for the coming year. Not only that, but Jessica identified several areas where all 10 parishes could share costs for goods and services at a significant discount, reducing expenses for everyone. It's what Michael called "leveraging scale."

And Jessica had done it all while cutting her own hours to about 50 a week. Of course, this meant being ruthless about how she spent her time. Making these choices was hard for Jessica, but she knew she needed to follow Groh's advice, not to mention the advice she was now giving other priests.

When he heard about the nine parishes' new budgets, Fox was thrilled. Once again, he called Jessica to St. Louis. She assumed he wanted to thank her in person.

"Mother," he said, "what you've done here in a very short time is remarkable."

"Thank you, Your Grace."

"What you've done for the parishes in Springfield needs to be done for our parishes throughout the archdiocese," he said.

He looked at her and smiled. Was he really thinking she might do the same thing for all the other parishes in Missouri? How could she possibly do that on top of her job as pastor of St. Joseph's?

She thought of Michael. She thought of their agreement about 50-hour work weeks. She thought about Josh and Emma. Her heart raced. She began to feel queasy.

"Don't worry," Fox said. "I wouldn't think of saddling you with that on top of your current role as pastor."

"Oh, good," she sighed.

"I have a different proposal."

"You do?"

"Yes, I do. Mother, you've got the talents and insights we need — not just to balance our parish budgets but to operate more efficiently as a single archdiocese. I mean how we pay people, how we hire people and so forth. You would work with our finance, IT and HR managers. Think of it as a COO position."

Jessica began to get the idea.

"Of course, you'd need to move to St. Louis because the resources you'd need are here," Fox said. "And that would mean you'd have to give up your parish in Springfield."

Fox paused. Jessica looked stunned.

"Well, what do you think?" he said.

Jessica felt like her head was about to explode. This was the last thing she was expecting. She tried to compose herself.

"I think it's exciting, and I'm honored," she said. "But Your Grace, I'm not just a pastor. I'm a wife and a mother too. I've already asked my family to move twice. I need to talk with them before I give you my answer."

"I completely understand," Fox said. "Take all the time you need and get back to me when you're ready."

Holy crap, she thought.

★

Once again, she stopped by to see Father John at SLU on her way home.

"Jesus, Mary and Joseph!" he exclaimed, throwing his hands up. "COO! He *is* grooming you. What did I tell you?"

"I'm starting to believe you."

"Are you going to do it?"

"If I can stick to a 50-hour-a-week schedule and Michael's okay with another move, yes."

Father John smiled.

"When does Fox turn 75?" he said.

"In three years."

"You'd better work fast."

★

Michael agreed to move back to St. Louis, his hometown, provided Jessica would continue to work about 50 hours a week. She then called Fox to tell him yes, with that proviso. He readily agreed.

Fox lined up a priest in Kansas City named Brian Connolly to succeed Jessica. The following Sunday, Jessica and Connolly announced their pending moves to their respective parishioners.

Jessica received a standing ovation at both Masses at St. Joseph's. Afterwards, parishioners formed a kind of receiving line to personally thank her and wish her well. There were lots of tears.

Two weeks later, the parish hosted a send-off for Jessica. It was packed, with a good number of residents from the community who were not parishioners.

Jessica recognized a lot of people from the food pantry. She thought of her mother's funeral reception not far from there and said a silent prayer of thanks to her mother for showing her the way.

★

Jessica started her new job in January of 2041. Josh was a sophomore in high school; Emma was in eighth grade. Michael decided he would stay in Springfield with the kids until the end of the school year. The three of them would then join Jessica in St. Louis.

In the meantime, Michael had already arranged to return to his old job at Anheuser-Busch that summer. Until then, on weekends, Jessica would come home for what Michael called "conjugal visits."

In St. Louis, Jessica dug in right away. She set several goals for a new "operating system" for the Archdiocese and developed a four-phase plan: (1) assessment, (2) recommendations, (3) engagement, and (4) implementation.

Fox reviewed her plan and approved it in minutes.

"Go," he said. "Just let me know what you need."

Jessica took full advantage of the time before her family moved to St. Louis to work long days. She got through the first two phases of her plan in less than three months.

Before she shared her findings and recommendations with Fox, though, she decided to share them with Ben Groh as a "reality check." She sent him her draft material, and they talked by phone.

"Bullseye!" Groh said.

Fox approved Jessica's recommendations with only minor changes. Two weeks later, with the archbishop at her side, Jessica presented her plan to the archdiocesan board of trustees. They approved it unanimously.

"Wow," said one CEO afterwards. "If she wasn't a priest, I'd hire her as *my* COO."

With the trustees' imprimatur, Jessica and the archdiocese's finance and IT managers then reviewed the new operating system with pastors throughout the archdiocese on a conference call. They'd all received the plan by email two days earlier.

"By now, you've all seen the plan," Jessica said. "Any questions or comments?"

They had a host of good questions and more than a few compliments.

"Most of all," said one pastor, "I appreciate you making all these administrative tasks simpler."

Others made similar comments. Jessica could hear the relief in their voices. As a former pastor herself, she knew what a drag these administrative tasks could be and how they made it all the harder for a priest to be a spiritual leader for his or her parish.

Jessica thanked the pastors for their partnership, especially on the initial assessment. She closed by letting them know she'd be sending them communication materials about the new plan which they could share with their parish councils.

The call ended with a chorus of thank yous.

Fox heard a lot of positive feedback from his priests. He was quick to share it with Jessica, who was delighted. She sent handwritten thank-you notes to everyone who had been involved in the process, more than 200 people in all. An email would have been much more efficient, but Jessica wanted all the participants to know her gratitude was heartfelt.

In June, her family joined Jessica in St. Louis. She'd found a nice, three-bedroom condo in the city. They could stay there until they found a house. Jessica was thrilled to have her family together again. She had missed them so much.

Over the balance of the year, Jessica worked closely with pastors throughout the archdiocese on implementing the new plan. They tracked progress on the main elements using a red, yellow, green scorecard. It was a system Jessica had learned from Ben Groh.

In August, Josh and Emma started the fall semester at the same high school. By then, Michael had settled back into his old job at Anheuser-Busch.

Jessica had to travel a bit to troubleshoot glitches at a few parishes around the state, but she still managed to spend time at soup kitchens and homeless shelters in St. Louis.

And most evenings, she was home for dinner. This made her heart feel light.

★

In February of 2044, Fox called Jessica to his office.

"It sounds like everything is going very well with our new system," he said.

"Yes. Overall, I'd say we're on-track. I'm pleased."

"I am too. Are you still getting interest in your model from other archdioceses?"

"Oh, yes."

"Good," Fox said, allowing himself a moment of professional pride.

He leaned forward in his chair.

"Do you know what October first is?"

"No."

"It's my birthday."

"It is?"

"Yes. I'll be 75. That's the mandatory retirement age for archbishops. That means I need to recommend my successor to the pope fairly soon. Of course, there's no guarantee he'll accept my recommendation. These appointments are completely his to make."

"I see."

"Jessica, I want to recommend you as my successor. I know you've been a priest for only nine years, but you've distinguished yourself. Our Church needs dynamic, experienced, young leaders like you. I think you'd do a great job leading this archdiocese. If the pope agrees, would you accept this responsibility?"

Even though Father John had called it more than two years earlier and this idea had been in the back of her mind, hearing Fox say these words stunned Jessica. Her face went pale.

"Are you all right?" he said.

"Yes, Your Grace," she said, feeling her heart race. "I am honored beyond words. My answer is yes."

"Wonderful!" he said, extending his hand across his desk. "Congratulations!"

"Thank you."

"I'd like to make an announcement around Easter," he said. "That will leave us a good amount of transition time. Of course, that means we'll need to go to Rome soon so I can present you to Pope Francis. Is your passport up-to-date?"

Jessica's head was spinning. Setting decorum aside, she put her head between her knees and took deep breaths.

Chapter 37

In 2044, Angelo Ricci had been pope for 20 years, making him one of the longest-reigning modern popes. He'd taken the name Francis II as a nod to his progressive predecessor. He then quickly proceeded to make the original Pope Francis look conservative by comparison.

As the pope who had allowed the ordination of women, Francis II was eager to see women take on important leadership roles in the Church. There were now scores of female priests, but no woman had yet been elevated to archbishop.

When Francis learned Fox would be recommending a woman as his successor, he was thrilled. He sent word to Fox that he looked forward to receiving both him and Jessica at their earliest convenience.

They flew from St. Louis to New York on a Sunday afternoon and headed for Rome that evening. Jessica hadn't traveled abroad. In fact, she'd flown only twice.

She was more than a little anxious. Her doctor had prescribed a sleep drug for the overnight flight. As soon as they left New York, she took it and fell into a deep sleep.

She was awakened by an attendant serving breakfast about an hour before they landed.

"Good morning, Jessica," Fox said, as she sat up.

"Good morning, Your Grace," she said, feeling a little groggy and very self-conscious about her tousled hair and puffy eyes.

They chatted over breakfast. Then Jessica grabbed her complimentary bag of personal care products and went to the bathroom to freshen up.

She returned to her seat just as the plane was about to begin its descent toward Leonardo da Vinci International Airport. Looking out her window, Jessica spotted the massive dome of St. Peter's Basilica rising up from the Roman skyline, gleaming under the rose-gold sunrise. She had seen it only in photographs. Now it looked even more spectacular.

In that moment, Jessica thought of her parents. She wished they were there with her to see this too.

A driver was waiting for them in the terminal. He took them to Casa Santa Marta, a luxury apartment building next to the Basilica.

A Franciscan nun showed Jessica and Fox to their rooms. They rested for about an hour, then headed to the Basilica on foot.

It was a sunny but chilly early spring day in Rome. They had lunch at a small restaurant near St. Peter's Square. Then they walked across the square and up the marble steps of the Basilica, bypassing the line of tourists courtesy of Fox's special pass.

Stepping inside and looking around, Jessica felt a little dizzy. The Basilica dwarfed even St. Patrick's Cathedral in New York, the largest church she'd ever seen.

"What do you think?" Fox said.

"It's magnificent," Jessica said, looking up at the arched ceiling, lined with gold, leading to the enormous dome. "Breathtaking actually."

They toured the Basilica for several hours. Fox, who had been there many times, enjoyed playing tour guide, telling Jessica the stories behind the architecture, statues and artifacts. He showed her through the Crypt, the lower level ringed with small chapels. He even showed her a few areas that were off-limits to tourists, including the Lady of Lourdes grotto, an artificial cave in the lush and perfectly manicured Vatican Gardens.

By early afternoon, Jessica could tell Fox was getting tired.

"Would you like to go back to the Casa and get some rest before dinner?" she said.

"That would be great," he said.

Over dinner at a bistro near the Pantheon, Fox tried to prepare Jessica for what to expect in the morning.

"Our session will be brief," he said. "It's a bit of a formality, I'm afraid. It's a long way to come just to receive a blessing, I know. But it's a blessing you'll never forget."

"Is there anything special I should say — or not say?"

"Not really," he said. "The pope's English is good. Just follow his lead. Oh, and always call him 'Your Holiness.'"

That evening, back at her apartment, Jessica called Michael.

"I almost can't believe this is happening," she said. "It's all so grand. I feel so small here."

"I'd love to see it with you one day," he said.

"You will. Next time, you're coming with me."

She hardly slept that night. In the morning, the sisters served them a hot breakfast. Their driver then took them to the Apostolic Palace. It would have been a two-minute walk, but their driver had to follow a circuitous route around the Basilica and the surrounding grounds.

A priest greeted them at the Palace. He escorted them through a series of hallways to a small room to await the pope.

"May I get you anything to drink?" he asked.

They ordered Caffe Americano.

Fox was wearing his vestments, standard attire for any bishop or cardinal visiting the Vatican. Jessica, as usual, was wearing a white pantsuit. They sat at opposite ends of a red sofa, facing a single chair, where Fox said Francis would sit.

Jessica dabbed the perspiration on her forehead. Her mouth was dry. She tried to sip her coffee, but her hand was shaking, and she had to set it down.

"Take a deep breath," Fox said. "Everything will be okay. Just be yourself."

Jessica closed her eyes. In that moment, she thought of Jesus, the man in the woods who had told her to follow him. Now here she was, inside the home of St. Peter's successor. She had done her best to follow Jesus, but she never imagined he would lead her here.

Someone knocked lightly at the door. It opened slowly. Jessica and Fox rose to their feet. There in the doorway stood Pope Francis II. He was smiling. He was small and thin, with white hair and dark brown eyes. His face was lined with wrinkles, but his eyes sparkled.

"Good morning," he said, with a thick Italian accent.

"Good morning, Your Holiness," they said.

Francis stepped over to Fox and extended his hand. The archbishop took it, then bowed. In earlier times, Fox would have kissed the pope's ring. But Pope Francis had done away with that ancient practice, and Francis II had followed his lead.

The pope then turned to Jessica, extended his hand and smiled. She took his hand and bowed.

"Your Holiness," she said.

"So let us sit for a moment," Francis said, taking his seat.

Fox and Jessica sat back down on the sofa.

"Did you get coffee?" he asked.

"Yes, Your Holiness," Fox said. "Caffe Americano."

"Of course," he said, smiling.

His smile seems so warm and genuine, Jessica thought.

"So," he said, looking at Fox, "happy birthday in advance."

"Thank you, Your Holiness."

"Your Grace, I see you have been a priest for more than 45 years. You have served the Church brilliantly. Thank you for your tireless dedication and exemplary leadership. I reluctantly accept your resignation, and I wish you continued happiness and good health. God bless you."

"Thank you, Your Holiness. It has been a sacred honor to serve."

The pope smiled and nodded, then looked at Jessica.

"And I see that you, Mother, have been a priest for only nine years. Archbishop Fox must think very highly of you to recommend you as his successor."

Jessica wasn't sure what to say.

"Mother Jessica has distinguished herself in her relatively brief time as a priest," Fox said. "Before that, she served as mayor of Springfield, a city near St. Louis. She's done wonderful work as a pastor and for our archdiocese overall. I know she will do an excellent job leading our archdiocese forward."

"Of that, I am sure," the pope said. "So I see you are also a mother and wife."

"Yes," Jessica said. "My husband Michael and I have two children, Joshua and Emma."

"What beautiful names," Francis said. "And are they all ready for you to take on this new responsibility?"

"Yes, Your Holiness, they are."

"You are blazing a new trail in our Church, you know."

"I am simply doing my best to follow Jesus," she said.

The pope smiled and looked at Fox. Jessica wondered if she had said the wrong thing.

"Jesus?" the pope said, looking back at Jessica.

"Yes."

Francis continued to look at her, saying nothing. He seemed to be studying her face. Then he looked at Fox and said, "Your Grace, will you please give us a minute?"

"Yes, of course, Your Holiness," he said, standing up.

"By the way," the pope said, "I agree with your recommendation for your successor."

"Thank you, Your Holiness," Fox said, smiling at Jessica as he passed by.

When he had gone, Francis said, "Mother, I have a few questions, if you don't mind."

"Certainly, Your Holiness."

"First, how are you finding it, I mean being a priest?"

"I love it."

"Good. And how are you finding the balance between being a priest and being a wife and a mother?"

She knew that was a big question, and she thought for a moment about how she should answer. Then she remembered Fox's advice to just be herself.

"It is a challenge, Your Holiness."

He nodded.

"I knew it would be," he said. "You are taking care of so many. I pray that you are able to take care of yourself too and that God will continue to take good care of you."

"Thank you, Your Holiness."

"So you are trying to follow Jesus."

"Yes."

"My namesake, Francis, tried to follow him too, you know."

"Yes," she said with a smile. "St. Francis has been a hero of mine since I was a girl."

"Is that so?"

"Yes."

"Why?"

"He too had visions of Jesus."

As soon as those words left her mouth, Jessica felt her body tense up. She felt she had said too much.

"You've had visions of Jesus?"

Again, she remembered Fox's advice.

"Yes, Your Holiness, when I was a girl."

"You saw him?"

"Yes."

"What did he look like?"

I'm all in now, Jessica thought.

"He had kind brown eyes and olive skin. He had long, black hair and a beard. He wore a robe."

"And did he speak to you?"

"Yes."

"What did he say?"

"Follow me and I love you. He called me by name."

"I see. And have you told others about this vision?"

"Only a few. My husband. My mother. My spiritual director and my mentor, a Jesuit priest."

"And now me."

"Yes, Your Holiness."

He looked at her with a gentle smile.

"Mother," he said, "I have a favor to ask."

"Of course."

"Will you pray for me? You seem to me a person who is very close to God, and I know I would benefit greatly from your intercession."

"Yes, Your Holiness. I will pray for you every day."

"Thank you. I know you will make a fine archbishop. The people of Missouri are blessed to have you as their new leader.

I hope you will continue to follow Jesus, and I thank you for your prayers."

He rose, and she did too. She was ready to shake his hand, but this time he opened his arms. She went to him, and they embraced. The pope was not much bigger than Jessica.

"God bless you, Mother."

"God bless you, Your Holiness."

Francis started toward the door, then turned around.

"Thank you for telling me about your vision."

Chapter 38

The following month, Jessica was installed as the new Archbishop of Missouri. On her first day, she called in her finance manager, Taylor Gibson, whom she had known for years.

"Good morning, Your Grace," Taylor said, black folder in hand.

"Good morning, Taylor. Please have a seat. I have an assignment for you."

"Certainly," she said, sitting down and opening her folder.

"I want to sell the archbishop's residence."

"Pardon me?"

"Yes, I'd like to sell it. As soon as possible."

"Why — if I may ask?"

"Well, for starters, my family and I won't be living there. More important, though, it's extravagant. I don't think the archdiocese needs it. We could use the money we could get for it to help a lot of people. How much do you think we could get for it?"

"Well, it was assessed last year at $1.4 million."

"Wow! Do you think we'll have a hard time selling it?"

"I doubt it. It's in good shape, and there are a lot of wealthy Catholics in St. Louis."

"Good. Will you call our realtor this morning and get things moving?"

"Yes, I can do that," Taylor said with a worried look.

"But what?"

"Well, I'm just trying to understand."

"What would you like to know?"

"Well, first of all, what are we going to do with the money?"

"I'd like to build food pantries, homeless shelters and job training centers where they're needed most around the state."

"I see. About how many did you have in mind?"

"I don't know. How much does it cost to build one or remodel a place? We don't need anything fancy."

"I'm not sure, but I suspect somewhere around $100,000."

"Great. That means, if we get $1.4 million, we could build or remodel 14 places."

"Yes, but we'd also need to cover operating costs, including staffing. That might double the cost."

"Well, even if it does, we could still afford seven new places."

"Your Grace, this is a pretty big deal. Don't you think we should talk about it a bit more before we move on it?"

"What more do we need to talk about?"

"Well, for one thing, I think we could make the proceeds on this sale go a lot farther."

"What do you mean?"

"I mean if we can get $1.5 million, we can probably afford to build or remodel 15 places."

"Fifteen? I thought we were talking about seven."

"We were. But why should we pay for everything? We could put up $100,000 for each place and ask local businesses to match us."

Jessica's eyes widened.

"Taylor, that's brilliant! Yes, we should definitely do that."

"Your Grace, that's just one example of why we should have a plan before we jump into this."

Jessica smiled.

"You're right, of course. Would you develop a plan for us?"

"I'd be happy to. When would you like to see it?"

"How about Wednesday?"

"*This* Wednesday?"

"Too soon?"

"No, Wednesday will work. I do want to consult with Bill on how we're going to announce this."

"Yes, we'll need to make an announcement. I guess as soon as we put the residence up for sale, we'll get attention. Will you ask Bill to draft a news release? Please invite him to join us on Wednesday too."

"Okay. I'll set something up with Kaitlyn, and we'll see you on Wednesday."

★

The following Monday, the archdiocese's 11,000-square-foot, castle-like mansion went on the market. This did indeed make news. By the end of that week, a St. Louis restaurateur had bought it for $2 million, furniture included.

What's more, more than two dozen businesses and individuals around the state contacted Jessica's office to say they were in for the matching gifts.

Jessica was thrilled.

"Now we can afford *20* places!" she said to Taylor.

"Maybe so," said Taylor, feeling both energized and exhausted at the end of Jessica's first two weeks on the job.

★

Next, Jessica began visiting the 428 Catholic churches throughout the state of Missouri. She knew it would take her years, but she felt a need to personally connect with all the priests and as many parishioners in the archdiocese as possible.

She spent extra time with female priests. She got to know them, coached them, encouraged them. She thought often about the time Charlotte Brown had spent with her when she was starting out.

As Jessica traveled the state, there was much to like about what she saw. Parishes devoting resources to ensure a good education for their children. Parishes with active prison ministries. Parishes providing fellowship for their members.

But she was disappointed to learn how little most parishes were doing to help the poor in their communities. Most didn't have outreach programs. What's more, only a handful of priests were active in their communities.

After six months of visiting parishes, she concluded the Church in Missouri should be doing much more to help the poor in the communities where its members lived, worked and prayed.

Jessica was now the leader of more than two million Catholics in Missouri. She knew she could simply proscribe the level of giving by all parishes in the state. But she well remembered the backlash when she tried to do that during her early days at St. Joseph's.

She decided to convene a two-day summit on poverty for all parish priests from the archdiocese. She opened it by sharing her perspective.

"We won't wipe out poverty," she said. "But that's not the point. Our aim should be to alleviate suffering, to lift people up. In the process, we can *begin* to end poverty. I've seen this happen. I've seen well-nourished children do better in school and graduate. I've seen men and women with a safe place to sleep and clean clothes to wear get jobs. I've seen people with new or updated skills get jobs. Most important, I've seen what happens when poor people are treated with dignity and respect. They feel that they matter. They begin to believe in themselves. They have hope. I've seen forgotten people rise up."

She paused.

"This is sacred work. We are Jesus' apostles, and this is our work to lead. We won't wipe out poverty, but we can help people, every one a child of God, break free of it."

Then she got personal.

"We, as priests, must lead the way," she said. "By the end of tomorrow, I'd like each of us to develop an action plan for how we'll step up in our parishes and communities. That includes me, by the way."

The first day of the summit was devoted to defining the problem and sharing stories about what was working well. The second was devoted to brainstorming solutions and giving each priest time to develop his or her personal action plan.

The mood was positive, the camaraderie energizing. Jessica got to see many of her former classmates who were now priests. It was a special treat to see Father Benjamin Lopez, who had befriended her on their first day at the seminary. He was now leading a parish in western Missouri.

Not once did Jessica have to mention anything that resembled tithing. She knew some pastors would need to ask for more from their parishioners. But she would leave it up to them as to how they would go about that.

The collective actions leading from the summit produced a new wave of contributions and community outreach throughout the state. Thousands of lives were improved, both the poor and those now helping them. Some people got the food, shelter, clothing, personal care products and medicines they needed. Others got job skills training. Young people, many of whom had become "spiritual but not religious," began returning to the Church, having finally found something meaningful to them.

Jessica was emerging as a strong leader on her largest stage yet. She was making a name for herself. This was not her aim. But she was the only female Catholic archbishop in the world, and what she did tended to make news.

★

Jessica's impressive achievements as archbishop came at a cost. Once again, she was seldom home. The 50-hour weeks she had been able to manage before becoming archbishop were long gone. Her work was now all-consuming, leaving little time for her family.

Michael did his best to fill the gap. But as Emma turned 16, curious and sensitive, she needed her mother. As Josh graduated from high school, aimless and hard-edged, he could have used his mother's direction and soft touch.

But even as Jessica was present for more than two million Catholics, she was increasingly absent from the lives of the three people who mattered most to her. This made her heart ache.

★

For years, Michael had done his best to connect with Josh. He had tried to talk with him, taken him to movies, taken him fishing. But nothing seemed to work. Josh seemed to care nothing for the things that Michael thought he should care about: doing well in school, going to college, getting a job, taking care of himself.

As soon as he graduated from high school, Josh told Michael he was moving out. Jessica was gone that evening.

"Where will you go?" Michael said.

"I'm going to live with some friends."

"Where?"

"Downtown."

"What will you do for money?"

"I'm going to sell my stuff and get a job."

"What kind of a job?"

"I don't know. Maybe I'll work at Starbucks."

"If you need money, Josh, we'll give it to you."

"Thanks, but I'll be okay."

Michael told Jessica when she got home that night. By then, Josh was asleep. Jessica hoped to talk with him the following day.

The following afternoon, when his parents weren't home, Josh took off. He told Emma to tell them he'd be in touch. He left on foot, with only a backpack and a sleeping bag.

When Michael got home that evening and Emma told him Josh had left, he tried to call Josh's cell phone but kept getting his voicemail message.

"I'm not sure what to do," Michael said to Jessica when she got home.

"Maybe we should file a missing person report," she said.

"Can you do that for someone who's 18?"

"I think you can do it for anyone who's missing."

Such was their uncertainty about what to do about their son. When it came to Josh, things were often unclear.

Michael did file a missing person report. The police located Josh by tracking his cell phone. He was in an apartment in the inner city.

They called Michael at work to let him know. He cut out early and drove to the apartment. Jessica was in Kansas City.

When Michael got there, Josh was sitting on the floor, watching TV with another young man and a young woman. They were all drinking beer.

"Dad, what are you doing here?"

"You weren't answering your phone, so I called the police. They tracked you down."

"Figures," he said, looking back at the TV.

"Josh, can we talk for a minute?"

"Sure."

Josh stood up, looking bothered, and stepped into the kitchen. He leaned back against the counter and crossed his arms.

"Josh, what are you doing?" Michael said in a low voice.

"What do you mean? I'm living here with friends, just like I told you."

"What are you doing for money?"

"I'm looking for a job."

"Do you need money?"

"No, Dad. I'm okay. But if I need anything, I'll let you know."

"Will you answer your phone when I call from now on?"

"I'll try. I don't always have it with me."

"Well, keep it with you. Your mother and I worry. We want to know you're okay."

"I'm okay. Really, Dad. Don't worry about me."

"All right. But stay in touch."

"I will."

Michael extended his hand. Josh took it, but his grip was loose, and he didn't make eye contact.

Michael called Jessica on his way home.

"Is he okay?" she asked.

"I guess."

"Thank you for going down there. At least we know where he is now."

"Yeah," he sighed.

★

Michael tried to call Josh every couple of days. Sometimes he would pick up. Most of the time, though, he didn't.

One Saturday, Michael went to Josh's apartment to see him, but he wasn't there. One of his roommates told him Josh had left that morning, but she wasn't sure where he went.

"Will you have him call me when he gets back?"

"Sure."

But Josh didn't call. Finally, the next day, he picked up.

"Yeah, Dad," he said, sounding distracted.

"Are you okay? I've been calling you. Did you get my messages?"

"Yeah. Sorry. I've been kind of busy."

"Doing what?"

"Looking for a job, I told you. Dad, I know you mean well, but don't worry about me. I'm fine."

"Okay," Michael said, sounding weary. "Okay. I'll back off, but promise me you'll take care of yourself."

"Okay, Dad. I promise."

★

As Thanksgiving approached, Michael and Jessica were hoping Josh would join the family for dinner. But once again, Michael couldn't get ahold of him. He figured if he kept calling, eventually Josh would pick up. That seemed to be the pattern.

One day at work, Michael got a call from the receptionist. He had a visitor in the lobby.

"Send him up."

"He said he would like to see you down here."

Michael went down to the lobby and saw a policeman standing there.

"Mr. Simon?"

"Yes."

The officer walked over to him.

"I'm afraid I have some bad news, sir. Why don't we sit down?"

★

Michael sat in an empty conference room near his office. He felt weak and sick to his stomach. He put his head down and started crying. He cried for a long time.

Then he got up, told his assistant he would be gone the rest of the day and drove to the archdiocesan offices.

Jessica was in a meeting. Michael asked Kaitlyn to interrupt her. He had never interrupted his wife at work.

He was sitting in her office when she got there. His face was ashen, his eyes swollen and red.

"Michael?" What's wrong?"

"Oh, Jess," he said, standing up. "It's Josh. He's—. He's gone."

She looked at him, searching his face, waiting for him to say something else, but he didn't. She didn't need to ask what he meant by "gone." She knew from the anguish on his face.

She gasped and brought her hands to her mouth. She felt dizzy, and her legs went weak. Michael caught her and helped her to a chair. Then he sat down beside her and put his arms around her.

"No," she moaned. "No."

He sat holding her. He whispered what the police officer had told him, that Josh was found in a homeless camp down by the Arch, that he had died of a drug overdose.

"There's no way to know whether it was intentional," Michael said.

"Ohhh," she groaned, taking in the awful significance of that thought.

They held each other and cried.

Finally, Michael said, "Jess, they need me to identify his body, so I have to go now."

"I'll go with you."

"Okay."

He helped her to her feet. She started for the door, but her legs went weak. Fortunately, he had his arm around her. Rather than lift her, though, he lowered her to the floor and knelt beside her. She was holding her hand to her chest and gasping.

"Are you okay?" he asked.

She kept gasping.

"I'm going to call 911," he said.

"No," she said. "I don't need a doctor. I need my son."

Chapter 39

They buried Josh near Jessica's parents. There was no reception. Jessica said she didn't have the strength. Everyone understood.

Over breakfast the following morning, after a sleepless night, Jessica said to Michael, "I need some time."

"Me too," he said. "What do you have in mind?"

"I'm thinking about taking the rest of the year off."

"Sounds good," he said. "Do you want to stay here or go away?"

"I think I need to go away."

"I understand."

"I think I want to go to Lake of the Ozarks. Will you go with me?"

"Yes," he said. "I should be able to work from there for a few weeks."

"Thank you."

Jessica stared into her coffee.

"What about Emma?" she said. "I'm worried about her. She's been so quiet. Do you think she's okay?"

"Yes. I think she's just trying to understand."

"You don't think she's at risk, do you?"

"No, I don't. Jess, she's like you."

"Sometimes that worries me."

"What do you mean?"

"I mean she needs to take care of herself."

"Jess, Emma will be okay. She'll be back in school next week. Only three more weeks until Christmas break. We can come back for Christmas. Emma could stay with Pete and Erin until then."

"What if she needs us?"

"If she needs us, I'll come back and get her."

"Well, she does love spending time with Hannah," Jessica said. "But I'd need to talk with her every day."

"Okay. We'll talk with her when she comes down. If she's okay with it, I'll call Pete."

"Okay. But Emma's really got to be good with this."

Michael put his hand on hers.

"We'll make sure she is."

"All right," she said. "If Emma's okay, will you rent a place for us?"

"Of course."

"I'll need to put someone in charge while I'm away."

"You have an auxiliary bishop, you know."

"Right."

"Jess, you need this time for yourself. You're a wonderful leader, but it's time to step away for a little while. The archdiocese will get by without you for a month and a half, and everyone will understand."

"I hope so."

They heard Emma coming down the stairs. She came into the kitchen.

"Good morning," she said, giving them each a hug.

They said good morning and told her what they had in mind.

"I think it's a great idea," she said. "You guys need this time out."

Jessica looked at Emma in her flannel pajamas. Her hair was a mess. Sometimes she still seemed like a girl. But that morning she seemed like a wise young woman, caring for her parents as they cared for her.

"I'd like you to call me when you get home from school every day," Jessica said.

"I will, Mom."

"And if you want to see us, I'll come home and pick you up," Michael said.

"Thanks, Dad. I might take you up on that."

★

The Saturday after Thanksgiving, Michael brought in the mail. Jessica was sitting on the sofa in their family room. Michael laid the mail down on the coffee table.

Jessica sat there, looking at the stack of envelopes. More sympathy cards, no doubt. She leaned forward and began leafing through them. She spotted an envelope with "Das" printed in the upper left corner. It was addressed to her. She opened it and pulled out a small, white card. On it was a handwritten note.

Jessica,
My prayers are with you.
God is with you.
Please let me know if I can help.
Peace,
Teresa

In all the years she'd known Teresa, it was the first time she'd ever written.

She read the card again. This time, she paused on "God is with you."

Jessica closed her eyes and thought about that idea. She knew it must be true. But the past few days, she had known only grief. For her, God had been strangely absent.

It was too much to think about. Jessica slipped the card back in the envelope and sat back on the sofa. She thought about going through the rest of the mail, but she couldn't take any more. Instead, she lay down, pulled a blanket over herself and fell asleep.

★

The following Monday, having seen Emma off to school, Jessica and Michael set out for Lake of the Ozarks. The sky was gray, and a light snow was falling. Jessica watched the snow cover the leafless trees. The land looked as dreary as she felt. She said little the whole way.

They arrived around noon. Michael had rented a cabin nestled in the woods near the lake. He knew Jessica loved that lake and thought being near it might be good for her.

When they had unloaded their things and unpacked, Jessica said, "I think I'll take a nap."

"Okay," said Michael. "I'll go out for groceries."

When he got back, he looked in on her. She was still sleeping.

He put away the groceries and began to make dinner. He had decided to make Jessica's favorite.

He blended tomato sauce, tomato paste and diced tomatoes in a pot, sprinkled in some oregano and set it on the stove to simmer. In a ceramic bowl, he kneaded ground beef and mixed in bread crumbs, parsley, eggs, oregano, salt and pepper. He formed six meatballs, which he placed on a cookie sheet and slid into the oven.

Jessica still wasn't up. Michael heard her phone ring. She'd left it in the main room. He answered it.

It was Emma. She'd just gotten home from school. She said she was fine. She was just checking in.

"Thanks for calling," Michael said. "We're fine too. I'm making dinner, and Mom's taking a nap."

"Is she okay?"

"Yeah. Just exhausted."

"I understand."

"Would you like her to call you when she wakes up?"

"No, that's okay. Enjoy your dinner. I'll call tomorrow. Just tell Mom I love her."

"I will. I love you, Em."

"I love you too, Dad."

Michael got a fire going and sat down in a leather recliner. The cabin was still a little chilly, and the warmth from the fire felt good. Michael leaned back, closed his eyes and fell asleep.

The sound of the oven door creaking open woke him up. He went into the kitchen. Jessica was pulling the meatballs off the cookie sheet with tongs and gently dropping them into the sauce. Michael had forgotten to set the timer.

"How did you sleep?" he asked.

"Fitfully."

"I'm sorry."

"It's okay. I got some sleep. Thanks for making dinner."

"You're welcome. Emma called. I told her you were sleeping."

"Is she okay?"

"Yes. She said she'll call tomorrow. She sends her love."

"I miss her," Jessica said, stirring the sauce.

Michael stepped over to her and put his arms around her waist from behind. She put her hands on his arms, then turned around, and they embraced. They held each other a long time, saying nothing.

They said little over dinner too. Each time he tried to engage her in conversation, she said a few words, then disengaged. They ate mostly in silence.

After dinner, they brought their glasses of wine into the main room. She sat down on the sofa. He added a few logs to the fire, then sat beside her.

Neither of them said anything for a few minutes.

Finally, Michael said, "Do you want to talk about it?"

Silence. Then she said, "I blame myself."

"Oh, Jess. How could you think that?"

"I was never there for him."

"Of course you were."

"Not when he needed me most."

"Jess, you're a great mother. We both did our best. He was simply beyond our reach."

"*You* did your best, Michael. I was too busy to care for him as I should have. He needed me. What kind of mother abandons her child?"

"Jess," he said, putting his arm around her, "please don't do this to yourself. You've suffered enough. Josh was troubled from the time he was a boy. Think of all the times we tried to help him. I'm quite sure he felt your love."

She wanted to believe him. She wanted to believe she was a good mother and that Josh felt her love. But at that moment, she wasn't sure what to believe.

After a few more minutes of awkward silence, Michael said, "Jess, I think you should see Teresa."

"Why?"

"I don't know, but whenever you see her, you seem to be more at peace. You need to find some peace."

Jessica stared into the fire. She watched the flames dance along the logs. She thought of Hell. She hoped Josh was in heaven. She wondered if she, having failed him, would ever join him there.

"Maybe you're right," she said.

★

Jessica hadn't seen Teresa Das in more than a year, since before she'd been appointed archbishop. Up to that point, she'd seen Teresa for spiritual direction every few months for nearly 15 years.

But the demands on Jessica as archbishop were so great that she kept putting off her meetings with Teresa. She even cancelled a couple. She felt bad, but meeting with Teresa was an investment in herself, and with so many people now in need of Jessica's time, tending to herself was no longer a priority.

Now Jessica realized that was a mistake. She missed her sessions with Teresa. She missed thinking deeply about her relationship with God. More than anyone, Teresa helped her explore that relationship.

The following morning, Jessica called Teresa. She thanked her for her card and, with some hesitation, asked if she would be willing to drive three hours to the cabin.

"I know that's a big thing to ask," Jessica said.

"I can be there the day after tomorrow," Teresa said.

★

Wanting to respect Jessica's privacy, Michael went out for the afternoon Teresa would be there.

She showed up early. Jessica heard her car coming up the gravel drive and met her at the door.

"Hello, Teresa," Jessica said from the doorway.

"Hello," Teresa said, walking up the stone path.

"Come in."

Teresa stomped the snow off her shoes, then stepped inside, and the two women embraced.

"I'm sorry," Teresa whispered.

"Thank you," Jessica whispered back. "I'm glad you're here."

Jessica took her coat and hung it up.

"Can I get you something to eat or drink?"

"Hot tea, if you have it."

"Yes, I do. You've had a long drive. Would you like to freshen up before we get started?"

"Yes," Teresa said, looking around the main room. "And I'd like to meet here, if that's okay with you."

"Yes," Jessica said. "The bathroom is the first door on the left down the hallway."

A few minutes later, Jessica returned from the kitchen with a mug of hot tea. She set it down on a softstone coaster on the coffee table just as Teresa was coming back in.

"Thank you," Teresa said. "Let's move these two chairs closer together."

They pulled two armchairs toward the fireplace, facing each other with a comfortable space in between. Teresa then grabbed a straight-backed chair from the corner and moved it next to the coffee table.

"For the Holy Spirit," she said. "He's still in charge."

Jessica smiled.

Teresa pulled a candle out of her bag, placed it on a coaster on the coffee table and lit it.

"There," she said. "Now let's sit."

They sat down. Michael had built up the fire before he left, and it warmed them.

"I'd like to begin with a prayer," Teresa said.

Jessica nodded. They closed their eyes and bowed their heads. They sat for a few moments in silence.

"Holy one, we come into your presence, and we thank you for this day and this time together. We ask that this time together be in the service of Jessica's highest good. We ask this in Jesus' name."

Jessica was holding her head in her hands. After a minute, she lowered her hands and opened her eyes.

"When you said that chair was for the Holy Spirit, I felt myself smiling," she said. "That was the first time I've smiled in a while. Honestly, I wasn't sure I could ever smile again."

Teresa nodded.

Jessica sighed.

"I feel so guilty," she said.

"Why?"

"I should have been there for him. Josh needed me, and I wasn't there."

"You hold yourself responsible for Josh's death?"

"Yes."

For a minute, Teresa didn't say anything. Then she said, "Jessica, tell me where you are right now."

"I'm in a dark place. I feel alone."

"Do you feel God's presence?"

"No."

"Please say more."

"I feel betrayed by God. I've given my life to God. I've sacrificed so much. I may not have been a good mother, but I didn't deserve this. How could God have taken Josh away from me this way? It's cruel. It must be some kind of punishment, the price I have to pay for being too selfish, too ambitious, for not being there for him. I've been thinking about Josh as a boy. Do you know there were nights when he threw tantrums, and I couldn't deal with him? Nothing I did helped. If anything, my presence seemed to set him off. Michael would go into his room and shut the door and somehow get him to calm down. To this day, I still don't know how he did it. Eventually, when Josh started acting up, I would just turn him over to Michael. I gave up on being able to help him. Imagine that. Imagine a mother giving up on her son. The poor kid was in trouble, and I stepped away. What kind of mother does that? If I had only been a better mother, Josh might still be here. I feel so guilty."

Teresa said nothing.

"I'm angry too," Jessica said, digging her fingertips into the arm of the chair. "I'm angry at God for letting this happen. I'm angry at myself for not being a better mother. I'm even angry at Josh. How could he be so selfish? Maybe he got it from me. But then I think: how can I be angry at Josh? And that makes me feel even more guilty."

They sat in silence for a few minutes, looking at the fire. Then Teresa said, "Do you believe God still loves you?"

"I don't know. I don't know anymore."

"What do you mean?"

"You know, I used to believe God loves us all, no matter what. But I'm not so sure anymore. I've failed my only son. I let him go even when I knew he might be in danger. I let him destroy himself. My only son. How in the world could that not be a mortal sin? How could I not be held to account for that?"

The fire crackled.

"Do you believe God is judging you?" Teresa said.

"Yes. I believe he is judging me for not being a better mother. I believe he is judging me for not being a better wife. I believe he is judging me for spending much more time on my career than on my family. I believe he is judging me for having the arrogance to think I can lead an archdiocese. Who am I? There must be a thousand people more qualified to do this job. How can I tend to all these souls when I can't even keep my own son safe? I should have stayed in Springfield. I should have raised my children there and never made my family move to St. Louis. That move was really hard on Josh. He was only three years old. He needed me, and I wasn't there for him. I was too busy studying theology," she said, slapping the arm of the chair. "I was too busy studying God to take care of his precious gifts to me. I was too busy to help my son learn to read or change my daughter's diapers. My mother-in-law and my husband raised my children. And as they grew up, it only got worse. I was home less and less. Michael did his best, but he didn't sign up to be a single parent. He needed me too, and I wasn't there for him either. Judging me? Yes, I believe God is judging me, and he must be so disappointed."

They sat in silence. Finally, Teresa said, "Do you think it's possible that God still loves you?"

"I don't know," Jessica said.

They sat quietly with their eyes closed, the fire warming them, the cabin protecting them from the falling snow, two women who had known each other for years, one of them having shared her inmost feelings, the other having listened patiently, without judgment, wanting nothing but to allow the Holy Spirit to guide them, praying only for the other's highest good.

"Jessica," Teresa said softly, "do you remember your experience of seeing Jesus when you were a little girl?"

"Yes."

"Is it possible for you to remember how you felt in his presence?"

Jessica closed her eyes and tried to remember. A few minutes later, she put her hand on her heart and began to cry.

"It was such a tender encounter," she said.

"How did it make you feel?"

"I felt loved."

"Do you think it's possible for you to access this feeling again?"

Jessica closed her eyes. She felt a cracking open deep inside herself, as if something or someone were breaking her apart.

"Maybe," she said. "Maybe it's possible."

Silence.

"Good," Teresa said.

They talked for another half an hour, mainly Jessica sharing more about how she was feeling. Then there was a long silence, and Teresa closed their session with a prayer.

Jessica asked her to stay for dinner, but she said she wanted to get home before dark.

Jessica walked her to the door. The two women embraced.

"God loves you," Teresa whispered.

It was the closest thing to an opinion Teresa had ever offered.

Jessica welcomed it.

★

The following morning, Jessica sat in an armchair in front of the fireplace, her hands wrapped around a mug of hot coffee. Michael was stretched out on the sofa, scanning news on his laptop.

They heard a vehicle crunching up the snow-covered gravel driveway. Michael got up to see who it was.

There were footsteps outside, then a knock at the door. Michael opened it.

"Delivery for Jessica Simon," a man said, handing Michael a box.

"What is it?"

"Flowers."

"Thank you."

Michael pushed the door closed with his shoulder.

"Flowers for you," he said, smiling at Jessica.

"I wonder who they're from," she said.

He set the box down on the coffee table. It was made of white cardboard, about a foot square and two feet tall.

"Open it," Michael said.

Jessica stepped over to the coffee table and sat down on the sofa. She pulled a piece of tape from the top of the box, opened it and peeked inside. She saw white tissue paper. She could smell the sweet aroma of fresh flowers. She reached in, pulled out a vase and set it on the coffee table. She peeled back the tissue paper, revealing a gorgeous bouquet of lavender roses, purple carnations, white lilies, green and orange magnolia tips, white cushion poms and green trachelium in a clear crystal vase.

"Wow!" Michael said.

"Aren't they beautiful?"

"Who are they from?"

Jessica looked through the box but couldn't find a card.

"I don't know," she said. "There's no card."

"Well, maybe you have a secret admirer."

She smiled.

"Here, let me get rid of this stuff for you," Michael said, gathering up the box and tissue paper and bringing it into the kitchen.

Jessica looked at the flowers. She had never seen an arrangement so lovely. She leaned in, closed her eyes and breathed in the scent.

She brought her hand to her heart. She thought of the flowers in her mother's garden in the backyard when she was a child. She thought of the day she walked to the edge of the yard and went into the woods and the man she had seen there. She thought of what he had said to her — "I love you" — and how, when he said that, she felt loved completely.

★

That afternoon, Emma called.

"How are you?" Jessica said.

"I'm fine, Mom. How are you?"

"I'm doing a little better, thanks. Do you have anything special planned for the weekend?"

"Well, that's kind of why I was calling. I was wondering if I might come visit."

"That would be wonderful, Em. Dad can come get you."

"Are you sure? I'd be happy to drive."

"I think Dad would actually like the diversion. You know he's an early bird. He can take off early tomorrow and pick you up by mid-morning. That way, you'll be here for the afternoon. We can go for a hike, do anything you like. Dad can bring you home on Sunday."

"That sounds great, Mom. I'll be ready. I can't wait to see you."

"I can't wait to see you, Em," Jessica said, her heart feeling a little lighter.

Chapter 40

Their cabin was on an inlet of the lake. It faced west. Jessica and Michael had begun a practice of walking down to the water in the late afternoon before dinner to watch the sun set.

They always held hands and usually said little. They were content to watch the ducks, geese and blue heron glide quietly across the tangerine sky, seemingly unconcerned about the gathering winter, as if the reservoir were their safe haven.

They also began taking hikes in the woods, sometimes together, sometimes by themselves. One afternoon, while Michael was taking a nap, Jessica decided to go for a short hike.

She went into the woods at an opening near the cabin and followed a path for about half a mile when she came to a fork in the trail. She and Michael had walked to that point and taken the trail to the right. Today, though, Jessica decided to go left to see where the path would lead.

Most of the hardwoods — maples, oaks and sweetgums — had lost their leaves, though some leaves still clung to branches and twigs. Jessica had noticed this during her winters in Springfield as a girl. She had always found it curious. Were the leaves hanging on, she wondered, or the trees holding tight?

She came to a bend in the trail where the path ascended slightly. As she looked up, she saw him. His presence startled her. She gasped.

He was standing on the trail just 10 feet away, facing her. His hair was long and black, and he had a medium-length beard. His skin was olive, his eyes dark brown. He wore a light brown, knee-length tunic and sandals. She recognized him immediately as the man she had seen in the woods as a girl.

Neither of them said anything for a minute. She stared at him. She wondered if he still knew her. It had been more than 40 years. She looked so different, though he looked the same. He even wore the same, warm expression. He smiled and looked at her as if he knew her well, as if they were old friends.

"You came back," she said.

"I never left you," he said. "I will always be with you, Jessica, and I will always love you."

How did he know? How did he know this was what she'd been seeking?

But just then, she thought of Josh, and her heart sank, and everything felt unresolved again.

He looked at her and said, "Jessica, your son is with our father. He is at peace."

Again, she brought her hand to her heart. How did he know these were the words she had longed to hear?

Overwhelmed, she fell to her knees and began to weep. She felt as though she were both empty and full. Then she felt a stillness, a peacefulness she had not known for a long time and thought she might never know again.

She looked up. He was gone.

Chapter 41

Walking back to the cabin, thinking about her situation and why she was there, Jessica still felt sad. But knowing God was with her and that he loved her made her feel hopeful too. Maybe there is a path out of this darkness, she thought.

When she got back, she told Michael about her encounter. When she told him what the man had said about Josh, Michael's eyes filled with tears.

"Oh, Jess," he said, embracing her and holding her tight.

Over dinner, she told Michael exactly how she'd been feeling. She'd been holding back. Not to keep anything from him. But what she'd been feeling had simply been too painful to share.

She told him she felt guilty about not being a better wife, about not being there enough for him over the years.

"I know it's not been easy being married to me," she said. "I'm sorry if you've felt ignored."

Michael listened carefully. Jessica expected him to say it's okay. He was always quick to forgive.

But this time he said, "We all make choices, Jess. The truth is I *have* sometimes felt ignored. I don't say that to be harsh, but if you want to make me a priority in your life, and if you want to make Emma a priority, you're going to have to make some different choices."

It was as direct as he had ever been with her. She looked at him and saw the pain in his eyes and realized that not being more attentive to him had wounded him deeply. She reached across the table and held his hand.

"I'm sorry," she said. "You're the most important person in my life, and I don't ever want to make you feel anything less than that again."

"Thank you," he said. "So what are you going to do differently?"

This was Michael at his best, she thought. Soft-spoken but determined. A man of action. It was what had first attracted her to him and what attracted her to him now.

"Well, to be honest," she said, "I've been so stuck, I haven't really given it any thought."

"I have an idea," he said.

"I'm all ears."

He filled their wine glasses, and they moved to the sofa, in front of the fire.

"You need a plan," he said.

"Yes, I do."

"I could help you develop it, based on everything I know about what works in the business world."

"That would be great."

"But it wouldn't be complete," he said, "because you don't operate in the business world. You operate in the realm of the Church, and I know very little about the Church. But fortunately, we both know somebody who knows a lot about the Church, somebody you trust implicitly."

Her eyes lit up.

"John?"

"Yes," he said. "I think Father John and I should work with you to develop your new plan. What do you think?"

"I think it's perfect," she said, raising her glass.

★

Father John arrived at the cabin two days later. He'd packed a bag, ready to stay "as long as it takes."

After a light lunch, the three of them moved to the main room. Michael and Father John moved two armchairs to the ends of the sofa, slanted toward the fireplace, forming a kind of oblong semicircle. Jessica sat on the sofa, and Father John and Michael sat in the chairs.

Jessica was holding a book. She opened it.

"I was reading a quote by Thomas Merton," she said. "He wrote: 'To allow oneself to be carried away by a multitude of conflicting concerns, to surrender to too many demands, to commit oneself to too many projects, to want to help everyone in everything, is to succumb to the violence of our times.'"

She closed the book and set it on the coffee table.

"I feel like Merton was writing about me," she said. "Long before Josh died, I felt as though I were being pulled apart. Since he's been gone, I've wondered if I can go on. It's been a dark night. But over the past few days, I've seen some rays of hope. I do want to go on, but I know I can't keep doing things the same way. I know I need to make some big changes, but I need help. There's no one I've relied on more over the years for good advice than the two of you. I'm so glad we're here together. I pray this might be a new beginning."

"Thank you for inviting me," Father John said. "I'm honored to be here."

"We love you, Jess," Michael said. "We're always here for you."

"Thank you," she said. "Where should we begin?"

Father John and Michael looked at each other. Each started to speak but then stopped in deference to the other.

"Father," Michael said, smiling, "please go ahead."

"Okay," he said. "Let me start with a question. Jessica, what is it you really want to accomplish as archbishop? I mean, what is the one thing you hope to do?"

"You do have a way of cutting to the chase, don't you, John?" she said.

Jessica had started calling Father John by his first name when she turned 50.

"Let me think for a moment," she said.

Silence.

"Okay," Jessica said. "I want to lead in a way that helps people understand Jesus' great commandment."

"Do you want them to follow that commandment too?" Father John said.

"Yes," she said. "Yes, of course. But I can't choose that for them. People will have to make their own choices."

"But ideally, as a result of your leadership, more people will choose to follow Jesus' commandment?"

"Yes."

"And what will make them want to make that choice?"

"I'm not sure," she said.

"Jess," Michael said, "you follow Jesus. Why?"

"Because I know it's right, and I see the results," she said. "I see the people who benefit, and I feel the difference inside myself."

"Like when you work with the poor?" Father John said.

"Especially then," she said.

"And how did you learn that?" Michael asked.

"My mother showed me," she said. "I went to the Well of Life and worked with her."

"Do you see a similar role for yourself, I mean as part of your role as archbishop?" Father John asked.

"I see that as my most important role," she said.

"Well, then it sounds like you need to make that your main focus," Michael said.

"Hang on," Father John said. "The leader of a large archdiocese can't spend her days in food pantries."

"Why not?" Michael said.

"Well, for starters, she has a lot of administrative responsibilities," Father John said. "She's in charge of a big organization."

"Jess, how much of your time would you say you spend on administrative work?" Michael said.

"Well, I hate to admit it, but some days, probably half of my time."

"Half?" Father John said, looking surprised.

"Sometimes more, John."

"Well, I guess you can't spend time in the community if you're sitting in an office," Father John said.

"You need a COO," Michael said.

"A COO?" she said.

"Someone to run your day-to-day operations," he said. "Someone who can free you up to lead."

"I hadn't thought about that," she said. "Someone like that would be a huge help."

"Is your archdiocese in pretty good shape?" Father John asked.

"Overall, yes," Jessica said.

"Give us the highlights," Michael said.

She said her parishes were in good shape physically and financially. Some consolidation was needed, but the number of Catholics in Missouri was growing. A number of parishes in the archdiocese were even building new churches and schools or expanding existing facilities.

She told them the majority of parishes were being run very effectively, though she would need to replace about 20 percent of pastors over the next couple of years because they would be retiring. Fortunately, the seminary in St. Louis was full, and there would be a good number of new priests ready for parish assignments soon.

Jessica also felt good about the progress most parishes were making in addressing poverty in their communities. However, some parishes still seemed to be hanging back.

"Why do you think that is?" Father John asked.

"I'm not sure," she said.

They decided to take a break. While Father John and Michael were in the kitchen, Jessica sat and looked at the fire. She remembered the impact of her work at the Well of Life on her parishioners at St. Joseph's. She thought of Jesus washing his disciples' feet at the Last Supper. She thought of St. Francis caring for the poor and sick people in Assisi.

It's not enough to urge my parishes to be active in their communities, she thought. I have to model the behavior I want to see in others. I have to personally lead the way.

Not that there wasn't any other role for her, beyond working in food pantries and homeless shelters, in helping the poor. She knew the impact an archbishop could have in seeking support from government and business leaders, for example. This was important work too. But she knew a *visible* role would be needed if she wanted to begin changing hearts.

But how was she going to do all this and still have time for her family? For herself? She wasn't sure. Her only thought was to limit the time she devoted to work and resist the temptation to "help everyone in everything."

When Father John and Michael came back, she said, "I want to commit to working 40 hours a week and spending half of that time helping the poor."

"Forty hours a week?" Michael said. "Jess, you've never worked 40 hours a week in your life."

She smiled.

"You asked me what I'm going to do differently," she said. "I'm going to spend 40 hours a week doing my job. And I'm going to spend half of that time serving the poor, working alongside my parishioners. I feel called to that. I'm going to pick a few administrative tasks that only I can do, like appointing parish pastors, and try to delegate the rest. And I'm going to have dinner with you and Emma at least three times a week, and that doesn't include weekends."

"You're serious?" Michael said.

"Absolutely."

"It's certainly admirable, Jessica," Father John said. "But do you really think you can do this?"

"I don't know, John. Remember what Jesus said. 'Enter by the narrow gate.' I think I'll try that for a change."

"Where will you start?" Father John asked.

She looked at Michael.

"You've got to hire that COO," Michael said.

"Exactly," she said.

"I know of an auxiliary bishop in Chicago who might be perfect," Father John said.

"No," Jessica said. "I don't want a bishop for this role. I want someone with a background in business or politics, someone who knows how to manage things, how to get things done."

Michael smiled.

"You want someone like Ben Groh," he said.

"Yeah," she said.

★

Father John spent another day with them at the cabin. They mainly talked about the nuts and bolts of how Jessica was going to pull off such a major change in her job.

Michael contributed a lot based on his business experience and knowledge of how to do things efficiently in an organization. He even came up with a "churchy" job title for Jessica's new COO: Auxiliary.

Father John had great insights and suggestions on how to make it all work politically, within the Church.

He also suggested Jessica write the pope a personal letter to share her bold new plan.

"Why?" Jessica asked.

"He's your boss," Father John said. "I suspect he'll be very supportive. But you know you'll have critics. Who knows how they might try to spin this. It's best the pope hear directly from you. You may need him in your corner."

The next day, after Father John left, Jessica drafted a letter to Pope Francis. It was brief, but she went through several drafts, refining her thinking about her new role in the process.

She then called Kaitlyn and dictated the letter. She asked her to type it, sign it for her and send it to the pope on her letterhead.

★

Jessica and Michael returned home on Emma's last day of school before her Christmas break. They made sure they were there when she got home.

Emma had put up Christmas decorations, including a nativity scene under the tree in the family room. They had a tradition of not laying the infant in his crib until Christmas morning. Now looking at the empty manger made Jessica think of Josh. She missed him so.

Chapter 42

When Jessica returned to her office, Kaitlyn greeted her with a hug, then pointed out a large basket on her desk filled with envelopes of various shapes and sizes.

"What's this?"

"Cards and letters that came for you. You might want to open these two first."

Kaitlyn handed her a small, square envelope and a business size envelope. The return address on both was simply the papal crest, embossed and in gold.

Jessica opened the small one first. Inside was a single piece of white card stock. On it was a handwritten note:

Mother,
I am holding you in prayer.
With love,
Pope Francis II

She slipped the card into her pocket, then opened the larger envelope. Inside was a typed letter from the office of the pope, signed by his secretary.

I am writing on behalf of the Holy Father, who has received your letter of December 8, 2045.
He is in full agreement with your proposal and says, "Please proceed with my blessing."

Jessica smiled and handed the letter to Kaitlyn.
"Keep this handy," she said.

★

The following day, Jessica called a man named Ethan Morelli. He was a vice president for Ascension Health, a large health care services company based in Clayton.

Father John had recommended him for her new Auxiliary position. Like Jessica, Morelli had been his student at SLU. Father John liked him and had stayed in touch over the years.

Morelli was 50 years old, a year younger than Jessica. He'd been with Ascension for 25 years. He was a member of the executive team, but he knew he was not in line for CEO.

Morelli had made plenty of money and was eligible for early retirement. A lifelong Catholic, he was active in his parish and community. He and his wife were now empty nesters, and he was looking for a change and a way to make a new contribution.

Jessica asked Morelli to lunch. Even without knowing why, he said yes.

They hit it off immediately, especially after Morelli told Jessica about his longtime involvement with Covenant House, which helps troubled youth. She thought of Josh.

She told him about the position, that it was really a COO role and why it was so important to her.

"You have quite a vision," he said. "I'd be honored to help enable it."

As they finished lunch, Jessica handed Morelli the job description. He called her the next morning to say he was very interested.

"I'm delighted," she said. "Of course, you know I'll need to post the position and consider other candidates too."

"I completely understand."

After interviewing half a dozen other candidates, Jessica was even more convinced Morelli was the right person for the job.

She invited him to her office and made him an offer, apologizing for the modest salary. He accepted on the spot.

"Wonderful!" Jessica said. "When can you start?"

"How about in three weeks?"

"That's perfect."

★

Morelli hit the ground running, immediately taking several big administrative tasks off of Jessica's plate. She had no interest in such "ecclesiastical bureaucracy," as she called it, but Morelli seemed to actually enjoy it. Jessica was thrilled.

"You were so right about my need for a COO," she told Michael. "Thank you."

"You're welcome," he said. "We'll keep his real title between us."

Just as she had hoped, Jessica was now able to focus more on the work only she could do as archbishop — pastor assignments, for example. She also had much more time for Michael and Emma. She was home for dinner most nights, and she began to learn to unplug. She began taking walks with Michael again.

She now had more time to work with the poor and enough time to visit at least one new parish a week, putting her back on track to visit every parish in the state.

One week, her plans called for her to visit St. Ann's Church in Carthage, a small town on the western edge of the state. It was a four-hour drive from St. Louis. It would be an overnight trip. Jessica was particularly excited about this visit because the pastor of St. Ann's was Father Benjamin Lopez, her former classmate in the seminary.

It was a perfect assignment for him, arranged by Archbishop Fox a few years earlier. Lopez and his family had moved to Carthage from Mexico when he was a boy. Nearly a third of the town's residents were Latinx. Many were Catholic. St. Ann's had been Lopez's parish growing up. He still knew many parishioners when he returned as pastor.

"Benjamin!" Jessica said when he greeted her on the sidewalk in front of the church.

"Welcome, Your Grace," he said, embracing her. "It's wonderful to see you."

"Please call me Jessica."

"Are you sure?"

"Yes. By the way, what do your parishioners call you?"

"Father Ben."

"Hmmm. Is it okay if I still call you Benjamin?"

"Of course," he said with a smile. "Please come in."

She followed him into the church. It was small but the ceiling was vaulted. It gave Jessica a feeling of being lifted. The sanctuary rose high into a rounded, Gothic arch. As they walked up the center aisle, Jessica noticed rainbows cast upon the rose-colored walls by sunlight streaming through the stained glass windows.

On the left side of the sanctuary, in an alcove, was a statue of the Holy Family. On the right, a statue of Jesus. Inset in the altar was a white, illuminated model of The Last Supper by da Vinci.

They genuflected in front of the altar.

"Your church is beautiful," Jessica said.

"Thank you. This way," Father Ben said, heading to a side door. "We're going next door to the parish center."

On the way, he said, "I've pulled together a handful of our parishioners who are involved in our community outreach. I thought we might have a conversation over lunch. I thought you might want to join some of them in their work in the community this afternoon. This evening, I hope you might celebrate Mass for us. Afterwards, we're planning a reception so you can meet everyone. How does that sound?"

"That sounds terrific, Benjamin. Will you concelebrate Mass with me this evening?"

"Of course."

They stepped into the parish center. It was a large, open room. In the middle was a single round table with a white tablecloth and a cluster of foods in the center. Half a dozen men and women were seated in folding chairs around the perimeter.

When Jessica and Father Ben entered the room, they all stood up.

"Your Grace, I would like to introduce you to our parishioners," he said.

Jessica smiled, stepped over to the group and shook hands with everyone. Then they all took their seats.

"Would you lead us in prayer, Your Grace?" Father Ben said.

"I'd be happy to."

They all bowed their heads.

"Thank you for this bounty before us," Jessica said. "We ask a special blessing for those less fortunate. May they too be fed. Amen."

"Amen," they all said.

Everyone took a seat.

"You'll have to forgive me," Jessica said, scanning the exotic-looking foods on the table. "I'm not as familiar with Mexican dishes as I'd like to be."

A woman named Isa explained them all. Jessica chose a chicken fajita with a side dish of crispy roasted potatoes. Isa fixed her plate for her. Then everyone served themselves.

"Each of these parishioners leads one of our ministries in the community," Father Ben said as they began eating. "I thought you might like to hear from them."

"I'd love that."

They went around the table and talked about their work in the community.

One man talked about working with a manufacturer of household durables based in Carthage to expand and upgrade the local homeless shelter. The company donated all the materials, and parishioners provided the labor.

Another man talked about working with several local food processors to donate foods to food pantries and soup kitchens.

In all these cases, the companies' employees, including executives, got personally involved.

"How has that been for them?" Jessica asked.

"It's changed them," one of the men said.

"How so?"

"One executive told me he had no idea so many people in Carthage were so poor. Another told me—"

The man clenched his jaw and cleared his throat. Everyone was silent.

"What did he tell you?" Jessica gently asked.

"He told me he felt he was looking into the face of Jesus."

Jessica smiled.

"Thank you for sharing that," she said.

One of the women talked about her work with local women to prepare them for job interviews, from teaching interviewing skills to securing proper clothes.

Then a woman named Gloria talked about her highly personal ministry.

"I cut hair," she said.

"You cut hair?" said Jessica.

"Yes, Your Grace. I've been cutting hair all my life. One day the woman who runs the crisis center in town called and asked if I would cut a man's hair. He wanted to find a job and knew he needed a haircut, but he couldn't afford one. So I went down to the center and cut his hair. When some of the others there found out, they asked if I would cut their hair too. So I did. That was 10 years ago. Since then, I've worked with local stores and salons to collect hair care products that don't sell so well. I use some of these products on people whose hair I cut at the center, and I give them the rest so they can take care of themselves. I cut several people's hair a day. I shave men or trim their beards too. Cutting hair is my personal ministry."

Jessica was fascinated.

"Why do you do it, Gloria?" she asked.

"The people whose hair I cut are often alone," she said. "They have no one. They have no one to touch them. Touch is so important for all of us, don't you think? Being touched by someone makes us feel human. Cutting hair, on your head or your face, is an intimate act. You trust the person who is cutting your hair. These people trust me. For some, I may be the only person they trust. When I'm cutting their hair, they tell me about themselves. They share their stories. They tell me about what they hope for, what they dream about. Sometimes they tell me what they regret, what they're sorry for. It's hard to put into words what this is like for me. All I can tell you is that it feels sacred. I think it's why I'm here. And so I cut hair."

Jessica was speechless. Everyone was silent, as if they had just heard a prayer. Finally, Gloria said, "Your Grace, would you like to join me at the crisis center this afternoon?"

"It would be an honor," Jessica said.

★

That evening, in her homily during Mass, Jessica talked about the time she had spent with Gloria at the crisis center that afternoon.

"I saw a man shuffle in looking shaggy and disheveled. Gloria gave him a shave and cut his hair. As she did, he talked with us. He told us about his childhood and, in the process of sharing his story, he seemed to come alive. When Gloria was finished, he looked like a new man. He told us it was the first 'real conversation' he had had in a long time.

"Our faith is important. But faith alone will not save us. Saint James, one of the first disciples to join Jesus, wrote this: 'What good is it, my brothers, if someone says he has faith but does not have works? Can that faith save him? If a brother or sister is poorly clothed and lacking in daily food, and one of you says to them, "Go in peace, be warmed and filled," without giving them the things needed for the body, what good is that? So also faith by itself, if it does not have works, is dead.'

"The work you are doing in this community is the work of God in our world. Jesus is alive in Carthage. He lives through you, through your hearts and through your hands, through your compassion for one another. You are living the Gospel. You are showing us the way."

After the reception for Jessica that evening, she went back to the rectory with Father Ben. He had offered her his guest room.

They sat in his small living room to catch up. He thanked her for spending so much time with his parishioners, especially Gloria.

"Gloria wasn't just cutting people's hair," Jessica said. "She was healing them. As I watched her, I felt as though I were watching Jesus. Your parishioners are truly doing the Lord's work."

"Gloria was cutting hair at the crisis center when I got here," Father Ben said. "But for the most part, this parish wasn't all that involved in the community then."

"Really? What happened?"

"Remember your summit on poverty? When you took over as archbishop and urged us to help the poor in our communities, we listened."

"Thank you, Benjamin. But I'm sure this wonderful work wouldn't be happening without *your* personal leadership."

"I feel like I'm in the right place."

She smiled.

"You know, there's not a day that goes by when I don't think of our first morning at the seminary and how you made me feel like *I* was in the right place. That meant so much to me, and I'm not sure I've ever thanked you."

"I knew then you were destined for greatness, Jessica. Thank you for being with us today."

"Thank you for the inspiration," she said.

Chapter 43

People did listen to what Jessica said, and not just Catholics in Missouri. Her dedication to the poor was catching the attention of other archbishops all around the country.

That, plus her ability to manage her archdiocese so efficiently, with balanced parish budgets across the board, attracted the attention of the US Conference of Catholic Bishops in Washington too.

The stated purpose of the Conference was to "promote the greater good which the Church offers humankind." But in reality, the group dealt mainly with matters of policy, from abortion to gay rights. It had become the main lobbying arm for the Catholic Church in the US.

The leaders of the Conference, all men, were self-aware enough to realize the group was seen as an "old boys club." Now that women were being ordained, they knew they needed to evolve.

This alone made them pay attention to Jessica. But they also admired the way she had managed to reorient the Archdiocese of Missouri and breathe new life into it. They admired her personal leadership. They knew the Conference had become stagnant, and they were eager to find a high-energy leader who could get it moving again.

The President of the Conference was Cardinal William Wright, who led the Archdiocese of Chicago. Jessica had met Wright but didn't know him well. She was surprised when he called her one morning.

They exchanged pleasantries. Then he said, "Your Grace, I'd like to invite you to Chicago for a brief meeting on an important matter."

"May I ask the purpose?"

"I'd like to discuss a possible leadership position with the US Conference."

Jessica was stunned. She was focused on her work in Missouri and hadn't really been thinking beyond that. But as a courtesy, she agreed to meet with Wright the following week.

She called Father John right away to get his read.

"They're going to ask you to lead the Conference," he said.

"Lead it? Me?"

"Why not you? Look at what you've done here in Missouri. The Church could use that kind of leadership nationally."

"But I've got a full-time job. How in the world could I lead the Conference too?"

"Jessica, have you ever been to the Conference's offices in Washington?"

"Yes, once."

"Well, then you know the place is crawling with people. All you would need to do is set direction. There's an army of people there to do the work."

"I don't know, John."

"Just go to Chicago," he said. "See what Wright has in mind."

She went home that evening and talked with Michael.

"Well, I suspect Father John is right," he said. "And what will you say if they offer you the lead role?"

"If I can figure out a way to do the job without compromising my role here, I guess I'd consider it."

"And if they ask you to move to Washington?"

"I'd decline."

"What about your time here at home?"

"That's not negotiable, Michael."

He smiled.

"I love you, Jess."

★

Cardinal Wright's office had arranged for Jessica to fly to Chicago. A driver met her at O'Hare and took her to the Archbishop's Residence in the historic Astor Street District in the central city.

On the way, the driver told her the archbishop's mansion was built in 1885, that Pope John Paul II and President Franklin Roosevelt had been among its many famous guests.

"It has 19 chimneys," he said.

Jessica tried to imagine a residence big enough for 19 fireplaces.

They pulled into the circular drive and drove through a large, red brick porte-cochere. Jessica felt as though she had been transported back to the Victorian Age.

She got out and looked up at the three-story mansion. Its towering chimneys, grand spires and angular bays gave it the look of an ancient castle, a giant version of the archbishop's mansion she had sold in St. Louis. It made her feel so small.

She walked up the wide stone steps and rang the bell, expecting a servant might answer. Instead, Cardinal Wright himself greeted her.

"Welcome, Your Grace," he said, clasping her hands.

Round. That's the word that came to mind when she saw him. His face was round. His body was round. The backs of his hands were round. His head was uncovered. He had a shock of white hair and bushy eyebrows. His face was pleasant, double chin and all. He looked like a Hollywood actor *playing* a cardinal.

"Thank you for inviting me, Your Eminence. Your residence is stunning."

"Thank you. It's an historic landmark, which means we can't really sell it."

She sensed this was his way of acknowledging what she had done in St. Louis and justifying his decision to keep this place.

"I see."

"I thought you might be hungry and we could talk over lunch," he said.

"That sounds wonderful."

She followed him through a large hall whose walls were adorned with portraits of previous cardinals and archbishops of Chicago. Jessica looked around for a cross or a painting of Jesus but saw none.

The dining room was large, with two fireplaces. They sat across from each other at a grand dining table under an enormous crystal chandelier.

A nun, an older woman in a white habit, entered through a swinging door to take their drink order.

"I'll have unsweetened iced tea, please," Jessica said.

She noticed the nun was staring at her.

"Oh, I'm sorry, Sister," Jessica said, extending her hand. "I'm Jessica Simon."

"Good afternoon, Your Grace," she said, blushing. "I'm Sister Teresa."

"What a beautiful name," Jessica said.

"Thank you. It's lovely to meet you."

Sister Teresa looked at the cardinal.

"The usual," he said.

She nodded and left.

"I can see why people have such affection for you," Wright said. "You have such a nice way about you."

Jessica wasn't sure if Wright's compliment was genuine or part of a build-up to a request.

They made small talk over their appetizer, smoked salmon with taro chips. Once their main course, pasta primavera, was served, Wright said, "Your Grace, I'm going to complete my term as president of the Conference next year, and we'd like to offer you the position. We think you would make an outstanding president. It would be a two-year commitment. Would you be willing to serve?"

"I'm honored you would think of me, Your Eminence," Jessica said. "May I ask a few questions?"

"Of course," he said, sipping his gin and tonic.

"Thank you. First, is there a certain amount of time I'd be expected to be in Washington?"

"No. That would be completely up to you. I myself typically spend one day a week there."

"I see. And what is the annual budget for the Conference?"

"This year, it's just north of $200 million," he said, looking proud.

"And what percentage of that goes to fund social services?"

"About 10 percent," he said, looking a bit chastened.

"I see. Would I have discretion to adjust that spending?"

"Well, any major shift in spending would require board approval, but the board would certainly be led by you."

"Very good," she said. "This perspective is all very helpful. I'd like to discuss this with my husband. I'll follow up very soon."

"Wonderful."

Sister Teresa came in to take their dessert order.

"I think I'll pass," Jessica said.

"I'll have the cherry pie," the cardinal said, "with a scoop of vanilla ice cream."

He looked at Jessica, who was staring at him.

"Please," he added.

★

Jessica prayed for guidance all the way back to St. Louis.

She talked with Michael when she got home that evening. She shared what Wright had told her. She sounded upbeat.

"You want to do this, don't you?" he said.

"You know, I didn't think I would, but I really do. I think I could make a big impact."

"And you think you can manage it, with everything else, and still have time for us?"

"Yes, I do."

"Well, then, I'd say go for it."

"Thank you, Michael."

She called Wright the next morning to accept.

★

A week later, Jessica and Michael attended Emma's graduation from Trinity Catholic High School.

Jessica was so proud of Emma. Proud that she finished in the top 10% of her class academically. Proud that she received a special award for exemplary community service. Proud that she too had decided to go to SLU, where she would major in social work.

Watching Emma stride across the stage to receive her diploma, Jessica could see her taking her first steps as a toddler.

She could see Josh as a toddler too. No one sitting around her realized Jessica's tears were for both of her children.

★

That fall, Jessica was elected President of the US Conference of Catholic Bishops. She began her term in January of 2048.

On her first day, she announced she would be convening a task force to examine and recommend ways the Church in the United States could do even more to serve the poor around the world, in line with the Conference's mission. That made the front page of the *Washington Post*.

In early April, the task force shared its findings and recommendations. The "big idea" was not to create any new programs but rather to invest more heavily in Catholic Relief Services, an agency established by the Conference in 1943 to help World War II survivors in Europe. It had since gone global.

Jessica recommended to the board that the Conference devote half of its annual budget to Catholic Relief Services. She also recommended making cuts in other areas, including administration, to free up the funds to enable this dramatic shift. Ethan Morelli had given her some great ideas.

After a brief discussion, the board unanimously agreed. The next morning, she announced the decision to Conference employees and all US Bishops. That afternoon, she held a briefing at the National Press Club to announce it to the world.

The announcement made international news. It was the first time many people, including most Americans, had seen Jessica. People weren't used to seeing a female Catholic leader. The image of this small woman, dressed in a white pantsuit, making such a bold announcement, was striking. Many stories portrayed Jessica as a "rising star" in the Church.

Jessica cared little for the personal attention, but she was grateful for the spotlight on the need to do more for the poor around the world. She hoped others would follow the Church's lead.

The announcement created a lot of buzz within the Church. Most of it was positive. It even won praise by the pope.

"Jesus is smiling," he said.

But some in the US questioned whether it was fitting for the Conference to be giving away "American dollars," which could be used to help poor Americans, to people outside the country. Others were openly critical of the move.

"This is the latest example of where the Church has veered too far left," Archbishop Penov told reporters in Bulgaria. "We must be vigilant against creeping socialism. Sometimes it comes in sheep's clothing."

Chapter 44

Over the next year, Jessica and her team at the Conference stepped up efforts by Catholic Relief Services all around the world.

The results were striking, especially in developing countries. Media coverage of Catholic Relief Services' work shone a spotlight on the plight of the poor in these countries. Feeling the pressure, many government leaders began directing more public funds to help the poor in their countries. Several large foundations and a handful of billionaires also stepped up with big donations and matching grants.

In the US, the results were visible too. The number of homeless people living in parks in some cities, for example, began to shrink as homeless shelters were expanded and new ones were built.

The world began to take note of the quiet leader behind all this work. Jessica's efforts to lift up the poor gained special recognition. In 2049, for example, the Archbishop of New York presented her with the Dorothy Day Award, named after the twentieth-century activist who worked for social causes through the prism of the Catholic Church.

But once again, not everyone was a fan.

"Dorothy Day was a Communist," Ivan Penov grumbled. "Day and Simon are birds of a feather."

★

One week after Jessica's term as President of the Conference came to a close, she received a certified letter from the Vatican. She assumed it was a note of congratulations for her service.

"Would you like me to open it?" Kaitlyn asked.

"Please, go ahead."

She sliced open the envelope and unfolded the single sheet of paper inside. As she read it, her eyes grew wide.

"I think you should read this," she said, handing the letter to Jessica.

Pope Francis II requests your presence at the Vatican at your earliest convenience. Please call to confirm the arrangements.

"Would you like me to call?" Kaitlyn asked.

"Not just yet."

Jessica called Father John.

"John, I need to see you. Yes, everything's fine. Is it possible for you to swing by this afternoon? Perfect. I'll see you then."

★

Father John glanced at the letter and smiled.

"He's going to make you a cardinal," he said.

"A cardinal? That's crazy, John. Why would you think that?"

"Look at this letter, Jessica. It's on Vatican stationery. It's addressed only to you. This is a one-on-one meeting with Francis. And you're getting this right after your amazing run as president of the Conference. That's no coincidence. There could be only one reason the pope would need to meet with you in Rome."

"Good Lord," she said. "What if you're right?"

"If? Trust me on this, Jessica."

A chill ran up the back of her neck. On things like this, she knew Father John was batting 1000.

★

Jessica left for Rome the following afternoon, this time with Michael beside her.

They landed in Rome the following morning. The Vatican had arranged for them to stay at Casa Santa Marta, where Jessica and Archbishop Fox had stayed six years earlier. After lunch, Jessica headed to the Apostolic Palace, and Michael headed for the Basilica.

Jessica was escorted to the same room where she'd last met the pope. This time, she was more acutely aware of its simplicity. Maybe the appointments had been this spare before. Or maybe, in her mind, she was now comparing this place with the Archbishop's Residence in Chicago. She wondered if the Apostolic Palace had 19 chimneys.

A nun came in to ask if Jessica would like anything.

"No, thank you," she said.

Then she extended her hand.

"I'm Jessica Simon."

"I am Sister Clare, Your Grace," she said, taking her hand and bowing her head.

"Like Saint Clare."

"Yes," the nun said with a smile. "My mother named me after her."

"What a beautiful name."

"Thank you, Your Grace," said the nun. "It is a pleasure to meet you."

Jessica wondered how she knew she was an archbishop. She was wearing a white pantsuit, hardly traditional garb for an archbishop. But then, this had become her trademark.

There was a faint knock, then the door opened slowly. Jessica got up. In shuffled an old man, smaller and slower than the one she'd met there six years earlier. He was nearly 90 now. His head was bent forward, his shoulders stooped, and he leaned on a quad cane.

Someone closed the door behind him. He stopped, looked up and smiled.

"Mother," he said in a soft, raspy voice. "How good to see you again."

"How good to see you, Your Holiness," she said, stepping forward, taking his hand and bowing. "Thank you for inviting me."

"Let us sit."

They sat in cushioned, straight-backed chairs facing one another.

"Would you care for something to drink? A Coke?"

"No, thank you, Your Holiness. My husband and I just had lunch."

"Your husband is here?"

"Yes. He is touring the Basilica."

"Please remind me of his name."

"Michael."

"Oh, yes. Like Saint Michael, the Archangel."

"Yes."

"Such a strong name."

"He is a good man."

"I would like to meet him sometime."

"And I know he would love to meet you."

Francis looked ill. His face was gaunt. He had withered away. Yet his eyes had not changed. They still sparkled.

His eyes searched her face.

"I am sorry for your great loss," he said.

"Thank you, Your Holiness. And thank you for your kind note. It meant so much to me. I carry it with me."

"I have continued to hold you in prayer," Francis said. "I hope you have remembered me in your prayers too."

"Yes, Your Holiness. I pray for you every day."

"Thank you."

He had been leaning toward her. Now he sat up straighter, as if suddenly remembering the purpose of their meeting.

"Mother, I have much admired the work you are leading in the United States. I have especially appreciated your focus on helping the poor."

"Thank you, Your Holiness."

"You are helping lead us down the right path," he said. "You have led so well as Archbishop of Missouri and President of the US Conference of Bishops. I have called you here to let you know I have decided to recognize both your exemplary contributions and your extraordinary promise by naming you a cardinal of the Church."

Once again, though Father John had called this, she was overwhelmed.

"Your Holiness, I am not worthy."

"Oh, but you are, Mother," he said, with a smile. "Like Jesus, you are showing us the way."

"Thank you, Your Holiness."

"Congratulations in advance. We will coordinate with your office to make the announcement. You will be installed at a consistory here next month. I am sorry this will require another trip to Rome."

"It will be a pleasure."

"Oh, there is one more thing," the pope said.

"Yes?"

"As a cardinal, I would like you to lead our Congregation for the Clergy. You have a clear vision of what it means to be a priest as one who is active in serving the community. I share that vision. We have too many priests who are content to stay within the walls of their churches. I'm afraid we have invested too much in our churches. We have become too comfortable there. We must be in the world. I need you to help me get more priests into the world. The Congregation for the Clergy offers a new way, and I can think of no one better to lead it. So we will make this part of your announcement."

Jessica didn't know much about these Congregations, the departments of the Roman Curia. But she knew there were only nine of them and that leading one was a "big deal."

"I am deeply honored, Your Holiness. I will do my best to lead this Congregation in line with your vision."

"I know you will, Mother."

She knew their session had drawn to a close, but she said, "Your Holiness, there is one more thing I'd like to mention."

"Of course."

"I've had another vision of Jesus."

"Oh? When?"

"He appeared to me soon after the death of my son. I was hiking in the woods, where I was on sabbatical. It was a most difficult time for me. I felt distant from God. I even wondered if I could go on. It was at that moment he appeared to me."

"Did he speak to you again?"

"Yes. He told me he loved me, that he will always be with me and that my son is with our father in heaven."

"How beautiful. I'm sure that was of great comfort to you."

"It was — and just when I needed it most."

"Thank you for sharing this, Mother. By the way, I still call you Mother because, no matter your title, you will always be a priest. Remember that. You have shown us the way as a priest, and now you will show all our priests a new way. How blessed we are to have you in the lead."

They got up. She began to step forward to shake his hand, but once again he opened his arms, and they embraced.

"May God be with you," Francis said.

"And with your spirit," Jessica replied.

★

Standing outside the Apostolic Palace, Jessica called Michael. He was still touring the Basilica.

She looked around to make sure no one could hear her and told him the news.

"Congratulations," he said. "Funny, I'm standing at the feet of a statue of one of your favorite people, St. Francis of Assisi."

"I feel very close to him right now," she said.

She walked to the Basilica. Michael was waiting for her at the base of the steps. When he spotted her on the plaza, he walked over briskly, and they embraced.

They went to an outdoor cafe to draw a breath and try to begin to comprehend the significance of this latest news and its impact on their lives.

"It's a lot more responsibility, especially leading the Congregation for the Clergy," she said.

"Won't they give you a staff for that?"

"Yes, I think so."

"Well, then pick your shots and delegate the rest. You're getting pretty good at that."

That afternoon, Jessica called Father John to share the news in confidence.

"Congratulations, Your Eminence," he said.

"Oh, John," she said. "I hope you'll always call me Jessica."

★

The Vatican announced Jessica's appointment two days after her meeting with Francis, once she and Michael had returned to St. Louis.

Jessica chose not to issue a news release from the archdiocese. Instead, she would rely on the Vatican to make the announcement.

"A news release from this office seems self-serving," she told Bob Wagner, her communication director. "We'll simply respond to any media interest."

"Are you sure?" Bob said. "This will be big news. I think we should get in front of it."

"But it's not our news," Jessica said. "It's the pope's."

Wagner was right. Jessica had greatly underestimated the newsworthiness of the appointment of the first female Catholic cardinal in history. Shortly after the Vatican made the announcement, it was one of the top-trending news stories in the world. And Jessica, not Francis, was the focus.

Wagner was deluged with media inquiries. He begged Jessica to make a statement. She relented, agreeing to a brief news conference at the archdiocesan office.

She showed up wearing her familiar white pantsuit.

"Thank you all for coming," she told the reporters packed into a small conference room. "I am humbled and grateful. I want to thank my husband, Michael, for all his love and support through the years; Pope Francis II for this new opportunity to serve the Church; and my mentor, Father John Dumont, for his wise counsel over many years. I also want to thank my fellow Catholics throughout Missouri for their exemplary work in helping the poor in every community in our state. I want to thank my mother and father for showing me the way. Most of all, I want to thank Jesus, who is my daily inspiration. Now I'll be happy to take a few questions."

"How does it feel to be the first female Catholic Cardinal in history?"

"Humbling."

"Will your priorities change?"

"Yes, but only in that I'll now be leading our Church's Congregation for the Clergy, which is responsible for the formation and ministry of priests. Otherwise, no."

"Some say this puts you in line for the papacy. What's your reaction?"

Jessica laughed. Not a small laugh, but a belly laugh, a long laugh, so long that everyone in the room began laughing with her.

Finally, she composed herself.

"I guess that's my reaction," she said with a smile.

Then Jessica cut it off because, as she told Michael afterwards, "It was getting a bit silly." Plus, she was beginning to feel uneasy in the limelight.

But now Jessica's image was everywhere. Her laughing hard at the idea of being in line for the papacy was played over and over on cable news and posted all over social media. Her self-effacing reaction was endearing. People weren't used to seeing religious leaders laugh, let alone one in a pantsuit.

★

The following month, Jessica was installed as a new cardinal by Pope Francis II in St. Peter's Basilica, the only American among 10 bishops so elevated. The image of her, smiling, sitting in the center of the front row of two rows of men, all of them looking serious in their new red hats, was flashed around the world.

One headline read: "No More Old Boys' Club."

The following day, Jessica convened her new staff for the Congregation for the Clergy. This group of 12 consisted of priests, retired archbishops and one nun.

Her first order of business was to thank the outgoing Prefect, the Spanish Cardinal Fernando Martinez. He was about to turn 75 and would be retiring. Martinez had led the Congregation for five years. His focus had been on raising standards for the formation of priests. This was much-needed after Francis II's removal of priests implicated in the sex abuse scandal.

The pope had already personally thanked Martinez for his service. Now it was Jessica's turn to do so before his staff. They were all gathered around an oblong conference table. Martinez was seated at one end, Jessica at the other.

"Your Eminence," she said, standing up, "we have a figure of speech in the United States. 'Raise your game.' It means to make things better. Of course, if we want to make things better when it comes to the clergy, we must begin in our seminaries, where our future priests are being formed. This has wisely been your focus these past five years. You've taken the long view of what can be done to raise our game as priests for years to come. Your impact has been immeasurable, and there is no way to fully express the Church's gratitude. But on behalf of our Church, I would like to offer a small gift which I hope will remind you of the original sacrament you have taken such great care to protect and advance."

Jessica turned around and stepped over to the wall. Leaning against it was a framed piece of art with the front facing the wall. Jessica picked it up, turned it around and rested it on the end of the conference table for all to see.

"Your Eminence, this is a limited edition reprint of the fresco Vocation of the Apostles by Domenico Ghirlandaio. It depicts the Gospel story of Jesus calling Peter and Andrew to become his disciples. We hope this painting will remind you of the great and lasting impact of your work on Jesus' modern-day disciples. We hope it will remind you of how you have raised our game."

Everyone stood and applauded. Martinez smiled and stood up. He pressed his hands together and bowed slightly. Then he walked to the other end of the table and embraced Jessica, kissing her on both cheeks.

"Thank you very much, Your Eminence," he said, his hand resting atop the artwork. "I already have a place in mind for this in my new apartment in Barcelona, where I can see it every day. Thank you for this most beautiful and thoughtful gift."

Then, looking around the room, he said, "And thank you all for your wonderful service these past five years. I know I leave this Congregation in very capable hands. I hope we will all stay in touch. May God continue to bless you all."

With that, Martinez picked up the painting, nodded toward Jessica and gracefully took his exit.

Jessica sat back down and looked around the table.

"I want to keep this meeting brief," she said. "Let's begin with introductions."

Going around the table, the staff members introduced themselves. Next to the seat where Martinez had been sitting sat a nun in full habit, the only woman in the room other than Jessica. When it was her turn, she said, "I am Sister Maria. I am the scribe for the Congregation."

"The scribe?" Jessica said.

"Yes, Your Eminence," she said. "I take notes in these meetings."

"Do you enjoy taking notes, Sister?" Jessica said.

The nun looked around the room.

"Not especially," she said softly.

"Sister Maria," Jessica said, "I'd like to ask a favor."

"Certainly."

"Please pass your notebook down to me," Jessica said. "I'd like to begin taking the notes for these meetings. I'll have my assistant back in St. Louis transcribe them and send them to all of you over the next few days. Okay?"

Sister Maria looked stunned.

"Si," she said, closing her notebook and sliding it down toward Jessica. "I mean yes."

The nun stood up and began to push her chair in.

"Where are you going, Sister?" Jessica said.

"I will take my leave, Your Eminence."

"I consider you a valuable member of this team," Jessica said. "Please sit down and join us."

Sister Maria gave Jessica a look of disbelief. Then, realizing she was serious, she smiled and sat back down.

"Thank you," she said.

Sister Maria then introduced herself, and the rest of the staff continued with their introductions.

"Thank you all," said Jessica. "What an impressive team. I very much look forward to working with you. I want to start with the purpose of this Congregation. It is, as you know, responsible for the formation, ministry and life of priests and deacons. How that has been interpreted over the past 600 years has varied widely. Of course, this body serves at the discretion of the pope. In asking me to lead this Congregation, Pope Francis II was very clear about his vision for the priesthood. He wants to make sure our priests are active in the community, serving the poor and disadvantaged, in line with Jesus' teachings. So that will now be our focus."

People looked at each other. There was a murmur around the table.

"Your Eminence," said a retired archbishop, "with respect, that sounds fine, but what about all the other work of this Congregation?"

"Such as?" Jessica said.

"Well, for example, our work to manage cases of where priests have violated their vow of celibacy and fathered children."

"And there is no one else to manage these cases but a small group of clerics in Rome, far removed from the violations?" Jessica said.

"Well, I suppose they could be handled at the diocesan level," the archbishop said.

"According to guidelines we might set?" Jessica said.

"Of course."

"Well, then let's do that," Jessica said. "Is there anything else we should continue doing?"

No one said anything.

"Here's what I'd like us to do," Jessica said. "I want to issue a recommendation that every member of the clergy and every seminarian personally serve disadvantaged people in the community every week. This isn't a requirement. It's a recommendation. Priests, deacons, nuns and seminarians can choose how they serve, where they serve and how long they serve. But the idea is to bring Jesus into the world, to help people and, in the process, deepen the members of our clergy."

"Your Eminence," said a priest. "Can you give us an idea of the type of service you have in mind?"

"Certainly, Father," she said. "Working in soup kitchens or homeless shelters, for example. Wherever disadvantaged people need help. I myself spend time working in food pantries whenever I travel around my home state of Missouri. In fact, that's what I'll do when I go back to St. Louis."

"I see," the priest said. "Thank you."

"You're welcome. Here's how I'd like to proceed. We will reconvene, via videoconference, in two weeks. By then, I want each of us to have spent time in our community, serving the disadvantaged in some way. During our call, I would like each of us to briefly share our experience. We'll then get to work on a plan to announce our new direction and help ensure every priest, deacon, nun and seminarian is working in their communities all around the world. I would like that announcement to be made and that work to begin over the next couple of months."

A few members of the group looked pensive, but most of them smiled. They began chatting among themselves, and there was even some laughter. Jessica sat quietly and watched.

Finally, the archbishop who had mentioned the violations of the vow of celibacy said, "Your Eminence, will there be anything else?"

"Not today," she said. "Are there any other questions?"

There were none. Everyone got up and left, smiling and nodding at Jessica on the way out.

★

Word of the reorientation of the Congregation for the Clergy quickly got out. It only added to the positive buzz about Jessica's new appointment as a cardinal. Clearly, she was taking things in a new direction — and wasting no time in doing so.

Progressive Catholics cheered her. Even more women applied to seminaries. Conservatives were suspicious. Hardline conservatives resented her. Some of them accused Pope

Francis of playing favorites. Others called Jessica's appointment nothing more than political correctness.

In Sofia, Ivan Penov was indignant. He told friends he was more deserving of being made a cardinal and raged the Church was being "hijacked by bleeding-heart liberals."

Chapter 45

As a cardinal, Jessica continued to visit parishes throughout Missouri. In September of 2050, she visited Immaculate Conception Church in Union, about an hour southwest of St. Louis.

She met with parish leaders in the morning. At noon, she said Mass for students, teachers and other parishioners, then had lunch with the students.

She moved from table to table around the cafeteria, carrying a small carton of chocolate milk, sipping it as she listened to the curious, high-energy children. Two girls told her they were thinking about becoming priests. She invited them to call her or come see her if they ever had questions or wanted to talk.

She spent much of the afternoon at the Second Blessings Food Pantry in downtown Union. It had the look and feel of an open-air produce market. Local farmers and grocers donated surplus fruits and vegetables. Booths were crowded with local residents eager and happy to get free, fresh, wholesome foods for themselves and their families.

Jessica joined Immaculate Conception parishioners and others in handing out ears of corn, tomatoes, berries, beans and bananas.

At first, the locals weren't sure what to make of this small woman dressed in white, working alongside men and women in

T-shirts and jeans. But she seemed to thoroughly enjoy giving out food and chatting with people. Some knew who she was, and they bowed as they thanked her. Some even crossed themselves.

The parish had offered to host a dinner for Jessica, but she politely declined. She said it was a "school night." That was true, but she really wanted to get home in time for dinner with Michael.

It was late September, and the days were growing shorter. By late afternoon, as Jessica was heading to her car in the church parking lot, the sun was already low in the sky.

What a wonderful day this has been, she thought. I must include these people in my prayers tonight.

Every night, Jessica gave thanks for everyone in her life. She gave thanks for all she'd been given. Sometimes she fell asleep giving thanks.

Yet at that moment, she felt grateful for something more.

She walked back to the church and went in. The windows were stained glass. It was nearly dark inside except for a single light in the sanctuary which shone up on a large, wooden cross.

She slipped into a pew. She looked up at the light and sensed the darkness all around her. She had known darkness in her life. But even in her darkest moments, there was always a light.

She felt grateful for the light, not just because it allowed her to see, but simply because it was there.

The light was God. The light was love. It was always there for her, and she knew it always would be.

"Thank you," she prayed in a whisper.

Chapter 46

Jessica was driving to St. Patrick Center, a homeless shelter in St. Louis, when she heard the news that Pope Francis II had died. When she got there, she sat in her car and said a prayer for him.

She debated whether to go in. She knew she would be called to Rome to elect a new pope, but she wasn't sure when she would need to be there. She decided to spend an hour at the center, serving breakfast.

Fifteen minutes later, though, she got a call from Ethan Morelli.

"We just got word from Rome," he said. "There will be a funeral for Francis in four days. Cardinals are not expected to attend. About two weeks later, the College of Cardinals will convene. That's when you'll be expected at the Vatican. So you have some time on this."

"But I consider Francis a friend," she said. "Would it be a breach of protocol for me to attend his funeral?"

"I don't know. Would you like me to check with the nuncio in Washington?"

"Yes, please. Just let me know."

Jessica resumed dishing out oatmeal and pouring coffee and orange juice. She tried to concentrate on her guests, but her mind drifted off to the man who had made her feel so at home in his residence in the Vatican.

★

The nuncio advised that, while it was unusual for cardinals to attend a pope's funeral, it was not strictly prohibited.

Jessica decided to check in with Father John too.

"Sure, you can go," he said. "But think of how it will look. You'll be one of the few cardinals there. Some might conclude you're campaigning for the papacy."

"You're probably right," she said. "But I greatly admired Francis, and he did so much for me. I'd like to pay my respects. I can't imagine *not* being there for him. I think I'll go."

"Okay," he said. "But you'll be all over the news."

"No interviews," she said.

"It won't matter."

★

Jessica flew to Rome by herself, knowing it would be a short trip.

For the funeral, she would wear the traditional scarlet vestments of a cardinal. She'd worn them only a handful of times in St. Louis. When she first tried them on, at home, she laughed looking at herself in a mirror.

Emma said she looked stylish. Michael said she looked elegant.

"I think I look like I'm ready for Halloween," she said.

Jessica let Bob Wagner issue a brief statement before she left for the funeral, simply saying that she would be attending out of deep respect for a leader she greatly admired and someone she considered a friend. She didn't want anyone to misconstrue her intentions.

However, no other American cardinals or archbishops attended the funeral, making Jessica seem like the *de facto* representative for the Church in the US, part of the official American delegation.

The pope's funeral Mass was said by Cardinal Abaeze Adeyemi of Nigeria. How he was selected to officiate wasn't clear. He was an ultraconservative and not especially close to Francis.

He seems like an odd choice for such a role, Jessica thought. But then, she was not all that plugged into Vatican politics. Nor did she wish to be.

★

When it came to media interest in Jessica, Father John was right. She was featured in much of the coverage of the funeral, especially on TV and social media.

Part of it was simply optics. Her short stature alone made Jessica stand out. Being dwarfed by most of the other attendees made her an appealing subject for the cameras.

Of course, her very presence at the papal funeral was newsworthy. It was the first time anyone had ever seen a woman dressed as a cardinal on a world stage.

Overnight, Jessica had emerged as something of a celebrity. When she returned to St. Louis, a group of about two dozen supporters greeted her at the airport. She shook hands with each of them. She wasn't used to a "fan club" and felt a bit embarrassed.

Michael was waiting for her too.

"Groupies," he said with a smile.

She gave him a hug and a kiss and said, "Let's go home."

★

Jessica returned to Rome for the papal conclave two weeks later. She had asked Michael to go with her, but he decided to stay home because Jessica would be sequestered during the election process. No hope of conjugal visits.

The intense media coverage of Francis' funeral quickly morphed into a frenzy of speculation about his successor. Experts' predictions were literally all over the place, with contenders identified from every region of the world.

Jessica's name popped up, although the odds of an American pope were considered very long. Many experts thought a cardinal from a developing nation was most likely to succeed Francis II.

Over 26 years, Francis had appointed more than half of the current 203 cardinals. Most were progressives, like him. Thus, he had effectively stacked the deck in favor of a progressive successor.

Yet there was a quiet momentum among the prelates toward a more conservative choice for pope this time. Francis had inspired many with his bold reforms, but he'd also caused many on the right to harden their positions. In general, they felt the Church was paying far too much attention to "secular matters." They wanted the Church to stick to "saving souls," not the planet.

The fastest-growing groups of these ultraconservatives were in Africa, Asia and Eastern Europe, where the Church was also growing at the fastest clip.

The names and images of cardinals from these regions popped up in news coverage, which began to take on the look and feel of a World Cup tournament.

★

Jessica was greeted at Leonardo da Vinci and driven to Casa Santa Marta. All 120 cardinals eligible to vote for pope would stay there throughout the process. They were the "younger" cardinals, under the age of 80.

On the afternoon before the conclave was to begin, the cardinals met to go over the election process and the rules. They gathered outside the doors of the Sistine Chapel, where they took oaths to faithfully observe the rules, including keeping everything to do with the election secret.

Then they processed into the chapel, two abreast, as the Latin command "*extra omnes*" — or "everyone out" — instructed all those not involved in the election to leave before the doors were closed.

The cardinals took their seats at one of two long tables on either side of the room to fill out their ballots in silence. Printed on the upper half of each rectangular, paper ballot were the words "*Eligio in Summum Pontificem*" — or "I elect as Supreme Pontiff." Below was a space for the name of the person chosen. The cardinals had been instructed to write the name in a way that does not identify them, then fold the paper twice.

Jessica had prayed about her choice for weeks. For her, it came down to whom had clearly followed Jesus' great commandment and had the skills and experience needed to lead an organization of more than two billion Catholics. Even then, though, it was a very tough choice. She had prayed for enlightenment at Mass that morning, still unsure about whom to choose.

Once the cardinals had marked their ballots, they walked one by one to the altar at the end of the room, held up their folded card and said, "I call on the Lord Jesus, who will be my Lord."

They then dropped their ballots into a lidded urn. Once all the ballots were counted and recorded in a ledger, a "scrutineer" called out the names of those cardinals who received votes.

After the first ballot, Adeyemi from Nigeria was in the lead with 41 votes. Jessica was shocked, and a little terrified, when her name was read aloud five times.

The scrutineer then pierced each paper with a needle, through the word "*Eligio*," and placed all the ballots on a single thread. This string of ballots was then thrown into an iron stove, which led to a chimney. A chemical was added to the fire to turn the smoke black, indicating a two-thirds majority consensus had not been reached.

The first two ballots that first afternoon produced no majority consensus. Two more ballots the following morning also yielded no winner, though Adeyemi remained in the lead, gaining ground with each ballot.

Jessica was getting more votes too. On the fourth ballot, she received 17 votes. At that point, she fanned herself with her blank ballots and took deep breaths.

Finally, after the seventh ballot on the morning of the third day, Adeyemi received 79 votes, pushing him past the two-thirds majority required for election. A different chemical mix was added to the fire in the iron stove, and the smoke turned white. The cardinals applauded, and the crowd in St. Peter's Square roared.

An hour later, the papal name Adeyemi selected was announced from the balcony overlooking the square, just before his appearance. It was Benedict XVII, in honor of his role model, Pope Benedict XVI. A few minutes later, under an overcast sky, the new pope emerged, smiling and waving to the cheering throng below.

He spoke in English for nearly an hour. His tone was stern, surprisingly so given the joyous moment. He spoke mainly of the need for the Church to return to its "conservative moorings."

"There is a time to return to venerated traditions and core beliefs," he said. "My papacy will be dedicated to re-centering the Church, to bringing us back to the standards and traditions which have served us well since the time of Christ. So much of the world is adrift. The Church must be a rock, a place where the truth is stated plainly and morality is not relative."

It's a shot across the bow of progressives, Jessica thought. Listening to the tough words of this new pope, she worried for the Church.

★

Benedict wasted no time in trying to bring the Church "back to center."

Within the first month of his papacy, he reminded Catholics that artificial birth control, abortion and homosexuality are mortal sins. He required all Church employees to sign affidavits renouncing such practices. He urged individual churches to consider saying at least one Mass in Latin each week. And he named three new cardinals, all of them ultra conservatives. One was Ivan Penov.

At first, the Church saw an increase in giving.

"Many conservative Catholics are wealthy," Father John told Jessica. "They feel they haven't been listened to for a long time. They're applauding Benedict with their dollars."

Within a year, though, Church membership, Mass attendance and giving began to decline. Parents started taking their children out of Catholic schools, in part because many teachers couldn't pass the new "purity tests" and had to leave. Catholic universities had trouble recruiting and even retaining administrators and faculty members. Seminary enrollment began to drop.

Within two years, 20 million Catholics worldwide had defected. Progressives felt abandoned, but many conservatives felt emboldened. They welcomed the idea of a "smaller, stronger, more devout Church," one of Benedict's mantras.

As the leader of her archdiocese, Jessica had a hard time explaining the pope's policy positions to her flock. She was careful not to criticize Benedict, but she continued to emphasize the importance of following the teachings of Jesus. She also reminded people of the Church's longstanding, if poorly understood, belief in the "primacy of the conscience."

"God is the author of our souls," she said. "Search your soul and choose what you know is right. Nothing is more important."

Personally, Jessica did not let up on her focus on the poor. She knew people were watching her and that she must continue to lead by example.

As giving continued to decline and the Church's budget began to feel the strain, some Church leaders, even within the Vatican, felt Benedict was going too far. They diplomatically tried to tell him, but he turned a deaf ear. He preferred to listen to right-wing archbishops and cardinals. Among these, Cardinal Penov had become a favorite papal sounding board.

It was rumored Benedict kept a "black book" of progressive and even moderate bishops. One anonymous Vatican source claimed he had a world map in his apartment with red and green push pins, each one marking a bishop.

Jessica shared her growing concerns about the direction of the Church with Father John.

"The question," he said, "is what are you going to do about it?"

"What do you mean? What *can* I do about it?"

"Jessica, do you think you're the only prelate in the Church who feels this way?"

"Hardly."

"Well, then, reach out to your fellow archbishops and cardinals who feel as you do. You know how to build a coalition. Benedict is certainly building one. But there are still far more progressives than hardline conservatives in the Church. Bring them together."

"Why me?"

"Why not you? Politics and religion are both in your blood."

"But I don't want to be seen as undermining the pope."

"Then be discrete."

"How?"

"Jessica, you're the Prefect for the Congregation for the Clergy. That gives you license to contact any member of the clergy you like. When you reach out, just make sure people know you're doing so in your role as Prefect."

She smiled.

"John, if you hadn't become a priest, do you think you would have gone into politics?"

"I would have made a lousy politician."

Then, looking serious, he said, "Always remember your sphere of influence is greater than your sphere of control. And your influence is more powerful than you realize."

★

Jessica made her own list of cardinals and bishops. Of the more than 5,300 bishops in the Church, she identified 100 who clearly shared her passion for helping the poor, the focus of her work for the Congregation for the Clergy.

This was a small fraction of the total number of bishops, but she knew that building successful coalitions begins with organizing the "true believers."

Jessica was mindful of how she might be perceived as she went about this work. She knew some might see her as trying to build a base for herself. In truth, she had no such interest. For her, reaching out to like-minded leaders was not about building anything. It was about preserving a light.

She started by visiting cardinals and archbishops in the US. She approached them for the express purpose of sharing best practices in outreach to the poor and disadvantaged. Her interest in this was sincere, and the dialogue she fostered was helpful for everyone involved.

Soon she was reaching out to bishops outside the US. She did this by videoconference to save time and money — and keep a lower profile.

In her interactions with other bishops, Jessica was always careful to not criticize the pope. But the more she reached out, the more attention she drew, and the more her fellow Church leaders began to see her as the "anti-Benedict."

One who took notice was Cardinal Penov.

"She's a trouble maker," he told Benedict.

"She's harmless," the pope said. "A woman and a small one at that."

"You ought not underestimate her, Your Holiness," Penov said. "She is a quiet but effective leader."

Jessica knew she was probably tempting fate by holding a conference call with Archbishop Oumarou of Bamenda in Cameroon, a heavily Catholic country in western Africa, bordering Nigeria, Benedict's home country. She had heard Oumarou was working with companies in Cameroon to train and hire low-income residents, with some very good results. She wanted to know more and see if Oumarou's innovative work could be reapplied in other developing countries.

Soon after that call, Oumarou was at the Vatican as part of a delegation of African bishops. In a meeting with Benedict, he mentioned Jessica's outreach. Benedict bluntly asked him whether she had said anything critical of him.

"No, Your Holiness," Oumarou said. "But she did mention she's doing quite a lot of this kind of thing with other bishops around the world."

Benedict was furious. He mentioned what he had learned to Penov, who was now visiting him every few weeks.

"She's a politician," Penov told him. "She's clever. She's trying to undermine you, and she's doing all this under the guise of her work with the Congregation for the Clergy. It's a pretext."

"Maybe it's time for me to meet this woman," Benedict said.

"With respect, Your Holiness, I think you need to confront her and tell her to stand down," Penov said. "She's not sharing best practices. She's leading a movement to give away our money and our power. She's leading a movement against you."

"You may be right," said Benedict. "I will summon her."

Chapter 47

Jessica was meeting with a group of young parishioners at Sacred Heart Church in Columbia, Missouri when Ethan Morelli called.

"I'm sorry to interrupt," he said. "You just received a letter from the office of Pope Benedict. He's asking you to come to the Vatican for a meeting."

"On what topic?"

"It doesn't say."

"When?"

"At your earliest convenience."

"Please ask Kaitlyn to book a flight for me for tomorrow afternoon."

★

The Vatican hadn't made any arrangements for Jessica in Rome, so Kaitlyn booked a room for her at the Residenza Paolo VI Hotel, a short walk from the Basilica. Jessica took a taxi from the airport.

She checked in, changed into her cardinal vestments and walked to the Apostolic Palace. She got a lot of looks along the way.

When she got to the Palace, Jessica was escorted to a conference room on the second floor.

"Please wait here, Your Eminence," a priest said. "His Holiness will be with you shortly."

Jessica took a seat and looked around the room. The furniture was in the Baroque style. Jessica wondered if the ornate pieces were authentic. Dark paintings of biblical figures, marked Rembrandt and Rubens, hung on the walls. Jessica assumed they weren't originals, but she couldn't be sure.

She looked at her watch. It was 45 minutes past the meeting time they had agreed. Jet lag was catching up with her. I could use a coffee, she thought.

The door swung open fast. Jessica got up. In stepped a priest, dressed in black with a clerical collar, carrying a black portfolio. He looked at Jessica but said nothing.

Then in stepped the pope. He was a large man, with a wide, round face, skin the color of milk chocolate and a full head of gray hair. He wore a white cassock and a skull cap, a large gold cross suspended from a gold chain and red shoes.

The priest closed the door behind Benedict.

"Your Eminence," the pope said, with a slight smile.

"Your Holiness," said Jessica.

He stood still and extended his right hand. She hurried over, bent down and kissed his ring, a practice Benedict had reinstituted.

"Let us sit," the pope said.

The priest stepped around the large conference table and pulled out a chair for the pope. Benedict sat down, and the priest pushed the chair in behind him. He didn't introduce himself or acknowledge Jessica in any way.

"Please have a seat," the pope said, extending his hand to the other side of the table.

Jessica sat down, and the silent priest took a seat near the end of the table. He opened his portfolio and pulled out a pen.

"You are no doubt wondering why I have called you here," the pope said.

Being much taller than Jessica, he was looking down on her.

"Yes, Your Holiness," she said. "How may I be of service?"

"It has come to my attention that you have been in contact with a good many bishops around the world lately," he said. "May I ask the purpose?"

"Certainly," she said. "My purpose is to exchange best practices when it comes to addressing poverty in communities around the world. I am doing this as part of my work for the Congregation for the Clergy."

Jessica could hear the priest writing.

"I see," said the pope. "Why this particular topic? Why poverty?"

"I believe helping the poor is in line with our mission."

"Our mission?"

"Yes, Jesus' great commandment."

"And you see this as your mission?"

"Yes, Your Holiness, I do."

"With respect, Your Eminence, who has told you this is your mission?"

"No one, Your Holiness. It is based on my own understanding of the Bible."

"In the Bible, Jesus says, 'The poor you will always have with you.'"

"Yes, Your Holiness. But Jesus also said, 'But you will not always have me.' I believe it is up to us to continue his work on Earth."

The pope smiled. Dimples appeared in his fleshy cheeks. He leaned back in his chair and looked down at his right hand.

With his left thumbnail, he pushed back the cuticle on his right middle finger. Then he looked up at her. His eyes were bloodshot.

"Your Eminence," he said, "I believe you do believe that. Let me tell you what I believe. I believe the Church is under siege. I believe it is under attack by a vast array of enemies, who aim to weaken it. Our job, your job, is to strengthen the Church in the face of these attacks. What you are doing may seem benign or even noble. But you are giving away our treasure at a time when we need it most. How you choose to run your archdiocese is your business. You are the king, or the queen as it were, of that kingdom. The Church can afford a small hemorrhage in Missouri. But your outreach to other bishops is bleeding us all around the world, and that we cannot afford. I must ask you to stand down. Tend to your own flock and leave everyone else alone."

Jessica felt her heart skip a beat.

"Your Holiness," she said, "I am sorry if you feel my outreach has in any way weakened our Church."

"Well, it has, Your Eminence," he snapped, leaning forward. "You are giving away our power, and you are undercutting my leadership."

"Undercutting your leadership?"

"Yes," he said, his voice rising. "I am trying to strengthen our position in the world, to reestablish the Church as a bulwark against evil. Abortionists, those who would prevent the very conception of life itself, those who are living in sin. I am trying to save souls."

"Your Holiness, with respect, you make it sound as if the Church is at war with the world."

"We *are* at war!" he bellowed, slapping the table. "And you are giving away our armaments. I have called you here to tell you to stop creating a distraction for my bishops. I would also urge you to carefully reconsider your own priorities."

Jessica almost couldn't believe this was happening, that the pope was sitting across from her, raising his voice and telling her to stop doing what she knew in her heart and soul was the right thing to do. The prelate in her was inclined to obey, but something deeper inside was telling her to resist.

"Your Holiness, I have no intention of creating a distraction for anyone," she said. "I am far from a perfect leader. But with regard to my own priorities, I am confident they are in line with Jesus' teachings."

"You dare to school *me* in Jesus' teachings?" he barked. "You defy me, woman, at your own risk."

Then he rose to his feet and leaned over the table.

"Leave my bishops alone," he scowled. "And I am relieving you of your duties as Prefect of the Congregation for the Clergy. You have served in that role long enough. I'll be announcing your successor shortly. In the meantime, no more outreach to my bishops!"

He stomped to the door, which the mute priest rushed to open for him, and they left.

Jessica was trembling. She closed her eyes and breathed deeply to calm herself. In the quiet of her mind, she saw a face. It was the face of the man in the woods, the son of God. His face was warm. He was smiling.

She opened her eyes and drew a very deep breath. Her heartbeat slowed, and she smiled too.

Then she let herself out.

★

Back at the hotel, Jessica called Father John and told him what had happened.

"Good for you," he said.

"I'm afraid I may have gone too far."

"Why do you say that?"

"John, I've pissed off the pope. Big time!"

"So?"

"What do you mean?"

"Are you going to stop your work with the poor?"

"No."

"Are you going to stop reaching out to other bishops?"

"Probably not."

"Jessica, Benedict is under tremendous pressure. The Church is falling apart, much thanks to him. But he can't blame himself, so he's lashing out at someone he thinks he can bend to his will. You *know* he's taking the Church in the wrong direction and what you're doing is right."

"You may be right, John. But what should I do?"

"Just be who you are."

★

Jessica returned to St. Louis — and changed nothing in her work as the leader of the Archdiocese of Missouri.

Beyond Father John and Michael, she confided in only one other person about what had happened in her meeting with Benedict: Teresa Das.

Jessica asked Teresa to come to her house. Michael left to run errands and give them some privacy.

Teresa lit a candle, pulled up a chair for the Holy Spirit and said a prayer for Jessica's highest good.

Jessica then proceeded to tell her exactly what had happened in her meeting with Benedict. She listened carefully, her face nearly expressionless.

"Has this changed your relationship with God?" she asked.

"Yes."

"How so?"

"It has made me feel even closer to him."

"Good," Teresa said with a small smile.

★

Word got out that the pope was angry with Jessica, that he had told her to stand down in Rome, yet she had not backed down. That silent priest must have leaked it, Jessica thought.

But if that was true, and his intention was to cast Jessica in a negative light, it backfired. The story did nothing but enhance Jessica's reputation and further endear her to Catholics and others around the world.

A few days after meeting with Jessica, Benedict announced his appointment of Cardinal Penov to succeed her as Prefect for the Congregation for the Clergy.

Penov immediately dismissed the entire team and hand picked his own people, all hardline conservatives.

This too made news. Most stories portrayed Penov as heavy-handed. One anonymous source called him "Benedict's henchman."

Chapter 48

The Church continued to spiral down. By 2053, the number of Catholics worldwide had dropped to just over two billion. Giving had dropped so dramatically that church and school closings had become commonplace around the world. The flow of new seminarians and priests had slowed to a trickle.

Benedict's core supporters weren't fazed. They felt these changes were the natural, even beneficial, result of the pope's efforts to bring Catholics back in line with Church doctrine. In their view, the Church had been overdue for a "cleansing."

But not all Catholics saw it that way. Many felt the Church was moving in the wrong direction. And while many had left the Church, most had chosen to stay. They had no particular affection for the pope, but their Catholic faith was important to them.

For many of these people, Jessica had become a light in the darkness, a beacon of hope. They watched her continue to advocate for the poor and personally lead efforts to help the disadvantaged. For a growing number of Catholics all around the world, Jessica embodied the spirit of their religion. She gave them hope for the future.

She did nothing to promote her work publicly, but the media took a dim view of Benedict and reveled in portraying Jessica as his foil.

Given all this exposure, Jessica was surprised she hadn't heard from the pope. She thought for sure he would come down hard on her once he saw she clearly hadn't "stood down." She wondered if she might even be dismissed.

But Benedict faced bigger problems, including personally. His health had been failing for years. In 2054, his doctors found an aneurysm in his aorta near his heart. They determined it was inoperable. His cardiologist told the pontiff that when his aorta eventually ruptured, he could not survive.

"How long do I have?"

"Months."

With that, Benedict seemed to give up the fight. He stopped making public appearances. He cut back his meetings, and he stopped talking about the Church as a rock.

On Christmas Day, he delivered his annual "*Urbi et Orbi*" message in writing.

"Repent, then, and turn to God, so that your sins may be wiped out, that times of refreshing may come from the Lord," he wrote, quoting St. Peter.

"He is writing to himself," Father John told Jessica.

★

Jessica and Michael were on their way to Emma's house for dinner when the news flashed up on the screen in their self-driving car.

Pope Benedict XVII dies at 85

"Good Lord," Jessica said.

A moment of silence.

"When will you have to leave?" Michael said.

"Not for a couple of weeks. I won't be attending the funeral this time."

Once they were parked in Emma's driveway, their car doors opened automatically. Michael went around to Jessica's side to help her out.

At 60, Jessica had begun moving a bit more slowly. Sometimes her joints hurt. Michael had always held her hand out of love, but now he did so for stability too.

Emma was now 27. She was a social worker in St. Louis. She and her husband, Lucas, lived in a small house in Benton Park, just south of the city. They'd been married for two years with no children yet.

Jessica and Emma talked every day. They went to movies together, went shopping together. Jessica had officiated Emma and Lucas' wedding. For the past year or so, they'd hosted Jessica and Michael for dinner once a week.

"Hello!" Emma called to her parents from her front porch.

"Hi, Em," Jessica said.

"Oh, Mom. I just heard the news. I'm sorry."

"Thank you," Jessica said. "We must say an extra prayer for Benedict tonight."

Michael squeezed her hand.

Over dinner, they talked about Jessica needing to go to Rome again and the prospect of electing another pope.

"You're getting pretty practiced at this, Mom," Emma said.

"I'd be surprised if *you* don't get quite a few votes this time," Michael said.

"Don't be silly," Jessica said.

"How long do you think the voting will take?" Lucas asked.

"A few days, I suppose," Jessica said.

"Maybe I'll go with you this time," Michael said.

"I'd like that," she said.

★

For years, Cardinal Ivan Penov had been seen as Pope Benedict's leading supporter, even his right-hand man, and Benedict had made no secret of his affection for Penov. It seemed natural, then, when Penov presided over Benedict's funeral Mass in the Basilica.

"Like St. Peter, Pope Benedict XVII was a rock," Penov said in his homily. "He saw the Church as a moral compass for the world. He stood up against moral relativism. He stood up for our traditions. He stood up for the truth."

The Mass was broadcast around the world. In much of the commentary, Penov was mentioned as a leading candidate to succeed Benedict. He said or did nothing to dampen such speculation. In fact, days earlier, the cardinal had informed the Vatican press office he was available for interviews.

★

When Jessica and Michael got to baggage claim at Leonardo da Vinci, several reporters and videographers were waiting. They asked Jessica to comment on speculation that she was a contender for the papacy.

"I look forward to the privilege of casting a ballot for the next pope," she said. "I pray for enlightenment."

Like all the cardinals, Jessica would be staying at Casa Santa Marta. They dropped Michael at the nearby Residenza Paolo VI Hotel.

"Goodbye and good luck," he said, kissing his wife as he got out.

★

At the Vatican, in the run up to balloting, Cardinal Simon's name was in the air. All the progressive cardinals now knew her well. They all admired her. Many of the more moderate cardinals admired her too. She was in disfavor only among the most conservative cardinals.

Yet many cardinals, even some of the progressives, were hesitant to vote for Jessica for pope. They worried privately the Church was not yet ready for a female pope. After all, Francis II had allowed women to become priests only 28 years earlier, a few ticks of the Church's ancient clock.

Of more than 5,000 bishops in the Church, only six were women, and Jessica was still the only female cardinal. In his five years as pope, Benedict had appointed no new female bishops.

Still, Jessica received 24 votes on the first ballot. It was far short of the 80 votes needed for a two-thirds majority and 10 votes behind Penov. But it put Jessica on the media's scorecard.

Though the cardinals had sworn an oath to keep everything to do with the election secret, somehow there were always leaks during these conclaves.

During the breaks between ballots, Penov was seen talking with various cardinals, trying to garner their support. Jessica spent her break time alone in her apartment, praying and trying to calm her nerves.

As the balloting progressed and the implications of their choice became ever clearer to the cardinals, there was a growing sense that the Church needed a strong, progressive leader to undo the damage Benedict had caused and bring the Church back in step with the modern world.

With each ballot, several progressive cardinals, including Jessica, began gaining momentum, and Penov began to fade. By the fourth ballot, on the afternoon of the second day, Jessica had taken the clear lead with 74 votes.

Late that afternoon, the cardinals returned to the Sistine Chapel for the fifth ballot. Regardless of the outcome, it would be the last ballot of the day.

After the voting, the names of the cardinals who had received votes were read aloud. Penov's total had dwindled to 18. Jessica had received 85 votes. She had won.

The cardinals gave her a standing ovation. Outside, white smoke billowed from the special chimney atop the Sistine Chapel. Jessica could hear the crowd roar in the square. Feeling humbled and overwhelmed, she stood and bowed deeply before her fellow cardinals.

A priest approached her and asked, "Do you accept your canonical election as Supreme Pontiff?"

"Yes."

"By what name do you wish to be called?"

"Francesca."

Again, the cardinals broke into applause. Then they formed a line. One by one, they bowed before Jessica, now Francesca, in an act of homage and obedience. But when Penov reached her, he only nodded.

Francesca was escorted to a room in the Palace of the Vatican to be fitted for her new robes. The papal tailor had prepared garments to dress a pope of any size, but he wasn't counting on a woman, let alone one so small.

He took her measurements, apologizing as he stretched his tape around her ample bosom. He then left to get to work making some serious adjustments.

Francesca stood alone. After a moment of quiet reflection, she pulled out her cell phone, which had been returned to her after the final voting. She called Michael, who was back in his room at the hotel.

"Jess?"

"Hello, Michael."

"Jess, how are you?"

"I'm fine."

"I'm watching the news," he said.

"Michael, I have something very exciting to tell you."

"Yes?"

"I've been elected pope."

"Oh—"

He cleared his throat.

"Oh, Jess. Congratulations. I'm happy for you. The cardinals have made an enlightened choice."

"Thank you, Michael. I'll see you soon."

"You will?"

"Yes. I want you to stay with me now in my apartment at Casa Santa Marta. In the meantime, you might want to go over to the square. I'll be appearing on the balcony shortly."

"Oh, my God, Jess. Of course. Yes, I'll be there."

"Great. Oh, will you let Emma know?"

"Yes."

"Thank you."

"I love you very much, Jess."

"I love you too, Michael, and I'll see you soon."

★

From the balcony of the Basilica, Cardinal Asahi Yamamato, the most senior of the cardinals, exclaimed: "*Annuntio vobis gaudium magnum ... habemus papam*!"

The crowd, a sea of hundreds of thousands of people in the square below, roared.

Then Yamamato called out, "Francesca!"

The shouting grew deafening as the first feminine papal name in history, and its significance, struck those gathered like a thunderbolt.

Moments later, the new pope appeared on the balcony. Fortunately, someone had thought to place a wooden box in front of the microphone. Francesca stepped up on it, holding tight to a portable railing. She waved to the crowd, which went wild.

"Francesca!" they chanted. "Francesca!"

She smiled and looked out over the crowd, aglow under the setting sun. She had never seen so many people in one place. She couldn't see their faces well, but she could see bodies swaying, jumping and dancing. She spotted more than a few American flags. She wondered where Michael was.

Francesca leaned forward to the microphone, the cornsilk strands of gray in her dark, shoulder-length hair glinting in the early evening sunlight.

"Jesus—" she said, but the crowd drowned her out.

"Jesus—" she said again, and people began to grow quiet.

She smiled.

"Jesus told us to love God and our neighbor as ourselves," she said. "This was, and is, his great commandment, and it will be my focus as pope. You are my brothers and sisters, and I love you. Tonight, I bless you all, and I ask for your prayers."

She made the sign of the cross over them, her first "*Urbi et Orbi*" blessing. Then, as the sun was setting, she went back inside.

★

The next day, back in Sofia, Penov dashed off emails to his inner circle of like-minded bishops.

"We are now the underdogs," he wrote. "We must fight like Hell to save the Church."

Penov was seething from Francesca's news conference at the Vatican that morning.

"World tour," he sneered. "Who does she think she is?"

He picked up a burner phone, which could not be traced, and placed a call to a most fervent acolyte in Houston.

"I need you to fly to St. Louis in a few days," he told Georgi Sokoloff. "Wait for instructions from me. Your ticket will be waiting for you at the airport when the time is right."

Penov hung up and disposed of his phone in the usual way.

PART 3

Chapter 49

August 2055

"I want to open Vatican III in January and conclude it by the following July," Francesca told Cardinal Angelo Salzano, head of the Roman Curia.

She had held a news conference announcing her intention to convene Vatican III the previous day, having just returned to the Vatican after her recovery in St. Louis. Now she was meeting with Salzano and a dozen other top officials of the Curia.

"I'll need your plan for how we're going to accomplish this by October," she said. "Please keep it simple. No more than 10 pages."

Under Pope Benedict, members of the Curia had grown used to studying things and issuing thick reports. They had become glorified paper shufflers. They weren't used to doing real work.

Now they needed to develop a plan for organizing and managing the most important Church gathering in a century in 60 days — and keep it to 10 pages.

Beyond the timeframe, Francesca gave the Curia very little direction, but the direction she gave was clear and specific.

- Vatican III should clarify the purpose and role of the Church in today's world.
- This ecumenical council should end with an action plan.
- There should be three major sessions, held at the Vatican. All bishops must play a meaningful role in the council and attend all three sessions.

That was it.

"Thank you in advance for your good work," Francesca told Salzano and the others. "I look forward to your plan in October. Please let me know if you have questions along the way."

Then she got up and left, leaving a dozen bureaucrats looking at each other and scratching their heads.

"I don't understand," one said. "What are we to produce?"

Others raised similar questions. They all seemed puzzled about how to proceed.

Finally, Salzano said, "Gentlemen, I have a suggestion. Let us take a fresh look at the process followed for Vatican II. Based on that, and taking into account Pope Francesca's push to simplify things, we can make a list of questions about our task. I will then meet with her to discuss those questions and secure additional guidance for our work. Does this sound reasonable?"

Everyone nodded in agreement.

"Good," Salzano said. "As next steps, please read up on Vatican II and write down your questions. We'll reconvene in one week."

Ten days later, Salzano met with Francesca in her modest office in the Apostolic Palace. They sat across from each other at a small table.

Salzano presented her with a list of the Curia's questions, five pages in all. She scanned it, then looked up at Salzano. He was at least a decade her senior. She slid his papers back across the table.

"Your Eminence," she said, "how long have you been a cardinal?"

"Ten years, Your Holiness."

"And when you were named a bishop?"

"Nearly 25 years ago."

"Congratulations. You have been a bishop far longer than I've been a priest."

"Thank you, Your Holiness."

"And how long have you led the Curia?"

"Eight years."

He was appointed by Francis II, she thought. How in the world did Benedict not let him go? *He must be really good at this.*

"The Church is certainly blessed to have a man of your talents and experience leading the Roman Curia."

"Thank you, Your Holiness. It has been an honor to serve."

Francesca sat up straighter. Even then, she was a head shorter than Salzano.

"Your Eminence, our Church is in dire need of renewal. Catholics need to know what it means to be Catholic in today's world. What is our purpose? By the end of Vatican III, I want every Catholic in the world to know what our common purpose is so that every man, woman and child can then decide how to bring our mission to life. And I want our leaders to have a say in that. We need to do all this in 18 months. There is no blueprint for how we should go about it. But you are a prince of the Church and a master of planning and administration. You know more about how to get things done around here than I will ever know, and I'm sure I can depend on you to lead the way. I trust you," she said, looking into his eyes, "and I look forward to reviewing your plan in October. Thank you in advance for your leadership."

"But—"

"Thank you, Your Eminence," Francesca said, standing up.

She came around the table. Salzano bent down to kiss her ring, but she opened her arms and embraced him.

"The Church is blessed to have you," she said. "I am blessed to have you."

Then she walked out.

Salzano went back to his office. He sat down behind his large desk, feeling a little disoriented. He was not used to such free rein in his work. He was not used to making his own decisions.

He looked up at a cross hanging on his wall. He closed his eyes and said a prayer for guidance. He wasn't sure he could do this. But then he heard Francesca's words in his head. "I trust you." He opened his eyes and felt his self-confidence growing, like water rising in a well inside himself.

Salzano called a meeting of his leadership team for the following day. Then he looked over the list of questions he'd shared with Francesca and started marking down answers.

★

Francesca finished reading the last page of the 10-page document in front of her and smiled. She looked up at the prelates sitting around the oblong conference table. They had been quietly watching her read their proposal, eagerly awaiting her reaction.

"Excellent!" she said.

"Do you have any questions or suggestions, Your Holiness?" Salzano said.

"None," she said. "It's perfect."

"Thank you. It was a team effort."

"I'd like to open the council in early January, on the Feast of the Epiphany," she said. "Your Eminence, will you please work with the press office to announce that tomorrow morning? I'll send a note to all the bishops this afternoon to let them know. I'll include your plan."

"Yes, Your Holiness," Salzano said. "Do you need anything else from us at this point?"

"Well, it would be helpful to have a bit more detail on the flow of the first session."

"Certainly. When would you like to see that?"

"How about next week?"

Salzano looked around the table. Heads were nodding.

"That will work well," he said. "We'll set up a meeting with your office."

"No need for a meeting. Just send me your proposal when you're ready. I'll turn it around fast."

"Yes, Your Holiness."

"Oh, and no more than 10 pages, please."

"Of course," Salzano said.

Looking around the table, Francesca said, "Thank you all for your wonderful work in setting the stage so well for the renewal of our Church. This might be the most important work of our lives."

Then she got up and left.

The prelates, who had grown accustomed to rework, looked both incredulous and relieved.

"Wait here," Salzano said. "I'll be right back."

He returned a few minutes later, followed by a man pushing a serving cart with several bottles of wine and a tray of wine glasses.

Minutes later, glasses filled, Salzano stood at the end of the conference table and raised a toast.

"To our liberation," he said with a rare smile.

★

A few evenings later, just as Francesca and Michael were finishing dinner, they got a video call from Emma. She and Lucas were sitting on their sofa, holding hands.

"Mom, I have some very good news," Emma said.

"What's that, Em?" Francesca said, reaching for Michael's hand.

"We're pregnant!" she said, beaming.

"Oh, Em! That's wonderful!"

"Congratulations, Em," Michael said. "And you too, Lucas."

"Oh, yes," Francesca said. "Congratulations to both of you. Do you know if it's a boy or a girl?"

"It's a boy," Lucas said.

"All right!" said Michael.

"How far along are you, Em?" Francesca asked.

"Three months. We're due in April."

"Wonderful," Francesca said. "Maybe Eastertime?"

"That's a possibility, Mom. Easter will be on the nineteenth. I'm due on the eighth. But you never know."

Francesca was so excited she could hardly get to sleep that night. When she finally drifted off, it was with a prayer on her lips for her daughter and her grandson.

★

From the moment Francesca became pope, people around the world began experiencing what many described as a "lift."

And not just Catholics. The previous five years had seemed heavy for everyone. Pope Benedict had been a scold.

Francesca was the opposite. She seemed to genuinely enjoy being with people. She seemed happy to meet people where they were.

On Sundays, rather than bless those gathered in St. Peter's Square from a window high above, Francesca came down and walked around the plaza, talking with people. She was usually holding Michael's hand.

"I almost couldn't believe I was talking with the pope," one woman told a journalist. "I felt like I was talking with a friend."

Chapter 50

On January 9, 2056, Francesca celebrated Mass for 6,000 people in St. Peter's Basilica. It was the prelude to the opening session of Vatican III.

All the Church's bishops were there. Nearly 1,000 others had come too: theologians, historians, sociologists, priests, deacons, nuns, lay Church leaders and representatives from all the other major world religions.

There was an hour break after Mass. Then everyone took their seats again. Francesca stepped up to the podium, and the cavernous cathedral grew calm.

"'Teacher, which is the greatest commandment in the Law?'" she said. "Jesus replied: 'Love the Lord your God with all your heart and with all your soul and with all your mind. This is the first and greatest commandment. And the second is like it: Love your neighbor as yourself. All the Law and the Prophets hang on these two commandments.'

"My brothers and sisters, this is our calling. And yet so much of our time, talent and treasure is directed elsewhere.

"And so we must ask ourselves: what are we about? What is the purpose of our Church in today's world? How can we best follow the greatest commandment?

"These are the great questions before us and the reason we are gathered here. Over the next 18 months, we will explore these questions together, and together we will clarify the purpose and role of our Church in today's world.

"In a moment, Cardinal Angelo Salzano, who leads the Roman Curia, will review our plan for doing this. But let me give you a snapshot.

"This ecumenical council will consist of three sessions. We are kicking off the first one today. Most of us will gather for all three of these sessions. Each session will frame the real work, which will be done *between* sessions. Most of this work will be done virtually. Many of you will be collaborating across the globe.

"The first session will be dedicated to assessing the landscape. Where are we, as a Church and as a world? What are our greatest needs? Where are we following the greatest commandment and where are falling short? The second session will define those areas where we need to focus our attention and efforts moving ahead. And the third session will be dedicated to developing an action plan for what we will *do*.

"By next July, we will conclude this council. We will announce the updated purpose and role of our Church and begin engaging every diocese, every parish and every Catholic in how collectively and individually we will bring our common purpose to life.

"All of this will require thousands of hours of work, work which, thankfully, Cardinal Salzano and his team have organized and will continue to organize for us. Success in this sacred endeavor will require the active engagement of every person gathered here today. It may be the most important work any of us has ever done, or will ever do, and I know we will do it with excellence and hearts that are full.

"In closing, I would like to share a quote by the great twentieth-century Trappist monk, Thomas Merton. He was a convert to Catholicism. Merton was an American who was born in France, lived in England and the United States and died in Thailand. He was truly a man of the world. 'You do not need to know precisely what is happening or exactly where it is all going. What you need is to recognize the possibilities and challenges offered by the present moment and to embrace them with courage, faith and hope.'

"This is the spirit with which I pray we will all recognize this historic moment and embrace our sacred task. Welcome to the Vatican. Thank you all for being here, for joining me and for helping ensure people all over the world, now and for generations, follow Jesus even more nearly."

With that, Francesca stepped down from behind the podium. As she did, everyone in the great church rose and applauded. They continued applauding for nearly 10 minutes. No one had ever heard such applause in the Basilica. But the Church had never had a leader quite like Francesca.

For five years, the bishops had grown accustomed to Benedict's long, dunning speeches. By contrast, Francesca was brief and uplifting. Everyone there knew it was a new day, and they felt happy to be a part of it.

As they applauded, Francesca stood at her seat and bowed slightly, pressing her palms together. Sunlight streamed in through the large, rectangular windows around the majestic dome high above.

Francesca looked up at the light and beheld the smiling face of the God-man she had seen throughout her life.

★

After Cardinal Salzano went over the process and everyone broke for lunch, they gathered in a hundred different meeting places set up throughout the Vatican, and the real work of Vatican III got underway.

Francesca joined for a working session in one of the chapels in the Crypt, near the tomb of St. Peter. About 25 people were there. They sat in the pews. Francesca sat in the center. Father Dominic Savio, a Vatican priest, kicked things off. He was one of scores of moderators trained by Cardinal Salzano's team to lead these sessions.

At first, everyone was looking at Francesca. Soon, though, they gave their full attention to Father Savio and took part in a lively discussion about what was working best in the Church. Like everyone, Francesca offered a few thoughts, but no more than anyone else.

She was heartened to hear a number of participants mention outreach to the poor. One woman, a priest, shared a story about her parish's work with the mentally ill and how they were helping people who were depressed and even suicidal. Francesca thought of Josh — and knew in her heart things were on the right track.

As she circulated among the meeting participants, Francesca was pleased to see a good number of female priests. She made a point of speaking with each of them.

She also made a note to herself to spend time reviewing all candidates for bishop positions around the world. She was mindful that she was still the only woman who had been elevated to bishop, even though women had been allowed to become priests in the Church for nearly 30 years. I need to understand that, she thought.

For now, though, Francesca's focus was on Vatican III. She actively participated in more than a dozen meetings over three days. For every moderator like Father Savio, there was an assistant, usually a deacon, who recorded highlights from the discussions using a special laptop computer.

Highlights from these laptops were automatically fed into a database, which Cardinal Salzano's IT experts had set up. It was a capability which Pope John XXIII and his Vatican II organizers could never have imagined.

After three days of meetings, most participants left and returned home. They would reconvene in teams at least once a month, virtually, and work in committees before returning to the Vatican for the opening of the second session that summer.

Everyone left feeling energized, valued and part of a vital cause. For Francesca, the exciting and productive first session exceeded even her optimistic expectations.

"I have a very good feeling about all this," she told Michael.

★

The morning after the first session of Vatican III had concluded, Francesca called Salzano to her office.

"Good morning, Your Holiness," he said, sounding upbeat.

Francesca had not told Salzano why she wanted to see him. He came prepared with his laptop and a binder full of reports.

"I need your help, Your Eminence."

"Of course."

"Let me ask you: under Pope Benedict and Francis II, were there regular personnel reviews?"

"Personnel reviews?"

"Yes, I mean reviews to determine who should be elevated to bishop."

"Well, Pope Francis tended to make those appointments annually. Pope Benedict tended to make them as he wished."

"Were they acting on recommendations?"

"Yes."

"By whom?"

"By the respective dioceses for given candidates."

She was familiar with this process, having recommended candidates herself as an archbishop and a cardinal.

"How many bishops are there in the Church?" she asked.

"About 5,000."

"Doesn't it strike you as a little odd that only one woman has ever been made a bishop?"

"Yes, now that you mention it."

"Your Eminence," she said, "I want to begin a new process for recommending, reviewing and approving candidates for bishop, and I need your help."

"Certainly. How may I help?"

"First, I want to make it clear to the Apostolic Delegates in every country that female priests should be seriously considered for positions as bishops if they are well qualified. Second, once a week, I want to review the files of all those priests being recommended for bishop positions. For these reviews, I'd like a one-page summary of the key accomplishments of each of these candidates and why they deserve to be considered for elevation to bishop. And third, I want to announce new bishops on a quarterly basis."

"I see," Salzano said, taking notes fast and looking a little overwhelmed.

"Your Eminence, I realize this is asking a lot," Francesca said. "I know you have many resources available to you, but I'm also mindful that much of the Curia is now devoted to Vatican III. Do you think you could put a small team in place to manage these personnel reviews without diverting attention from Vatican III?"

"Yes, Your Holiness. I suspect it will take a few weeks to set it up, including informing the Apostolic Delegates about your new expectations, but we should be able to manage it."

"Good. I want to set aside a couple of hours every Sunday afternoon to review recommendations. If it wouldn't be a hardship, I'd like you to join me for these reviews."

"It would be an honor, Your Holiness."

"Very good. I will greatly appreciate your advice, Your Eminence. Let's plan to meet for the first of these reviews in about a month."

"I will look forward to that," Salzano said.

★

April 8 came and went without Emma feeling any contractions. An exam by her obstetrician showed she was one centimeter dilated. But she advised Emma that full-term women can remain slightly dilated for weeks without giving birth. This was not what Emma wanted to hear.

Ten days later, late in the evening Rome time, Emma texted her mother to let her know her water had broken and she and Lucas were on their way to the hospital. Francesca went into the small chapel in her apartment, knelt down and said a prayer for Emma, her baby and her doctor.

Francesca and Michael were up all night, pacing and waiting for texts that did not come. Finally, just after 6:00 in the morning Rome time, Emma and Lucas called from their hospital room in St. Louis. Their image flashed up on the widescreen in Francesca and Michael's apartment. Emma was sitting up in bed, holding a baby.

"Mom, Dad, meet your grandson, Joseph," she said, smiling through her tears.

"Oh, Em, he's beautiful," Francesca said, laughing and crying at the same time.

"Thank you, Mom. He's healthy too. I had a tough labor, but everything's good."

Francesca squeezed Michael's hand.

They talked a few more minutes, then Francesca and Michael said goodbye.

It was Easter Sunday. Between the happy birth of her grandson and the exciting start of Vatican III, Francesca felt as if she herself were being born again.

Chapter 51

July 2056

Council participants returned to the Vatican for the second session. Once again, Francesca celebrated Mass for everyone. She then made brief remarks before turning things over to Salzano.

For this session, though, Francesca decided to step back from the meetings. She had loved participating in the first session. But she was mindful that she was not just another participant. She might have been unassuming, but she was still the pope, and she didn't want her presence to inhibit or unduly shape the discussions.

But while stepping back may have well intended, Francesca's absence from the meetings left a gap which others stepped in to fill.

One of them was Ivan Penov. Over several days, he sat in on more than a dozen meetings. In each, he pushed the need for the Church to reassert its authority on matters of doctrine and dogma. He tried to discourage discussion of greater involvement by the Church in "secular realms."

Some participants tried to push back. But Penov dominated, and most deferred to him as a ranking prelate. He also urged a legion of other conservative bishops to take a similar tack in their meetings. In this way, in short order, Penov and his allies began to cripple the momentum for change that had been building and sow division throughout the council.

Of course, this was merely the latest episode in Penov's work to oppose Francesca. Now he was simply more visible.

He had led a resistance effort against Francesca behind the scenes since she had been elected pope. It was he who organized a global network of conservative "not my pope" priests who refused to recognize Francesca as the rightful heir to St. Peter. It was he who encouraged "Francesca-free zones" in certain seminaries. And, of course, it was he who had sponsored Sokoloff.

Francesca had heard about all these antics, but she dismissed them as "dirty politics."

However, because she had chosen to step back from the meetings of the second session of Vatican III, Francesca didn't realize the serious disruption Penov had caused until that session was over. Salzano brought it to her attention in his debrief.

Francesca was livid. She immediately called Penov back to the Vatican. She was still fuming when she got home that evening.

"Damn it!" she said when she saw Michael.

It was one of the few times he had ever heard his wife swear.

"What's wrong?" he said.

She told him everything.

"Jess, it will be okay," he said. "You can still nip this in the bud."

"You don't know that."

"Jess—"

"I've had it with this guy, Michael! He's been trying to undermine me for years. I can take that. But trying to wreck Vatican III? He's gone too far. It's time for him to go."

★

Francesca had Penov meet her in the same conference room in the Apostolic Palace where she had met Benedict several years earlier. When she came in, he was seated midway down the conference table.

He got up and walked over to her.

"Your Holiness," he said.

She held out her right hand, and he bent down and kissed her ring. She normally shook hands but, under the circumstances, she welcomed Penov's gesture of subservience.

"Your Eminence," she said. "Let us sit."

He went back to his seat, and she sat down across from him. He had set a black portfolio on the table. It was closed. She had brought a black portfolio too and set it down in front of her. It too was closed.

Francesca had seen Penov many times at the Vatican, including when he nodded instead of bowed right after she'd been elected pope. But they'd never actually met.

Now she looked at him across the table. He was quite handsome. His hair was thick and gray. His eyes were dark brown, almost black. His eyebrows were dark. His jaw was square. His lips were pursed, and the ends of his mouth curled up, as if he wore a perpetual smile.

He looked so familiar. And then it dawned on her. He bore a wicked resemblance to Jeffrey Epstein.

She hadn't thought of the notorious sexual predator in years. She remembered thinking, when Epstein was charged for his heinous crimes 30 years earlier, that he was the very face of evil. Now, looking at Penov, who could have passed for his brother, her skin crawled.

But she composed herself.

"Thank you for coming back so soon," she said.

"Certainly, Your Holiness. How may I be of service?"

He opened his portfolio and picked up his pen.

"Your Eminence, it has come to my attention that, during our most recent council meetings, you were making statements which many found disruptive and not at all helpful to the process."

He feigned a look of surprise.

"I can't imagine what statements those would have been," he said.

She glared at him.

"Don't play games with me," she said, putting her hand on her portfolio. "I have the verbatims right here."

He looked down at her portfolio, then looked away, saying nothing.

"Let me ask you something," she said.

"Certainly, Your Holiness."

"Are you supportive of Vatican III?"

He looked her in the eye and leaned in a little.

"No."

"Why?"

"I believe it is unnecessary."

"Unnecessary? Would you have our Church continue to shrink?"

"I believe the Church was overdue for a cleansing."

"A cleansing? A cleansing from what?"

"From years of liberalism that took us in the wrong direction and eroded the Church's power."

"Are you talking about the policies of Francis and Francis II?"

"Yes."

"Cardinal Penov, do you see me in that same vein?"

"I think your track record speaks for itself."

"And what do you think of my track record?"

"I think you are—"

"That I am what?"

"Naive."

"Naive?"

"Yes. I believe you are well intentioned, but misguided."

Francesca felt blood rushing to her face. But again, she composed herself.

"I am sorry you feel this way, Cardinal. I am sorry you are not supportive of Vatican III. And I am sorry you have caused a needless and unfortunate disruption to what has otherwise been a most productive process.

"Now let me tell you what I believe. I believe it is time for you to give up your leadership position in the Church. You are very close to mandatory retirement age. I would like a letter from you stating your intention to retire immediately. I expect this letter in the morning."

He sat back in his chair.

"And if I do not furnish such a letter?"

"Then I will be forced to relieve you of your duties."

"I see," he said, the curled-up corners of his mouth drooping slightly. "In that case, you will have my letter in the morning."

"Thank you."

"Will there be anything else, Your Holiness?"

"No."

They got up. He came around the table, bowed to her and kissed her ring.

"Good day, Your Holiness," he said, averting his glance.

"Goodbye, Your Eminence."

Penov left, and she sat down.

In 40 years of managing others, she had never had to let anyone go. She disliked even thinking about the prospect.

But sacking Penov felt good.

★

That afternoon, she heard the news that the trial of her assailant more than a year earlier in St. Louis, George Sokoloff, had concluded.

He was found guilty and sentenced to life in prison. He would spend the rest of his life in the Federal Correctional Institution in Greenville, Missouri, about an hour east of St. Louis.

Francesca had visited many prisoners there over the years. If I get back to St. Louis, she thought, I'll visit Sokoloff.

I wonder if he's sorry, she thought. I hope he is, but it doesn't matter. I forgive him.

★

No sooner was Penov's retirement announced than a dozen other conservative bishops announced their retirements too. They constituted Penov's inner circle.

News stories reported that Penov's retirement was really a resignation, that Francesca had forced him out for being critical of Vatican III and that the other bishops had "retired" out of solidarity.

Soon stories began to report that Vatican III was in trouble. Critical comments by anonymous sources about both Vatican III and Francesca fueled the negative coverage.

"Revolt by the right?" read one headline.

"Vatican III meltdown?" read another.

Francesca was concerned all this publicity could indeed put Vatican III at risk. She was inclined to make a statement. But what could she say that wouldn't simply add to the swirl?

She wasn't sure what to do. So she did what she'd always done in times of trouble and uncertainty: she called Father John.

Chapter 52

Francesca had a driver meet Father John at Leonardo da Vinci. She was waiting in the courtyard to greet him when he arrived at the Vatican.

"John," she said, as he slowly got out of the car.

He stood up straight, then bowed.

"Your Holiness," he said.

She went to him, and they embraced.

She hadn't asked him to come to Rome. He insisted, and she didn't object. She hadn't seen him since she'd left St. Louis a year earlier. At his age, she wasn't sure she'd ever see him again. Now just the sight of him began to calm her.

She had arranged for him to stay in Casa Santa Marta. He had flown through the night. He went to his room to take a nap and freshen up. Francesca sent an aide to escort him to the Apostolic Palace for lunch.

They dined in the same small, spare room where Francesca had twice met with Pope Francis II. She liked that room.

"So how are you, John?"

"I'm fine, Jessica. But I'm starting to slow down."

She smiled. This man was a marvel. He was in his eighties, and he was *just starting* to slow down.

"Truth be told, I'm feeling my age too," she said.

"You look fine. Is your health good?"

"As far as I know."

"And Michael?"

"He's fine. In fact, I was hoping the three of us could have dinner tonight."

"I'd love that."

"So have you seen the latest headlines about Vatican III?" she said.

"Well, they're hard to miss."

"I know. What do you think?"

"Honestly?"

"Yes."

"It looks like all Hell's breaking loose over here."

"That's what I think too," she said.

"What do your advisors say? I mean you must have PR people."

"They think I should weigh in, set the record straight."

"Why haven't you?"

"Because there's nothing to correct."

"But you didn't let Penov go," he said. "He retired."

"Yeah, knowing that if he didn't, I'd fire him."

"Okay. But what about all the talk about a revolt by the right?"

"That's true too," she said. "The hardline conservatives hate Vatican III. They don't care much for me either."

"Well, putting all that aside, how do *you* feel about the way Vatican III is going?"

"Honestly, John, until all this stuff with Penov, I felt great about it. Everybody seemed so positive. The work done during the first session was excellent. But I'm concerned Penov and his friends may have really screwed up the second session. That session is vital. It's where we really began to converge on our focus areas. If we don't get that part right, we'll never be able to come up with the right action plan."

"So you want my advice?"

"Yes, John, I do."

"You're overreacting."

"Overreacting?"

"Yes. Don't you remember that town hall you held at St. Joseph's years ago? Penov and his gang *want* you to step in. They know that any reaction by you to denounce the unrest they've caused will put wind in their sails. It will energize their supporters. They're waiting for you to react."

"And so what I am supposed to do? Sit idly by and watch the whole thing unravel?"

"Jessica," he said with a smile, "you've put a very thoughtful process in place, and there are thousands of dedicated men and women now discussing the right focus areas for the Church. Let them do their job. Let the process take its course. Soon enough, the naysayers will be drowned out."

"How can you be so sure?"

"I can't be sure," he said. "But you yourself said Vatican III is a matter of faith. Trust the process, Jessica. Trust in God."

"That's it?"

"Well, I would also suggest you not opt out of any more meetings. Your presence is important."

"So you think it was a mistake for me to have stepped back during the second session?"

"Yes, I do."

"Well, why didn't you tell me?"

"You didn't ask," he said with a smile.

"Oh, John," she said. "What would I do without you?"

"I don't know," he said, looking around. "It looks like you've done pretty well."

★

Francesca and Michael hosted Father John for dinner in their apartment that evening. Afterwards, Michael left to give them some privacy. He knew the priest would be leaving in the morning.

"John, I can't thank you enough for coming here," Francesca said. "Are you sure you can't stay a little longer?"

"Thanks, but at my tender age, I like to sleep in my own bed."

"I understand," she said with a smile. "John, before you leave, I have one more request."

"Of course."

"Would you hear my Confession?"

"Your Confession?" he said with a look of surprise.

"Yes."

"Of course. Right now?"

"Yes."

"Okay."

They were sitting across from each other in cushioned arm chairs. Francesca scooted her chair in a little.

Father John lowered his head.

"Bless me, Father, for I have sinned," she said, crossing herself. "It has been far too long since my last Confession."

"Go ahead, Jessica."

"Mine is a sin of omission."

"Please tell me about that."

"I've focused on others for as long as I can remember, but I've neglected myself in the process."

He waited for her to say something else, but she didn't.

"Is that your sin?" he asked.

"Yes. John, I've not told anyone this, not even Michael. But I've been experiencing shortness of breath and heart palpitations off and on for the past year or so. At first, I thought it was just exhaustion. But now I'm concerned there might really be something wrong with me. I know it doesn't make any sense, but I can't bring myself to see a doctor."

"Why?"

"I don't know. It feels selfish, and I guess I'm afraid of what a doctor might tell me. You know my parents died of heart attacks in their sixties. I'm 62."

"Do you consider not seeing a doctor a sin?"

"Yes."

"Well, then there is only one thing you can do."

"What's that?"

"You must see a doctor. You must take care of yourself."

"Okay. I will."

"Good. Is there anything else?"

"No."

"All right. Please bow your head."

He placed his right hand on her head and gave her absolution.

"Thank you," she said, crossing herself.

"Please take care of yourself, Jessica. Not to add to your stress, but the world needs you."

★

In the days that followed, several more hardline conservative bishops announced their retirements. This sparked another round of news stories about "defections" within the Church and more speculation that Vatican III was at risk.

Again, Francesca was tempted to speak out. But her mentor had counseled patience, and she refrained.

She did ask Cardinal Salzano for regular updates on the meetings and activities coming out of the second session. He assured her everything was progressing well.

She wanted to believe this was true, but how could she know for sure? What if Penov was still causing trouble from the sidelines?

Jessica was tormented by the idea that the seeds of discord Penov had sown might have taken root.

There was so much at stake. Her head ached. Her heart ached.

Chapter 53

As Francesca and Michael were getting ready for bed, they got a video call from Emma.

"Em, is everything okay?" Francesca asked, looking at her daughter holding Joseph on her lap.

Francesca was on edge these days.

"Yes, everything's fine, Mom," Emma said with a smile. "I just thought you'd like to know Doctor Goodman told me it would be okay for Joseph to fly now."

"Oh, Em! Are you coming to see us?"

She sat up straighter and squeezed Michael's hand.

"We'd love to, Mom. Whenever it's a good time for you."

Francesca looked at Michael.

"Anytime is good for us, Em," he said. "Just let us know what works best for you."

"How about next week?"

"Great," Michael said.

"Yes," Francesca said. "Next week is good."

When they hung up, Francesca reminded Michael she had a trip to Russia planned for the following week.

"I know," he said. "But the Russians have been waiting more than 1,200 years for a pope to visit. It's taken them that long to extend an invitation. Surely they can wait another week."

★

Michael greeted Emma, Lucas and Joseph at the airport. Francesca didn't come with him to avoid creating a scene. Few people recognized Michael on his own.

Emma was carrying Joseph, who was asleep. She picked up her pace as she approached her father, who gathered his daughter and grandson in.

"He's beautiful," Michael said, looking down at Joseph through his tears.

"Thank you, Dad."

"Welcome to Rome," Michael said to Lucas, extending his hand. "I'm so glad you're all here."

★

Francesca did her best to keep her schedule light that week. She returned to her apartment at least twice a day, letting go of the rest of the world to hold her grandson. If Joseph wasn't sleeping, and sometimes when he was, she would hold him.

She loved holding him. It reminded her of holding Josh as an infant. Joseph looked a lot like Josh. His blue eyes, his small nose, his brown hair were all so similar. Sometimes Francesca would let herself imagine she was back in Springfield, holding her own infant son again.

One afternoon, she was holding Joseph as Emma, Lucas and Michael all dozed. He looked up at her, studying her face and cooing.

She looked into his eyes, then beyond them. She saw Emma and Josh as babies. She saw herself as a baby being held by her mother. She saw her mother being held by her mother and her mother by her mother. They were all holding one another and being held by God, and she felt one with all of them.

That night, she said to Michael, "Holding Joseph this afternoon, I had the most amazing experience."

"Really?"

"Yeah. I don't think Josh has gone away at all. I think he's here as surely as Joseph and Emma are here — and Jesus, for that matter."

Michael smiled.

"You really are one who walks with the Lord," he said.

"I hope so."

"What do you mean?"

"I mean we're at such a critical point in Vatican III. I really need his help."

"He's with you," Michael said. "He's walking right beside you."

They got into bed. He turned to her and kissed her on the lips.

"Good night," he said. "I love you."

"I love you too."

She closed her eyes and remembered what Jesus had said as he held her in his arms after she'd been shot in St. Louis.

"I've got you."

As she faded into sleep, Francesca felt her worry about Vatican III ebbing away.

Chapter 54

January 2057

A year after she kicked off the opening session of Vatican III, Francesca celebrated Mass in the Basilica for roughly the same 6,000 people, clerics and lay people, Catholics and non-Catholics.

And yet not one of them was the same as before. The process of reflecting on and praying over the needs of others had made them think hard about the real world, the world outside the walls of churches. It had cleared their eyes, opened their minds and softened their hearts. They, the leaders of a transformation, were themselves being transformed.

After another hour-long break after Mass, Francesca once again stepped up to the podium. She looked out at those seated all around her.

"Home stretch," she said with a big smile.

Laughter reverberated throughout the cathedral.

"We've come so far," she said. "Let us finish strong."

Everyone applauded.

"I am so heartened by your work over the past year, and especially these past six months. Your latest task was to identify those areas where our Church needs to focus our attention and efforts moving forward. Your conclusion, in every region of the world, in every country, is clear. While we must tend to every person, we must do more, much more, for the poor and disadvantaged in our communities.

"Defining what this means and how we should go about it will be our focus over the next six months. But we've already gotten some great ideas precisely because so much of the work you yourselves have been doing has *been* in the community.

"Let me read from a letter I received from Father Carlos Fernandes. He is the pastor of Santa Cecelia parish in Sao Paolo. Father Carlos has been an active participant in this ecumenical council. He is here with us today.

"'Our parish is relatively wealthy, at least by local standards. We have a beautiful church, having just completed a major renovation. Our parish is growing. We are thriving. But the questions we are asking as part of Vatican III prompted us to take a fresh look at what we are doing for others in our community, including the neighborhood where our church is located. We were all surprised and a little embarrassed to learn that very little of our time, talent and treasure was devoted to the poor people all around us. So we began reaching out, helping serve people in soup kitchens and homeless shelters. We looked into the eyes of these people. We talked with them, and we made a choice. We chose to spend one real, the equivalent of about 20 cents in the US, on the poor and underprivileged in our community for every real we spend to maintain our church. This may not seem like much, but it has been a huge change for us. Although it is still early, I can tell you the changes I am seeing in our parish are dramatic. We have always talked about helping others as part of our mission, but now we are really doing it. Many of our parishioners are now personally involved in our community. This has brought a new spirit to Santa Cecilia. More people have joined our parish over just the past few months than joined over the past few years. It is as if we are being reborn, and all because we looked outside of ourselves.'"

"Father Carlos, his parishioners and the people in their community in Sao Paolo are not alone. Many of you are sharing similar stories of transformation by more fully helping those less fortunate in your communities. Your experiences will inform our choices as we enter the third and final phase of this ecumenical council.

"In a moment, Cardinal Salzano will go over logistics for the next few days and the process we'll follow over the next six months. Before he does, though, I would like to read something from the Gospel of Matthew for all of us to keep in mind.

"Then the righteous will answer him, 'Lord, when did we see you hungry and feed you, or thirsty and give you something to drink? When did we see you a stranger and invite you in, or needing clothes and clothe you? When did we see you sick or in prison and go to visit you?' The King will reply, 'I tell you the truth, whatever you did for one of the least of these brothers of mine, you did for me.'

"We all know this Gospel passage. We may know it by heart. But how can we live it more fully? Two billion Catholics are looking for the plan.

"My brothers and sisters, developing that plan is the task before us. It is the most important work we will ever do. Let us enter into it with loving hearts."

★

Over the next few days, dozens of groups met in rooms all over the Vatican. Participants began to shift gears, from assessing needs and identifying focus areas to setting priorities and developing action plans.

Francesca personally joined every group at least once. This time, she was there to listen. She was listening for ideas; she found many. She was listening for enthusiasm; she found much. She was listening for discord; she found little.

In the process, she relearned an old lesson. Leadership is personal. It means showing up.

Her presence, even if quiet, was inspiring to the participants, who had come to the Vatican as much for inspiration as instruction. Seeing her there, so small and unassuming, made them all the more mindful of the least of their sisters and brothers.

At the end of three days, Francesca sent them off with a blessing.

"May the God of hope fill you with joy and peace. Jesus said, 'You are the light of the world.' And so we are. Let us go forth and light up the world."

Chapter 55

July 2057

"Crunch time," Francesca said to Cardinal Salzano and his top team.

"Pardon me, Your Holiness?" Salzano said.

"Sorry," she said with a smile. "It's an American expression, I suppose. It means a time when the pressure to succeed is great, usually near the end of a game."

"Well, then, this is indeed crunch time," Salzano said to laughter.

As keeper of the proceedings, insights, ideas and recommendations of the council over the last 18 months, Salzano brought to mind another term, which had its roots in Silicon Valley: big data. Now it was time to bring all that information together, in an organized way that ultimately enabled Francesca to make choices about the Church's path forward.

Fortunately, Salzano had been born for this. He might have been a prelate and a diplomat, but his passion was researching, organizing and presenting things. Being Francesca's "organization man" for Vatican III was the highlight of his long career.

Naturally, he condensed everything into a PowerPoint presentation.

"My apologies in advance, Your Holiness," he said. "I have exceeded 10 pages."

"I will allow it this time, Your Eminence," she said playfully.

Salzano's PowerPoint consisted of nearly 100 slides. Going through them took two days because the key points sparked so much constructive and, at times, spirited discussion by the group, discussion which Francesca welcomed and encouraged.

These Curial administrators had dedicated their careers to the Church. They provided valuable insights with helpful context — and great passion. What a contrast with my first meeting with this group, Francesca thought. It was as if they'd awakened from a slumber.

On the morning of the third day, Salzano boiled everything down to three big ideas.

First, the Church should maintain, develop and evolve those things required to bring Jesus' teachings to life in the world. These things included everything from church buildings to doctrine and the sacraments.

"This is a stewardship role," Salzano said.

Second, the Church should make a "hard pivot" toward the poor and disadvantaged. Parishes, the backbone of the Church, would be encouraged to give up to half of their revenue to the help the poor, from food pantries to job training centers. What's more, parishioners would be encouraged to get personally involved in their communities.

To help enable this second big idea, churches, schools, including universities, and hospitals would be streamlined to cut costs. Some of the church's property, including its art and architecture, would be sold. The proceeds would be redirected to the poor. Some participants even suggested beginning with some of the Vatican's holdings.

The third big idea fit with the second. It was to streamline bureaucracy wherever it existed in the Church. The organization of the Church should be flattened, with far fewer bishops and cardinals, and the Church itself should be much more inclusive.

"Wow!" Francesca said. "I'm so impressed."

Then drawing on her political experience, she said, "So what are the key issues?"

Ever the bureaucrat, Salzano was prepared.

"We see three key issues, Your Holiness," he said. "First, resistance from more traditional bishops and priests. Second, how to balance maintaining what's important to preserve while pivoting toward the poor. Third, the very definition of 'Church.'"

Francesca thought for a moment.

"I understand the first two issues," she said. "What do you mean by the third?"

"If we enact this plan," Salzano said, "much of what we have defined as 'Church' through the centuries would be dramatically changed. We would need to reset expectations."

Francesca smiled.

"Your Eminence," she said, "I had two concerns as we embarked on this ecumenical council. The first was that we might go too far. The second was that we might not go far enough."

Salzano looked anxious.

"I am happy to tell you, to tell all of you, that you've hit the bullseye. Your plan is outstanding. Well done!"

Everyone smiled. Salzano looked relieved.

"However, before we do anything with this, I need three more things from you."

"Yes, Your Holiness," Salzano said.

"First, a plan for how to communicate our new direction. Second, a plan for how to manage the changes — at least over the next few years. And third, your thoughts on how to best address the key issues you've identified."

"When would you like these?" Salzano said.

"How about by the end of the week?"

"*This* week?"

"Yes," she said with a smile. "Just keep it to 10 pages."

★

Francesca bounced the Curia's plan off her two most trusted advisors: Michael and Father John.

Independently, they had similar reactions. The plan is excellent, and some in the Church will revolt.

She asked them how she might minimize backlash and defections.

"You can't," Michael said. "It's the price of reform."

"You're asking people to adopt a new mindset," Father John said. "That will take time, and not everyone will stay on board."

"But I don't want to cause people to leave the Church, John."

He knew she was conflicted.

"If history teaches us anything, Jessica, it's the power of getting an organization focused, or refocused, on its mission. That's what you're doing here. We all make our own choices. You're choosing to lead."

Francesca didn't like the prospect of Vatican III driving anyone away from the Church. But she believed in the reforms being proposed, and she was grateful to Michael and Father John for telling her the truth.

She was doing her best. She thought of her first failed attempt to push through her agenda as a new city councilwoman in Springfield nearly 40 years earlier. She learned then that doing things right was as important as doing the right thing.

Francesca knew Vatican III was the right thing to do. She prayed she was doing it right.

★

The following week, Francesca met with Salzano to review his team's recommendations for resolving the key issues and rolling out the plan.

Simply put, Salzano and his team proposed announcing the new plan boldly but starting slowly, giving people time to understand and digest the called-for changes and allowing them flexibility in how to best implement them.

This spoke to the hard reality that both Michael and Father John had articulated.

"The key, Your Holiness," Salzano said, "will be how *you* present these changes. You must be clear and then personally lead Catholics down this new path. You will need the support of many, to be sure. But there will be no substitute for your personal leadership."

"I agree," she said. "What do you have in mind?

"A global tour."

Francesca smiled. At last, she thought.

They talked briefly about when and where she might go and agreed to reconvene to discuss a specific plan the following week.

As Francesca was getting up, Salzano said, "There is one other thing, Your Holiness."

"Certainly," she said, sitting back down.

Salzano turned to his colleagues and said he would see them outside shortly. They took their leave.

He then said, "This doesn't have anything to do with Vatican III per se, but it might be helpful with the rollout."

"You have my attention, Your Eminence."

"Your Holiness, you have been in office for nearly three years, and yet you haven't issued any encyclicals."

"That is true," she said, giving him a quizzical smile.

"Well, whether you issue encyclicals is certainly your prerogative. But I was thinking that a well-timed encyclical on the right subject might be helpful as you enact the reforms of Vatican III."

Francesca knew an encyclical was one of the most powerful forms of communication available to her as pope, a way to instantly reach bishops and priests all around the world. She had actually thought about one early in her papacy but dismissed the idea because it seemed too bureaucratic.

Now, though, she was intrigued. She knew Salzano wouldn't suggest issuing an encyclical unless it were strategic.

"Did you have a specific subject in mind?"

"Serving the poor."

She blinked, thinking about it for a moment.

"That's brilliant."

"I am pleased you think so."

"The only question is when."

"When?"

"When would such an encyclical be most helpful to our cause?"

He thought for a moment.

"Probably at the conclusion of your global tour," he said. "That way, you can draw on insights from your travels, from what various countries are actually doing in their communities."

"And their biggest challenges."

"Yes. That would put teeth in it."

She smiled.

"Your Eminence, I think my American idioms are wearing off on you."

He laughed.

"Would you draft this encyclical for me?"

"I would be honored."

"Thank you. I'd like to review your draft when I get back. Feel free to share any drafts you might have along the way too. I'd like to issue this encyclical as part of my Christmas Day message to the world."

"That sounds perfect."

"Thank you for proposing this, Angelo."

It was the first time she had called him by his first name.

"You are most welcome, Your Holiness," he said with a look of delight.

They both got up.

"Would you like me to go with you?" he said. "I know most of the other secretaries of state."

"No, but thank you," she said. "I think you'll be most helpful right here. It would be a great comfort to me to know a man of your experience and capability and someone so devoted to Vatican III is here while I'm away."

★

That evening, Francesca reflected on the idea of an encyclical on serving the poor and how helpful that could be in promoting the reforms called for in Vatican III.

She thought of Salzano, a Vatican bureaucrat, proposing such a conventional idea just now, nearly three years into her papacy. He knew about her lack of interest in "the system." Maybe that's why he hadn't proposed the idea sooner.

She thought of St. Francis of Assisi. He too had little interest in the system. He even refused to be ordained a priest. Yet he chose to stay in the Church, broken as it was, and rebuild it.

Maybe I've been too quick to dismiss the Church's traditions, she thought. Maybe I should be embracing more of them.

How to renew the Catholic Church without losing Catholics? Francesca's heart was on fire with reform, but she knew she needed to step carefully.

★

Francesca spent the month of August getting ready to announce the outcome of Vatican III.

On Saturday, September 3, she held a videoconference with all 5,000 bishops of the Church to go over the main conclusions and the new plan. The following day, she addressed Catholics worldwide in a video played in every church.

"Nearly two years ago, I convened all the bishops of the Church and many others to clarify the purpose and role of our Church in the world," she said. "Today I want to share the outcome of deep thought, extensive dialogue and fervent prayer and tell you about our exciting path forward."

Francesca then went over the highlights of the new plan.

"I realize these changes are big," she said. "Understanding them and embracing them will take time. It will require all of us to adopt a new mindset when it comes to what we mean by 'church.' By church, I don't mean a building or even a religious denomination. Church should be about union, our union with God and one another, and our efforts to bring God into the world. Church should be about love. Church should be a place where we all belong because, although we may be a chosen people, we are not really a people set apart. We are all the sons and daughters of God."

Francesca said the changes called for by Vatican III will take time to make.

"But this should not keep us from acting boldly."

She said: "I will take the first step. The podium near the altar in St. Peter's Basilica is made of wood, but it is decorated with elaborate, golden reliefs, which have been added over centuries. This gold is worth about one million US dollars. I have decided to sell it and use the proceeds to feed the hungry throughout Rome. The wooden podium will remain, tens of thousands of hungry people will be fed and we will be in more perfect union with God and one another.

"I do not intend to sell off the treasures of the Vatican. But we must all ask ourselves: how much of our treasure do we really need and how can we use at least part of it to help those less fortunate? Is it not possible to share our gifts?

"As we embark on this new path together, I want to be in union with you. Two years ago, when I was elected pope, I intended to travel the world to be with you, but my trip was cut short. Now I will begin again. In a few days, I will start over, this time talking with you about the exciting and important changes coming out of Vatican III. I will begin in Bethlehem, the birthplace of Jesus, because in a real way our Church itself is being reborn. I expect my journey will take about three months. I will visit as many countries as I can and talk with as many of you as I can. I hope to return to the Vatican in time for Christmas. I ask for your prayers for a safe journey.

"I want to close with something Saint Teresa of Calcutta said. 'If you can't feed a hundred people, then feed just one.' When I was a girl, my mother took me with her on Saturdays to help feed poor people in a food pantry just a few miles from our home. We didn't wipe out poverty in our town. But we fed hungry people, one at a time, and both we and they were blessed. May God bless us all as we embark on this new journey together. I love you, my brothers and sisters, and I will see you again soon."

★

That afternoon, Francesca held a news conference to tell the world about the changes coming out of Vatican III. At the same time, thousands of bishops and priests around the world began engaging their parishioners, using materials Cardinal Salzano and his team had prepared.

Media coverage was immediate and global. Most stories praised Francesca and the Church. But some raised questions about how the changes would be implemented. Some quoted bishops who felt the changes were too radical. Some stories cast Francesca as a modern-day St. Francis. Others called her a zealot.

"In his day, people thought Jesus was a zealot," Francesca said to Michael. "I guess I'm in good company."

As Francesca got ready for bed that night, her heart raced. It had been racing a lot lately. She attributed it to all the recent excitement.

But now she also felt dizzy. She sat down on her bed and took a deep breath. She wondered if her cardiologist at Barnes-Jewish in St. Louis had ever connected with her doctor at the Vatican. No one had ever mentioned it to her.

She thought of her Confession and the promise she'd made to see a doctor about her heart. She felt bad she still hadn't done that. She made a mental note to try to see someone before she left for Israel.

She thought about saying something to Michael but didn't want to worry him, especially on a day as glorious as this.

Chapter 56

Francesca awoke in the darkness and looked at the iridescent numbers on the clock on her nightstand. It was 3:17 in the morning.

She'd been dreaming about being in the Well of Life food pantry with her mother. They were serving guests. Being with people, helping them, had given her a warm feeling.

She looked up at the full moon through the window. Remembering her dream, she thought of how long it had been since she'd been in a food pantry.

Francesca had spent so much time on Vatican III, so much time *advocating* for the poor. Yet she'd spent virtually no time lately with anyone who actually was poor. In the Vatican, she had become a captive of the "ecclesiastical bureaucracy" she had for so long managed to avoid.

She felt an urge to break free. She felt called to help a poor person at that very moment. She felt drawn to the city.

She quietly got out of bed, took off her pajamas and slipped on some "old clothes" from St. Louis. She put on a black jacket and pulled on a wool cap, stuffing her hair up into it.

She went over to the desk and wrote a note.

Good morning, Michael.
I'll be right back.
Love, Jess

She put the note on the corner of the desk, where he would see it. Then she opened a lower drawer, pulled out a thin pouch and slipped it inside her jacket. Michael stirred but didn't wake up.

She made her way out of the apartment, took an elevator down to the first floor and walked to the back door.

A security guard was sitting at a small desk, reading a book. She startled him.

"*Buon giorno*," she said.

"*Buon giorno*," said the guard.

Then he looked at her more closely.

"Your Holiness?" he said, rising to his feet.

"Shhh," she said, putting her finger to her lips. "Please don't tell anyone. I'll be right back."

The guard stepped out from behind the desk.

"But Your Holiness, you cannot go out alone."

"It's okay," she said. "I'm just going down the street. I'll be gone only a little while. Will you still be here when I get back?"

"Yes. I'll be here all night."

"Good," she said with a smile. "You can let me back in then."

"But Your Holiness—"

"It's okay," she said again, pushing the door open. "I'll see you soon."

She slipped out. The air was cool. It was dark, but the full moon lit up the square. No one else was around. She stepped almost noiselessly across the smooth stones of the plaza toward the rows of shadowed buildings just beyond.

She crossed a brick road at the edge of the plaza and stepped onto the sidewalk, which led down a street lined with shops. No one else was walking about, but she spotted two men under blankets at opposite ends of the broad doorstep of a shop that sold religious items.

She approached them. They were asleep. They both had beards and wore wool caps. The air near them wreaked of wine and urine. She stepped over quietly and sat down between the two men on the stone doorstep.

The one on her right stirred. He was squared up in the doorframe, his knees drawn up to his chest, facing Francesca. He opened his eyes.

"Hey!" he said.

"*Buon giorno*," she whispered.

The man stared at her, sitting up a little.

"*Tu chi sei*?" he said.

"I am a friend," she said.

He squinted.

"*Americano*?"

"Yes."

The other man stirred.

"*Che cosa avvenimento*?" he said.

"*Esso e okay, Leo*," the first man said. "*Torna a dormire*."

Leo lay back against the doorframe and closed his eyes.

"Do you speak English?" she asked.

"Yes, a little," the man said.

He stared at her.

"What are you doing here?" he asked.

"Just resting," she said. "Is it okay if I rest here for a moment?"

"*Si*," said the man.

"*Grazie*."

He leaned back against the doorframe. His eyes were still fixed on her.

"My name is Jessica," she said, extending her hand.

He leaned forward, slipped his hand from under his blanket and took her hand. He gave it a funny look.

"My name is Antonio," he said.

"It's good to meet you, Antonio."

He leaned back again and pulled his blanket back up.

She looked at him in the moonlight. His beard was a bramble of black and gray. His eyes were dark and small as beads. His face was thin, his cheeks lined and sunken, like dried fruit.

"Do you always sleep here?" she asked.

"Not always, but often lately. The woman who runs this shop kicks us out when they open, but she is kind. Sometimes she even gives us something to eat."

"I see. Do you have a home?"

"No."

"A family?"

"No. Only Leo. He is my brother."

"I see."

He continued to stare at her. They were both silent. A mourning dove cooed. A car bumped slowly, quietly down the cobblestone street.

"Do you ever go to the Basilica?" she asked.

"Oh, no."

"Why?"

"I am not worthy."

"Not worthy?"

"I am unclean. No one wants to be near me."

"Do you ever go to the Square?"

"Yes. I beg there. People give me money. But that is not why I go."

"Why then?"

"I go to be near people. Many of them have just come from the Basilica. That is a holy place. I go just to touch them as they pass by."

"Oh, Antonio. God loves you."

"Maybe so. But I need to feel his touch."

"We all need that, don't we?"

"Yes."

Again, they were silent.

"Antonio, will you do me a favor?"

"Yes."

"I'm going to give you some money. I want you to buy some new clothes for yourself and Leo and go someplace where you can clean yourselves and sleep in beds. Then I want you to go into the Basilica. Spend the day there. It is a place of holiness, but so are you. God lives in you. I want you to remember that and to know that, wherever you go, you bring God with you."

He was staring at her.

"Will you do that for me, Antonio?"

"Yes," he said.

"Then here," she said, unzipping her coat and pulling out a thin, fabric bag. "This is for you, for you and Leo."

She handed it to him. He took it.

"Thank you," he said.

"You're most welcome."

He closed his eyes and ran his thumb and forefinger over his eyelids, clearing the tears that had formed.

Then he looked at her and said, "Why are you doing this?"

"Because I love you, just as God loves you."

She stood up, and he got up too. Now, under the light of a street lamp, he could see her face much more clearly. His eyes opened wide.

"Are you—?"

"I am Jessica," she said with a smile.

Then she opened her arms, and he stepped forward, and they embraced.

"I will see you, Antonio," she said. "And remember God loves you."

"I will," he said.

Chapter 57

Francesca and Michael landed at Ben Gurion Airport in Tel Aviv on Friday afternoon. They would stay at the Vatican embassy there that night and travel 35 miles southeast to Bethlehem in the morning. There, Francesca would celebrate Mass in the Church of the Nativity, the very place where Jesus was born. At last, her world tour would begin.

That evening, Francesca and Michael hosted a dinner at the embassy for a group of local Catholics, Jews, Greek Orthodox, Anglicans, Muslims, Buddhists, Sikhs and Hindus. As their guests entered the building and looked around in awe, it was evident to Francesca they had not been there before.

"How good of you to invite us here tonight, Your Holiness," a rabbi said.

"The doors of our Church are always open to you," she said. "And to all of you."

After dinner, Francesca and Michael returned to their room. She decided to call Father John.

"Hello, John. I thought I'd call you before I begin my tour tomorrow."

"I knew you'd find a way to do that world tour sooner or later," he said with a chuckle.

"I just want to thank you for helping me get to this point."

"Well, I appreciate that very much, but I'm not sure you needed much help from me."

"Who knows where I'd be without your good advice."

"Jessica, I knew the day we met that you'd do great things. But I could not have imagined you would almost singlehandedly save our Church."

"Well, that's exaggerating just a little," she said, laughing.

"Remember when you weren't sure about whether to go into politics or religion?"

"Yes. What a tough time that was."

"Well, when you picked politics, I was happy for you. But I have to tell you I was also praying you would one day choose religion."

"Sometimes it takes us a while to discover our truth," she said. "I felt a little lost back then, but I just kept trying to follow Jesus. Eventually, I found my way."

"You most certainly did."

"I should get to St. Louis by Thanksgiving. Let's get together then."

"I will very much look forward to that."

"Be well, John."

"Godspeed, Jessica."

After she hung up, Francesca let her mind linger for a moment on the idea of being back in St. Louis. How she had missed that place and those people, Emma most of all. She couldn't wait to see them all again.

She hoped to see Teresa Das too. Francesca had managed to talk with her by phone or video every few months, but it wasn't the same as sitting with her. She looked forward to being with Teresa in person again.

★

Francesca and Michael got into bed. He leaned over and kissed her good night.

"I love you," he said.

"I love you."

They faced each other in the dark and, as they did every night, held hands for a moment before they fell asleep.

They had been married for 40 years. But every time Francesca held Michael's hand, to her, it felt like the first time, when he reached across the table at Avanzare's. How blessed she felt to have someone to love and who loved her, someone whose hand she could hold, all these years.

She was tired. She closed her eyes and began to drift off to sleep.

Then she saw him, standing near her bed. She knew him right away.

His robe was now radiant. It lit up the whole room, as if it were morning. His face was radiant too.

She pulled back her covers and sat up.

He smiled and opened his arms.

"Peace be with you, Jessica," he said.

She stood up and went to him, and he embraced her. His arms were strong, his garments soft, and he gathered her in.

She heard voices, familiar voices, the voices of loved ones. She heard laughter.

Then her heart was still, and she was filled with a joy beyond anything she had ever imagined.

★

In the morning, Michael got up to go to the bathroom. When he came back, Jessica was still in bed.

"Jess," he said. "Time to get up."

But she didn't move. He stepped around to her side of the bed and sat down. She'd been sleeping so soundly lately, and sometimes he had to wake her up.

He bent down and kissed her face. It was cold.

He sat straight up, his heart pounding, and looked down at her.

"Jess?"

She still didn't move. He felt her neck with his fingers. Her skin was cold, and her neck was hard. There was no pulse.

"Oh, Jess," he moaned in agony.

★

The coroner in Tel Aviv examined Francesca's body and reviewed her medical history. The Vatican had given him access. He concluded the cause of death was a heart attack.

Vatican authorities demanded the body be flown to Rome immediately. They'd already begun preparations for the funeral.

As soon as Francesca's body arrived at the Vatican, it was prepared to lie in state in the Basilica. In the fog of the moment, amidst the flurry of funeral arrangements, no autopsy was performed.

★

Michael asked that Father John say Francesca's funeral Mass. It was an extraordinary request, as papal funeral Masses are traditionally said by cardinals.

However, no other pope had ever left a spouse with wishes to follow. Cardinal Salzano himself granted Michael's request. He called Father John, who agreed to come to Rome and say the Mass.

Meanwhile, the whole world mourned. Vigils were held and memorial Masses said for Francesca in every country. Tens of thousands filed by her open casket in the nave of St. Peter's Basilica to pay their respects.

Perhaps predictably, conspiracy theories about the cause of Francesca's untimely death sprung up almost immediately, no doubt fueled by insolent comments by Cardinal Penov and others of his ilk.

"The Church is better off without her," Penov callously told friends.

But they were the outliers. The world at large felt bereft. Every leader of every religion and every head of state made the sad journey to Rome for the funeral of a leader who had inspired everyone.

"I talked with Francesca just a few days ago," Father John said in his homily. "She reminded me that sometimes it takes us a while to discover our truth. It has taken us, the Church, a while to discover *our* truth, that our purpose is to love God and our neighbors. Francesca helped us see that, and then she left us too soon. And there is only one way to honor her. We must continue on the trail she was blazing for us, the one she followed all her life."

"Amen," whispered Antonio, who was standing next to Leo in the last pew.

★

Most popes are laid to rest in the Vatican. Some are even on display there, entombed in glass coffins.

But Michael instructed that Francesca's body be returned to Springfield, in accord with her wishes, and buried in a casket made of pine next to her parents and their son.

Michael, Emma and Father John accompanied her body. In a simple graveside service, Father John recited the prayer of St. Francis over her, as the 10,000 people who had gathered at the cemetery bowed their heads and prayed for her too.

Chapter 58

The red granite obelisk in the center of St. Peter's Square shimmered in the morning sun, which cast shadows in the shapes of the stone saints atop the colonnades of the Basilica.

Though it was still early, the square was buzzing with people who had gathered in anticipation of the election of a new pope.

Inside the Apostolic Palace, a throng of cardinals, wearing red robes and gold crosses, gathered outside the entrance to the Sistine Chapel, where the conclave would begin shortly.

Cardinal Luciani of Calabria spotted his fellow countryman and old friend Cardinal Salzano standing by himself, looking down at the marble inlay floor. Luciani walked over to him.

"*Buon giorno, Angelo,*" Luciani said.

Salzano looked up, as if awakening from a daydream.

"Gianni," he said. "It's good to see you."

The two men embraced and lightly kissed one another on both cheeks.

Salzano was known for his stoic demeanor, but now he looked troubled.

"Are you okay?" Luciani asked.

"I am sad," Salzano replied.

"I am sorry, Angelo. I know you were close to her."

Salzano simply nodded.

"May I ask you something?" Luciani said.

"Of course."

"What was she like?"

Salzano sighed.

"Working with Francesca was a joy. She was the most empowering leader I've ever known. She was kind but tough and very clear about her purpose. She wanted to lead us back to the great commandment, and she was so close to doing that, Gianni. She was so close."

Salzano's voice was trembling, and his eyes were moist. Luciani had never seen him this way.

"Do not give up hope, Angelo," he said, putting his hand on the older man's shoulder. "With the grace of God, we will choose a new pope who will advance the sacred work Francesca had begun."

"That is my prayer," Salzano said.

"Mine too."

The large, paneled doors creaked open.

"I suppose it is time," Salzano said.

"Yes, my friend. Let us go."

They stepped into the forming line of cardinals and processed slowly and silently into the ancient chapel, past a row of Swiss guards standing at attention. A few minutes later, a monsignor called out "*extra omnes,*" and the great doors were closed.

Inside, 120 cardinals searched their souls. Outside, Vatican III, Francesca's legacy, hung in the balance.

About the Author

After a long career in the corporate world, Don Tassone has returned to his creative writing roots.

Francesca is his sixth book. The others are the novel *Drive* and four short story collections: *New Twists, Sampler, Small Bites* and *Get Back*.

Don and his wife Liz live in Loveland, Ohio. They have four children and five grandchildren.

Made in the USA
Monee, IL
01 June 2021

69941483R00215